# TRACKER HIVE

## ACADEMY

SEMESTER 1

# AVERY SONG

Cover Design by Melody Simmons

Editing by
Incantation Ink
Format: Yumoyori Wilson

## ACKNOWLEDGEMENTS

### *Thank you for purchasing THE TRACKER HIVE ACADEMY.*

*Thank you for giving Avery Song a chance! This was a spur of the moment decision, and I'm so glad I decided to create/write as Avery Song.*

*Special thanks to my amazing Mom for blessing me with the gift to write and supporting me in all aspects. I pray to continue making you proud as I strive towards success.*

*Finally, I thank God for giving me the strength to achieve my goals. Without Him, I would be nothing.*

**AVERY SONG**

## BLURB:

*I've dealt with my share of homelessness. I've endured being the bad gal in the room. I've taken a lot of life's punches on the chin. But never did I expect to be forced to attend an academy full of power-hungry delinquents.*

Born with powers far too great to control, I ended up homeless at eight years old. With my family gone, I lived on the streets, learning quickly that the world was just as cold as my beating heart.

Because I carry all eight magic elements, enemies sought me out from every dark corner. Luckily, I was saved and taken in by Alaric Masters, headmaster of Tracker Hive Academy.

*My name is Jade Storm, and I'm the youngest recruit to become a Tracker.*

Now that I'm eighteen, Alaric is insisting that I attend the academy. I'll do it but on my own terms. My only goal is to learn just how powerful I am and breeze through the next four years. I have no interest in joining any cliques, and I'm not here to make friends. If there's one thing life has taught me, it's that I work best alone.

However, the Troubled Four — Zeke, Zion, Zackery, and Zeus — have other plans. Quadruplets who together carry all eight elements, the boys are desperate to make me submit to their trickery. They're stupid to think I'll play by anyone's rules but my own.

I can handle whatever threats, traps, bullying, and schemes are thrown my way because I'm not here to be a good student. I'm here to keep my secret safe from those who will do everything to see me perish.

***Game on.***

# SOLACE IN HOMELESSNESS

R*ain...*
The thundering sound of multiple droplets hitting the cement floor soothed my lonely heart.

The cold trickled past the thin layer of cloth that clung damply onto my skin.

The rain never bothered me. It was a reminder, like many of the harsh conditions I'd endured, that this was my life now.

No more warm, homemade meals. Goodbye to loving hugs and cheerful laughter.

Forget about the roof that once hovered over my head, shielding me from the grim, unpredictable weather and the darkness that accompanied every corner of the city I currently stayed in.

There weren't many options for me.

I had chump change, but not nearly enough to take me on the bus ride out of this scary place.

Being only eight got me enough to get one big meal at the local fast food joint, with the occasional sympathetic tip for a hot beverage to keep me going through the tough nights.

Within this part of the city, I had three spots where I'd hidden the emergency items I'd gathered, things like water or warm sets of donation clothes for the rare occasions I got hurt and tainted my current set with bloodstains.

***Being homeless sucked.***

But at least I was alive.

I'd had to grow up fast, or else I'd be dead along with my mom, dad, older brother, and sister. People were still after me, and being a lone kid on the streets only made it easier for them.

Hugging myself tighter to combat the cold, I rested my head on my knees, staring at the buzzing street only a few inches away from the alley.

Watching everyone walk to and fro made me wish to be like them. I was too young to have a job, and the only time I was walking or running somewhere was to get away from the evil men.

Since my family's death, I'd been hunted. No place was safe for too long. After the police reports and the attempts to put me in foster care, I'd discovered the truth.

I'd overheard the adults who were supposed to protect me offer to trade me to those same men who wanted me now, all for a little cash.

That was when I took the donated backpack, a few sets of clean clothes, the first aid kit, and my documents from the foster care lady's desk and bolted out of there.

I felt like a criminal, but I was a little girl trying to survive the grim, bitter world.

On weekdays, I stayed in the library, thankful to the librarian who took pity on me. Reading was one of the few activities that brought me solace. No one would ask where my mom or dad was, or spit and laugh at my predicament.

The room was filled with numerous book-shelves, stuffed from top to bottom with knowledge that I could learn, absorb, and use to my advantage.

The greatest benefit was the magic section, one that carried many spells that had aided me in my fight for survival.

Our world was made of magic; the gods up in the sky blessed us humans with a fraction of their essence for us to use and learn. Some used their magic to heal, while others used it to destroy.

Not everyone was worthy of carrying these gifts

and magic wasn't distributed evenly. Though many had hints and bits of power, others carried a lot more than the average person should.

The world of magic had eight elements: fire, water, earth, wind, thunder, ice, spirit, and darkness.

No individual on record had all the elements; the most powerful mentioned in the history books had five out of eight at their disposal.

*I am the first one with all eight.*

From what I remembered of my mother's loving words, every birthday I'd obtained an element. Now that I was eight, darkness, the final and most compelling power of them all, was mine. It was the company I needed to live another day on the streets.

With each year that I gained an element, I became more and more dangerous — and hunted. My family members were the only people I could rely on, but they were eradicated from this earth.

*All because of me.*

The sadness bore into my heart, and the darkness was my saving grace.

Now I was growing, learning about things eight-year-olds shouldn't, but it was for the best. If these men wanted me, they would have to fight really hard to catch me.

It was a game of hide-and-seek, and for ten months, I'd been winning.

Tonight worried me. I was tired from yesterday's long chase. Sitting here in the dark alley while the rain poured upon my shivering body only made things feel more ironic.

My arms and legs ached, coated in bruises and scratches, and the emptiness of my stomach made it feel like something was biting my insides.

*Tired, thirsty, hungry, and cold. The usual cycle of my new world.*

Closing my eyes, I waited for morning to come, glad that my soaked hoody could give me a bit of shelter.

My black hair with white highlights was tied and tucked in the inner layer of the t-shirt that I wore underneath. My black leggings were baggy but helped me run the fastest rain or shine, and my black Converse sneakers were slowly deteriorating but still holding on — for now.

A suffocating flow of energy began to bubble inside me, strong enough for my eyes to dart open and have me standing up the next second.

That was the darkness's way to warn me of danger. I had to get moving.

Slipping my little hands in my pockets, I headed farther into the alley, only to bite my lip and push off the ground. The swift call of the wind shot me up, securing my rise to the top of the building, seconds before five men rushed into the alley I'd been hiding in.

The darkness came to my aid, wrapping around my body and hiding my presence completely.

I stayed frozen in place, not caring about the rain that beat harder against me or how the frigid steel plates of the roof aided in the cold's mission to give me frostbite.

"Shit! Where did the brat go?! We're not going home until we got her!"

"Boss, she's just a brat. What's so special about her?"

"Did you not see the sign in the Black Market? She apparently has six elements. She could even have seven! There's some big money on the line for us to retrieve her. Stop bickering and find her!"

The Black Market. I'd yet to figure out what the place was. There were no books on it in the library and I was too afraid to ask the librarian. There was no need to risk getting kicked out.

Holding my breath, I eyed their movement as they walked deeper into the alley, looking around the narrowed path. When they lifted their heads up, I prayed the darkness hid me well enough.

My nose caught onto the distinct scent of

smoke when I silently took an inhale, and another scent bugged me, reminding me of metal.

*Or blood.*

They continued searching the alley for another minute. "She's not here. Let's go!"

Tracking their every step until they moved out of the alleyway and into the crowded night streets, I let out my breath and rose up.

*I need to run away.*

I spun around, and the darkness continued to cloak me protectively, like a chameleon who shifts its skin to match the color of its environment.

Who knew how effective it was, but I took advantage of it, making my way to the next roof. The rain was getting harder, pouring down with anger and strong enough to make people start running for shelter.

I wished I could be like them, running from the rain and not from all these people who were desperate to find me.

Dropping to the ground, I thought I was safe, but in five seconds two men came to stop ten steps away on my left, their hands lifting up and pointing in my direction.

"There!"

*Oh, no.*

Springing into a run, I raced in the opposite

direction. I picked up the pace when I heard their footsteps picking up, darting my eyes from left to right to get a grip on my environment and where I was going.

The only advantage of being homeless was that I knew this city like the back of my hand, and the adrenaline thrumming through my veins was giving me the determination to lose these guys.

Turning a corner, I ran through another alleyway, ready to jump over the large fence, but a man came out of nowhere, leaving me no time to avoid crashing right into him.

"Oomph!" I hit him hard, falling back toward the ground, but was caught at the last second.

My wide eyes looked up at the man, who had long golden hair. There were hints of silver that reminded me of how my short black hair had a number of white strands.

This man was tall and wore a black suit with a gold tie. He looked rich, like someone you'd associate with the higher-class men and women in the city who had the privilege to do whatever they wanted.

I noticed he held a gold cane in his other hand, as well as black leather gloves.

I swallowed as I looked up at him in horror,

recognizing that I was in his domain and could potentially be a prisoner.

"RIGHT THERE!"

I lowered my head back to see the upside-down view of the two men who were chasing me earlier. My heart stalled when the remaining three showed up, making it five against me and this new man — and I had no clue which side he was on.

"Well, well, well. Isn't it far too late to be chasing after little children?" the man questioned. He easily lifted me back up, placing me on my feet and taking a step forward.

His hand reached back, knowing exactly where I stood, shivering and out of breath. Ever so gently, he moved me to stand behind him.

Protectively, like I was someone of value to him.

*And not in a negative, selfish way like these men glaring at us.*

"Get out of our way! She's our bait. We sought her out first!" the leader of the group roared, stepping up in front of the four men who crowded behind him.

Together, they were fierce-looking and made me tremble, but I tried to remain strong. To prove I wasn't afraid of their large, muscled frames and the tattoos along their arms and legs.

Yet I was still a kid, one who didn't have the

strength of these men to fight back evenly, and that was scary.

They wanted me for my powers, for the magic that came to my call when I needed it the most, but I didn't know how to control it, leaving me just as useless as someone who had no powers at all.

I could run, fly with some wind, and hide in the midst of the shadows, but an uneven battle like this was a lost cause. I'd lose if this man changed his mind.

"Children should not be used as a pawn in adults' silly games. This girl has done nothing to you. What would you need from her?"

"We don't need to answer you, rich scum. Get out of the way or you'll just have to be another victim of our wrath," the leader spat, conjuring a ball of ice in his hand and smiling wickedly at us.

Out of instinct, I moved closer to the man. Gripping his expensive coat, I whispered, "Go. They'll hurt you. I-I don't need your help. I can fight on my own."

My tiny voice held little conviction, but I didn't want this man's help. Well, deep down I did, but that would leave me having to do a favor in return, and that was something I *definitely* didn't want.

*No one helped someone out for free.*

His head tilted slightly to the left, giving me a chance to see his tiny smirk.

"Do not fear, Tracker. Today I'm feeling a little generous."

He looked away and raised his cane up slightly. "These men don't deserve mercy."

He slammed his cane down.

The ground shook and a wave of energy burst from both ends, hitting me and the five men waiting for this man's answer.

My legs grew weak and I fell back on my butt, but I noticed the cement wasn't drenched.

*That's impossible. The ground is still wet. It's still...raining.*

Glancing up with wide eyes, I noticed the raindrops suspended in the air. I lifted my finger to poke one of the tiny droplets. I expected it to burst into mini particles, but instead, I merely felt its firm outer shell.

*Did this man stop time?*

I'd never read in any spell books of anyone having the ability to pause time, but when I peered at the man before me, he was walking forward and the men who were chasing me were frozen solid.

Lifting his cane up, he tapped each of the men's heads. I was unsure what his actions would do as he reached the final guy and swirled back around, walking to where I sat on my butt in wonder.

When he stood before me, he offered a hand to help me up. Staring at it, I pouted my lips and fought my aching body to stand up on my own.

"I'm strong. I don't need your help," I said defiantly.

"I'm aware that you are strong, dear. It is always nice to learn to trust those willing to help. Even if it's a rare occurrence."

"Trust is earned," I voiced.

"Big words for a child."

"I'm eight," I argued.

The man looked happy with my response and tapped his cane against the ground. Just like that, time started again, and the five men dropped to the ground.

My jaw fell open as I stared in horror, leaning to one side to get a better look at the men who lay unmoving on the ground.

When I noticed the pools of dark liquid, I gulped but knew without a doubt the men were now dead.

"Now that those men are out of the picture, I best be going. I do recommend you find solace else-where. There are many shelters that would take you in and maybe protect you from the dangers of living on the streets," he advised. "Unless you'd like to come with me?"

I took note of his offer, but his statement made me mad.

"There's solace in being homeless!" I argued proudly.

It was stupid that I was being presented a chance out of this life, and here I was defending it.

The man's warm laughter was soft yet calming. He knelt down on one knee before me. With a sincere smile, he bobbed his head.

"You're correct, but there's also solace in having a roof over your head. There's peace in knowing you can sleep in peace and not in fear. There's comfort in living in a safe environment. Most importantly, there's hope in learning just how powerful you are."

He presented his open palm, and I watched in shock as eight balls appeared. Each was a different color, but even I knew what each symbolized and the power harnessed within its thin walls.

"Eight...elements," I whispered in awe.

"Just like you."

My eyes bore into his, wondering if he was good or hiding behind his saving grace.

"You know that I have eight?"

"I do. The same way those men know how

special you are. The only difference is I can help you and they want to use you for money and power."

I liked how this man didn't treat me like a kid. He showed a sense of respect toward me, which very few people did.

They didn't know what I'd learned and experienced. What I'd done to grow fast and smart.

"I'm not good to be around."

"I wasn't either when I first gained my magic. I got better with time and training."

"I don't trust you."

"You don't have to in the beginning. This offering is all I can do to prove I'm not like those men who have been chasing you for months."

"Months. How do you...?" I blinked at him.

"You are what many refer to as a Tracker. Individuals with massive magic power. It's one of my duties to keep an eye on Trackers who have no knowledge of who and what they are. I've protected you from afar, but things have become too dangerous."

Lowering my head, I felt annoyed at his dangerous comment. Every day was dangerous for a homeless person like me. What did he know?

"Every alley has been blocked off with magic," the man announced, shifting my attention from my annoyance. "If you had jumped up to go over that fence, you would have hit an electric wall that would have dosed you with enough electricity to kill you instantly. I'd personally rather you live than die with a bounty on your head."

"I don't know what a bounty is," I mumbled, but I understood his point.

My head fell in shame, as frustrated tears formed in my eyes. "If I'm some special Tracker, why can't I be stronger? I never asked for this. I want to live like a kid. To have fun again...but I can't have that anymore."

Biting my lip, I stomped the ground, my frustrated tears running down my flushed cheeks. "Mom, dad, brother, sister. They're all dead! If I'm so important, why couldn't I protect them? Save them! I'm tired of running. I can fight. I can hurt those men too, but I'm only eight. I don't have the strength and it's annoying."

I sniffed and lifted my hands up to rub my eyes. The man very slowly pressed his hand on my head, gently stroking my wet hair without caring how mucky it must have been from the rain and weeks of not washing it.

"You're tired, aren't you?"

I sobbed and cried harder. "I'm so tired, sir. I'm trying hard. I want to live and make my family happy in heaven, but I need to be stronger. To work hard and be able to protect myself. I'm tired of being afraid. I just want a nice bed. A warm meal. A place to stay...and books to read. I won't bother anyone. I'll stay out of everyone's way. I...just want to stop running away."

That was exactly it. My inner thoughts that had run through my head every day since my family died.

*Was there no place for me?*

The man's hand left my head and hovered before me in an offering gesture.

"A child should not be fighting in adult games. It takes the little innocence you have left. However, I can help you. I may be an adult like these other men, but I ask nothing in return. Your abilities as a Tracker will only grow from here, but if you remain as you are, you won't survive against these people chasing after you."

I opened my watery eyes to look up into his gold ones, watching them shimmer and glow against the dark hollow of the alley.

"I can offer you protection, and when you are eighteen, you can enter a place with people like you. It's a long time from now, but during that time you may live at my home. You'll be given food, shelter, clothes, and be trained to protect yourself.

You'll have the freedom to come and go, and all I'll ask of you is to respect the decisions I make regarding your education. Does that sound reasonable to you?"

He was giving me a choice I surely wouldn't receive from anyone else.

"You'll be like a dad?" I asked.

"If you want to put it that way, then yes. I'll take responsibility for you as your father and mother would," he reasoned.

Staring at his hand, I thought about it long and hard. *I won't ever meet a man like this again. If I'm this Tracker, that means I'm important. I won't need to sleep in the cold anymore.*

"If I say yes, will I get to know your name, Mister?" I asked.

"Certainly," he acknowledged with a tender smile.

A warmth filled my chest, and that told me that he was telling the truth. It was the spirit element telling me so.

I placed my shaky hand in his large one, amazed that he was so warm given the cold of the night.

"Jade. My name is Jade Storm. I'm eight and like mushroom and cheese soup."

The man's smile widened, and his fingers wrapped around my hand in greeting.

"My name is Alaric Masters. I'm the headmaster of a school called Tracker Hive Academy. Mushroom and cheese soup sounds swell. Let's have that for an early morning treat when we get home, shall we?"

"Home," I whispered, the word almost foreign to me.

Alaric rose up but kept my hand in his as he nodded.

"Yes. Let us make our way to your new home."

## 2

# HAPPY BIRTHDAY AND TRUST IN ME

"Mr. Masters....don't you think she should slow down?"

I gave the maid a look, which shut her up real quick. Returning to the delicious food in front of me, I went back to digging in like this was my last meal before death.

A year of being on the streets had made me appreciate food. In the cold environment, you never knew which day would lead you to three amazing McDonald's meals...or a single cup of coffee.

I always got the question of, 'Why not go to a shelter?' People didn't understand. The people who ran the shelters were the same ones who were in charge of child aid, like foster care. Seeking out a place to sleep at night and grab a warm bowl of soup would land me in the hands of the bad people, and I couldn't have that.

*I had to live. Fight to breathe the oxygen my family was unable to. They deserved that much.*

Scooping up the last bit of soup and moving on to the second bowl of rice, I filled my mouth and actually smiled in happiness at the rich, tasty texture flooding my mouth.

"It's fine, Annabelle. You may leave us," Alaric assured the maid.

This Alaric man was peculiar to me. I wasn't sure if I trusted him yet, but he seemed very easy-going. And that was what was strange.

The most notable factor about him so far was that he was rich.

Rich people were mean. The ones I met walking past me on the streets while I minded my own business were the ones who degraded me the most. Laughing at my plight and shaming me for not being in school. They didn't take a second to know my story.

They couldn't have cared less.

Rich people were busy being rich and letting others do their work for them. I doubted every single rich person on the planet was like that, but all the ones I'd encountered were like photocopies of one another.

*All but this man.*

Even now as I downed my food, he didn't give me a look of pity or sadness like the maid. He looked pleased that I was eating and drinking water. It was different and throwing me off my game.

I couldn't be fooled. This all could have been a trap to give the people that were after me what they wanted. They needed my power — the magic growing and beating through me — to expand and prove how dangerous of a weapon I could be with them molding me into what they wanted.

Thinking about his offer was one of the few things that motivated me to be patient.

Being a Tracker sounded interesting. A worthy position or job. I still wasn't sure what I'd have to do, and we were ten years away from me reaching eighteen and attending the school he spoke of.

There were a lot of questions, but I wanted to enjoy this amazing food and fill my belly. Pausing to drink a large glass of milk, I noticed Alaric's smile as he worked on sipping his coffee.

Lowering my glass, I stared at him. "Aren't you going to eat, sir?"

"It's pretty early for me. I'll eat a bit later," he assured me. "Are you enjoying the food?"

"Very much, sir." I nodded and stared at my glass.

Licking the milk residue from my lips, I glanced back at him, noticing he still looked pleased with me.

"It's okay for me to eat more?"

"Yes, Jade. Eat as much as you want. Just don't get a stomachache." He winked at me, ridding me of the bits of worry I had regarding my rather quick eating habits.

With a nod, I went back to eating, finishing the food in a few minutes. The maid brought dessert, a little chocolate cake with white icing and a scoop of vanilla ice cream with chocolate syrup.

I stared at its beauty, not wanting to ruin it by eating it.

"Is the dessert not to your liking, Jade?"

"It's not that, sir," I whispered, trying not to get emotional. Meeting his gaze, I gave him the tiniest smile I could muster. "The last time I had cake was with my family." My voice was but a whisper and I lowered my eyes back to the delicate piece of dessert. "Mommy made me a nice cake. There was a candle, and they all sang...my brother, sister, dad, and mom. They clapped their hands like this." I demonstrated by clapping a few times. "Happy birthday to you. Happy...birthday to you...happy birthday...dear...Jade. Happy birthday to you."

My tears hit the floral place mat, and I used my

sleeves to wipe my cheeks. "I wish they could see how pretty this cake is." My lips quivered as the sight of the cake blurred from my tears.

The screech of the chair moving back, followed by footsteps, told me Alaric was walking to my side of the six-seater table. I felt his gentle hand rub my back as I cried.

"There, there, Jade." His words were point-blank, but they were perfect. Whether he knew that or not, I'd never know, but I didn't crave the typical, 'What's wrong? Why are you crying? I'm sure your family loves you,' speech.

They were dead. It was all because of who I was, and the power bestowed upon me.

No one could confirm that they could see me from where they were. No one could say they were watching me at this very moment or had seen my struggle in the last year.

*No one could give me the affirmation that my family could forgive me. Not a single person.*

"I wish it had a candle," I whispered, remembering how amazing the candles on my birthday cake looked. "It's not my birthday, though."

"Do you remember when your birthday is?" Alaric asked.

"No..." I trailed off. "It's on my documents, but

I...marked it up with a black marker." There was no point in lying.

Seeing my birthday merely reminded me of my existence and that I was too young to do anything.

I erased it from my memories, not wanting to remember the dreadful day.

If I were older and stronger, I could have changed the path I was walking and hurt the people trying to take me for their own benefit.

"Hm. That won't do then."

I looked at Alaric, noticing how he fixed his glasses and looked at me with a soothing smile.

With a snap of his finger, a single stick appeared in the middle of my cake. I stared at it, knowing for sure it wasn't a candle because it was far too thin.

"Today is June first, 2504," he announced.

"June...first." Had I really lost track of the months when living on the streets?

With how cold it was, I'd assumed we were already in fall or even early winter, but our weather was unpredictable due to global warming and magic influencing the seasons.

With his reassuring nod, I watched as he snapped his fingers. The single stick lit up and sparkled brightly like a dandelion on fire. It was stunning, and something I'd never seen before.

He cleared his throat and sang. "Happy birthday

to you. Happy birthday to you. Happy birthday, dear Jade. Happy birthday to you." His voice was deep, reminding me of the jazz and blues music the library played during the evenings.

The song was in tune, and the emotion suffusing every word had tears rolling down my flushed cheeks.

His smile widened, and he gently patted my head. "June first is the day I found you. Therefore, we'll make it your birthday to remind you of how strong you were to survive the streets on your own."

I didn't know what to say. No words could describe the multiple waves of emotions within me. The sadness that revealed itself through my tears.

The heartache of missing my family. The sheer happiness at finding one person who didn't want to kill me.

*He cared. He actually cared about me.*

Swallowing the lump in my throat, I whispered, "Thank you...D...Dad."

The word was hard to say, and I waited for the backlash I'd receive for calling him that. But it never came.

He looked overjoyed by the title, and he gave me a light hug. "You're welcome, Jade. Remember, you are now my daughter and will remain in my protection for as long as you want."

Letting me go, he pointed to the cake. "You should eat it before the ice cream melts. They go well together."

I grinned and quickly nodded, picking up my spoon to start, but paused. Glancing at him, I asked, "Would you share with me?"

"You don't want the whole thing?" he inquired as he rose up to stand at his full height. I thought about it for a bit, wondering if my next response was unnatural, but I replied, "Sharing cake with loved ones always makes me feel happier. It also tastes better."

Avoiding his gaze, I took a tiny piece of the cake and a bit of the ice cream, plopping it into my mouth. The combination was heavenly with the perfect balance of chocolate, leaving me no choice but to have another bite.

I noticed the second spoon that dove into the other side of my cake. Looking up, I beamed at the sight of Alaric sitting down in the chair on my right, his spoon taking a bit of the cake and then the chocolate-drizzled vanilla ice cream.

He took it into his mouth and sighed. "You're right," he praised and glanced my way. "Cake is better with company."

A wide smile formed on my lips, and I nodded quickly in response. "Yes."

With a little bit of happiness, I continued to dig into my cake as we both worked on finishing the dessert.

*This man...Alaric Masters. Could I really trust him with my problems like I would my own dad?*

𝕺𝕶𝕯

CREEPING THROUGH THE DARK HALLS, I BIT MY lip nervously, the action beginning to tear through the layer of flesh and make it bleed. The metallic taste reminded me of the problem at hand, leaving me to wonder about how angry Alaric would be.

It hadn't been twelve hours and I'd done something bad. As I walked quietly through the large home, I debated whether to run away. He'd fed me, sung to me, made me feel like an actual human being in this world and not discarded trash.

I feared his rejection. Worried that I'd have to leave the comforting home for what I had done.

*Not necessarily me, exactly, but would he understand? No one understood. My family had, but look where they ended up.*

Passing the library, I heard a quiet call. "Jade?"

I stopped, my heart plummeting in fright as I slowly shuffled back to the doorway of the library.

Turning to peer inside, I saw Alaric was at a desk with a lamp on, an open book displayed on his desk. He still had his glasses on, but he looked pretty tired.

*It only made me feel worse.*

Moving to stand on the left side of the doorway, I tried to hide, allowing Alaric to only peer at my peeping head as I avoided his puzzled eyes.

"What's wrong, Jade?"

*He doesn't sound mad, but he doesn't know what I did.*

Watching carefully as he pushed his desk chair back and rose, I made myself as small as possible, while blinking back tears.

*He's going to send me away.*

Once he reached me, he knelt down to be on my level. Petting my head gently, he observed me as I trembled.

"Jade?"

"I'm sorry," I immediately apologized, fearing the consequences.

Deep down, I wanted to stay. This rarely happened, and when it did, the police could never find the true culprit. In the vast city, there was freedom to do what you needed. If something bad happened, I was able to slide out of it because the evidence wasn't enough against a homeless girl.

Alaric didn't say anything, but he looked down the hall when the sound of something crashing echoed through it.

"Do you want to show me why you're upset?"

"You'll send me away."

"I won't. I promise." His sweet smile was back, and he lifted his pinky up in offering. I stared at it, knowing exactly what it meant.

Lifting my head slightly to look into his eyes, I saw the truth in them. They weren't in the least intimidating and I still felt safe, even with the fear sinking in my gut.

Raising my hand, I offered my pinky and locked it with his, giving it a firm shake.

"Pinky swear?"

"Pinky swear," he replied with a small smile.

He rose up and offered his hand, and I took it and led the way back to the temporary room I was staying in.

When we arrived, I waited at the doorway while Alaric took a step inside to view the full extent of my trouble.

Everything was a mess like a tornado had passed through. The window was shattered, the bed sheets were torn, books and furniture were turned upside down, and the culprit was sitting in the middle of the room on the tiny round table that hadn't been destroyed yet.

*An identical silhouette of me.*

"Destroy. Destroy. Lalala. Destroy. Destroy!" the pure black shadow of me sang happily, focused on a book that was still in one piece and in her hands.

She didn't seem bothered by our presence, looking far more intrigued with whatever was written in the book.

Alaric's silence left me in a bundle of nerves and watching him walk deeper into the room to view the damages had me trembling in fear.

My phantom copy lowered the book, finally acknowledging us. She was a shadow, but her eyes glowed a light purple and they were staring at Alaric.

"Destroy?" She tilted her head in curiosity, but the action would be defined as eerie by most people.

I personally knew that was just how she was, but her abnormality was what people feared.

*That and her destructive qualities.*

"You've definitely destroyed a lot," Alaric replied.

His tone confused me, and my shadow was just

as confused. She flipped the book and presented it to Alaric.

"Me."

I gathered the courage to step into the room, avoiding any debris on the floor that appeared sharp.

Stopping by Alaric's side, I zoomed in on the page my shadow was referring to, noticing the title DARKNESS at the top.

"Ah. That explains it." Alaric nodded.

My shadow bowed her head once and closed the book. Sliding off the table, she walked to me.

"Me also." She pointed to me. Then she moved to hug me. "Sad?"

"Alaric is going to be mad at us. This isn't outside where no one can find you," I mumbled.

"Sad?"

"Yes, I'm sad," I whispered. "I want to stay here."

"Home?"

"I wish it was."

"Home!" She lifted her hands up.

"No. Not home. We destroyed everything."

"Not? Home?" She blinked, and I gave up trying to explain, feeling more pity for the both of us.

She was my dark power. She'd been taking this

form as often as twice a month and I couldn't even make up an excuse for her at this point.

Alaric watched our debate. We peered at him in unison, waiting to hear the bad news.

"Do you want this to be your home?" he asked my shadow.

"Home! Our...home?" she questioned, lowering her hands and walking around to hug me from behind. "Together."

"You're her dark element, correct?"

"Darkness. Me. Destroy. Protect," my shadow replied.

Alaric nodded, and I lowered my head, my tears falling to the tile floor.

"We'll leave in the morning," I concluded.

"Why are you leaving?"

His question surprised me enough for me to glance back up. He had that genuine, kind smile on his face.

"We destroyed the room."

"Yes," he replied.

"That means we have to go away. We damaged your property."

"It's *our* property," he corrected as his eyes softened. "This is your home, too." He used his hand to gesture around the room. "Material things can be replaced. This isn't something serious enough to let you leave your home."

My shadow was intrigued. "Stay? We stay. Home?"

Alaric smiled, giving us a firm nod. "Yes, you stay. This is your home, and this can be fixed with a bit of magic. We'll work on it in the morning."

He opened his arms up, inviting us to give him a hug.

"Nothing to cry about. Come. I'll take you to another room closer to mine."

My shadow and I stared at one another. My shadow smiled, a sight I'd never seen before. It showed her hollow mouth that glowed the same purple as her eyes, and she skipped into Alaric's arms.

"Home! Home!" She looked back at me, presenting her hand. "Me."

A flow of gratitude flooded me, and I let my tears fall as I placed my left hand in hers. She tugged me forward, and into Alaric's arms. He hugged both of us, removing any last bits of worry that assaulted my senses.

"Yes, this is your home and you two are the same. Nothing is wrong. We'll work through this little bump and I'll help you learn more about what this is called."

I rested my head on his chest, listening to his steady heartbeat.

*He means it. He'll help me?*

"You'll help me? You're not scared of my shadow?"

"Your shadow is your dark element claiming a physical form. It's a rare trait, which tells me your dark magic is one of the strongest. I'll teach you exactly how to control it and give it a better form."

"That means there's nothing to worry about. I can stay."

"Yes, Jade. You can stay. We're family now." His reminder made me smile, and I let my body rest against his as he scooped me up.

My shadow was gone, her play time was enough for her.

My body was tired, but instead of feeling the usual dread of it all, I felt happy. Relieved. Hopeful.

Closing my eyes, I decided to give this man, Alaric Masters, a chance. I wanted to be a Tracker and do anything I could to return the favors he'd done for me.

*Most importantly, I'd learn how to control the eight elements bestowed upon me.*

## ৩ ৩

### WEIRD LOVING FAMILY

# ~ TEN YEARS LATER~

**"KILL? KILL? KILL?"**

*You know, when you keep repeating it like that, it really makes me want to do it just to shut you up. You also make me feel like I should be in a mental institution rather than on an assignment.*

My mind was silent for all of five seconds.

**"Not kill?"**

I mentally groaned.

*Never mind. You can return to singing the Kill song.*

**"Kill. Kill. Kill."**

Taking a turn into a narrow alleyway, I put my hand into the pockets of my leather branded jacket, moving my hips in a more seductive manner while my steps slowed on purpose; the sound of my feet stepping into the small pools of water on the ground made me grin in anticipation.

My senses were on high alert, just like the elements that surrounded me.

The musky air, the droplets of water that fell back into their rightful puddles, the strength of the earth beneath me, and my adorable dark self who had been singing the Kill song for the last two hours in my head.

*Today was a good day.*

Most people didn't understand me. Didn't get my dry sense of humor or my "dark" viewpoint on the wonderful thing called life.

I viewed everything like I was playing a video game.

The stakes were always high, and the consequences of failure were up there with death itself. It was what had gotten me this high in the Tracker rank.

*It's what made me their top lead underdog of the junior division, which I was being upgraded from.*

I wasn't the eight-year-old homeless girl anymore. I was Jade Storm, daughter of Alaric Masters, and a Tracker in his organization.

Many people attempted to belittle my acceptance into this Tracker organization. I was the pitiful child who got lucky. I got in because Alaric was my father.

Excuse after excuse of why I was here and favored, but with my competitive personality, many realized I was nowhere near a pushover.

I had goals. Dreams of becoming the best and making Alaric proud, though I'd never say that to his face. He'd grow an even bigger ego and when it came to defeating him in combat, well, let's just say I struggled to get even his cane out of his grasp.

*Annoying.*

How could an old man still look like he was in his thirties and kick ass better than me? I was younger, a female, more flexible, blessed with eight elements...need I say more?

All I lacked was experience and whatever amount of training Alaric had under his belt.

*Didn't mean I wasn't going to keep trying.*

Either way, I'd proven a point long ago that I wasn't someone to mess with. A girl who secretly carried eight elements wasn't someone you could push and shove.

To everyone but Alaric and his trusty teammates who trained us on the regular, no one knew how powerful I was. The only element I commonly displayed was the darkness.

*Only because she made me act crazy half the time and she loved to randomly appear as my dark twin.*

The whole twin thing always amused me, though. My dark element — aka Shadow Jade — loved to appear in my exact image and taunt people. If it wasn't for her erratic thought process and repetitive speech, I would be getting in a lot more trouble than I already did on the regular.

What I did love about my shadow, though, was her loyalty. She couldn't be manipulated by others or their elements. She'd do whatever I told her, even if she didn't necessarily like it.

*Except eat chocolate pudding. She'd kill anyone who forced her. Even me.*

Having her around made growing up as a Tracker easier. She was the support I needed when the fear sunk into my bones and did its best to divert me from my path.

Coming to a stop at the end of the alley, my eyes scanned the stained cement, wondering what body fluids had darkened it today. I tapped my foot impatiently, moving to the melody of Shadow Jade's Kill tune.

Who knew you could make an entire song with one word?

**"Target!"**

Shadow Jade's enthusiasm stilled my tapping

foot. The person we needed to kill was in the same closed-off alley.

"There you are, sexy. You're hard to keep up with."

Taking my sweet time, I twirled around, putting some extra effort into swinging my hips seductively as I turned to face my target.

It was a middle-aged man in his late thirties. One who got his kicks kidnapping girls and selling them on the Black Market to those who traded in sex trafficking or element manipulation.

*All the bad, illegal things that could make you a millionaire.*

"Am I?" The question rolled off my tongue like maple syrup glazing the top of freshly baked pancakes. "I love a little fun."

Seducing men was fun, especially when they thought of me as someone they could sweep into their grasp like an innocent child.

Though I was eighteen, when I didn't wear makeup, I looked far younger. Even now with my simple black outfit, a short skirt and leather jacket, I looked like a young teen on the wrong side of town out for the night.

*One that wanted a good fucking.*

Perfect impression to give off when you're trying to seduce a bad guy.

This wasn't the typical case a Tracker like me should be working, but with Alaric out of the office and no one else close to qualified to deal with this case, I'd been "forced" to take it.

*Forced, as in I accepted it in exchange for a day off and shopping money.*

"Fun, huh?" The man began to walk down the alleyway, which felt a lot longer than before. "We can do something fun here."

"It's a little unsanitary here," I pointed out with a pout of my lips. "Can't we go somewhere warmer? A cozy place where we don't need to wear so many layers?" I suggested, pressing my legs together.

The man noticed my deliberate move; his lust was beaming out of his eyes, while he licked his lips like I was his next snack.

"I can do all that and more, cutie."

His reply made Shadow Jade stop her singing. ***"Weird."***

*From my singing shadow in my head.*

"What if I can't trust you?" I questioned when he stopped in front of me, the smell of alcohol and smoke flooding my senses. A typical scent for guys like this.

"And why would you think I wouldn't be trustworthy, cutie?"

I smirked, closing the distance between us as I leaned upward, my lips just inches from his.

"Well...for starters, you're a complete stranger." I leaned over to his right ear. "A dangerous one who's been tailing me for an hour and a half."

His rough chuckle would have sent shivers through me if I were actually afraid of him. "You're valuable, cutie. I'm sure you know that. But I'm trustworthy. I can protect you."

I inched back slightly, my black eyes meeting his. "I can trust you in exchange for your protection." My voice held a vulnerable aspect to it, low but trembling with emotion. "This dark world won't protect me. These buildings don't shield me when the rain comes down, for I don't belong in them. I don't deserve their protection. Yet, a stranger, one with no ties to me, is willing to protect me. A girl who could be playing him this entire time."

A sinister smile crept onto my red lips. I noticed his amusement at first, his mind taking in my words like I was a child. When I didn't move or say a word, his smile turned upside down.

"What?"

"This world is a cruel one. To find one person who will love and protect you is like finding a needle in an endless layer of muck, debris, and lies.

Oh, the lies people will feed to others to gain the trust they desperately need. You need my trust, but only until I'm in the hands of your boss to use and abuse while the money runs into your bank account. Just like all the other girls you've sold."

His eyes widened, but an eerie giggle hovered in the air, particularly on his left side.

"Lies and deceit."

The man slowly looked to his left, where my exact copy stood behind him, her lips right next to his ear. His body grew rigid, frozen from his acknowledgment of both of us.

"Now, Professor A. Roland. You have five seconds to tell me why you're trying to catch a Tracker like me."

"Y-you're a Tracker?" he stuttered with fear, making Shadow Jade giggle.

"Idiot. Idiot," she sang joyously.

"You're right, Shadow twin. This guy is an idiot. You followed me this whole time, but didn't do your research? What would possibly make me so valuable, hmm?" My finger trailed down the side of his face. "I think we both know my body isn't what appeals to you."

"I'm not supposed to tell you why," he whispered, voice shaking.

"We know," Shadow Jade and I said in unison.

Turning around, I flicked my hair and looked over my shoulder, taking in every detail of this man before me.

"It sucks that it's too late now."

"What? Too late. Wait. You're not going to kill me, right? I...I have information."

"Just because one has information doesn't make them any more valuable than a piece of shit." My flat tone had him trembling.

He wasn't paying attention to Shadow Jade, who was looking less like me and more like her true shadow form. Her purple glowing eyes had taken over, but she remained behind the man, who didn't dare look back.

"Besides. You just told me you're not supposed to tell me why."

"I-I was just joking," he laughed nervously. "There are rumors that a girl with black and white hair carries the eight elements. Been on the run for years and there's a hefty reward for anyone who brings her to the Black Market."

"Intriguing. The Black Market is a million-dollar underground industry with multiple sellers and bidders. If I was that particular 'girl' you're referring to — which is pretty preposterous, because I'm a woman, to begin with — who would you be delivering me to? The Black Market square?"

I watched him gulp and I turned around, crossing my arms as I began to laugh. "Ah. Professor. You really think I'm stupid." I lost all emotion as I glared at him.

"No. I-I don't. I swear that's the truth." He put his hands up defensively, shaking them to support his claim. "I-I never said you were stupid."

"Of course not." I smiled. "Or you'd be dead by now."

He fell to his knees, his hands in a begging position as he bowed his head.

"Please, don't kill me. I'm only the messenger. I had no clue you were a Tracker. I'm listening to orders."

"Indeed you are." I sighed dramatically, pinching my nose. "Well, Professor, I have to be on my way. Though my dad is on vacation, I still have to follow my dreadful curfew."

"Curfew?"

"I know, right?! I'm eighteen and I have to follow curfew. Sucks really, but I can see why my dad does it." I gave him a happy smile while I tilted my head. "To make sure I don't have to deal with lying assholes like you."

"I wasn't lying!" he argued, attempting to get up. Instead, he fell to the ground, two black tendrils wrapping around his ankles.

He looked back in horror, his eyes growing wide as he saw Shadow Jade standing next to me in her pure black form. His jaw dropped, looking between the two of us.

"Kill. Kill. Kill?" Shadow Jade looked at me, her mouth turned up in a wide smile that showed her pure white, sharp teeth.

"Hmm. I'm not sure, Shadow Jade. Maybe before that, we can prove to Professor Roland that he's a liar." I clapped my hands.

"I'm not...I swear on my mother's grave!"

"Bad move, my friend. Your mother would not be happy hearing that from you, but you'll be meeting her very shortly. She can tell you what she thinks about your behavior herself."

He tried to fight the tendrils, only adding to his misery as two more burst from the ground and wrapped around his wrists, forcing him down to the ground.

With a sigh, I looked at Shadow Jade. "Want to reveal what we know?"

Shadow Jade squealed, skipping up to Professor Roland, who lifted his head up to look at her in shock.

Clearing her throat, Shadow Jade stood up straight and put her hand on her chest like she was about to sing the national anthem.

"Professor A. Roland. Thirty-nine, male. Works for Leonardo Denzel, who is the leader of the mafia and currently on the Tracker Hive list of top criminals in this area. Purpose of Professor Roland's interference is to kidnap the targeted girl, bring her in for experimentation, and sell her to Leonardo in exchange for a clean slate for all his crimes in the last ten years. He also had the intention of conducting forced sexual intercourse."

Professor Roland was speechless, his gaze slowly moving from Shadow Jade to me. I stroked my chin in thought.

"Hmm. When you talk like that, you sound exactly like me," I muttered.

"Me!" Shadow Jade declared, her childlike responses back. "Kill now?"

"H-How?! What the fuck are you?!"

"Me or her?" I asked, pointing to Shadow Jade, who blinked her purple glowing eyes innocently.

"Me?"

"N-no! Dammit, how did you read my mind?"

"There are common spells for that, but it's child's play for the element of darkness. If you'd done your research, you would have known that."

He tried to speak but I answered his thought. "You think that's not possible? Well, those who can use the dark element well enough can send tiny little tendrils into the brain that deliver the host's thoughts back to the Shadow. And before you started following me, we bumped into each other at the bar by accident. That contact was all I needed for my Shadow to connect and listen in on every one of your thoughts. Pretty cool if you ask me. I'd be a brilliant CIA agent. No, FBI? Ah, right. I'm a Tracker! I almost forgot." I laughed, shaking my head.

"Kill?" Shadow Jade asked again, pouting her lips impatiently.

I sighed. "Yes, my Shadow. You may kill him now. You can even sing the Kill song all the way home. Just don't make a mess." I gave her permission.

"You can't kill me! I'm protected! I'm valuable! You'll regret this!"

I took two steps forward, Shadow Jade moving out of my way to give me a moment. I crouched down and stared into the man's eyes, noticing my black eyes began to turn a shocking red.

*As red as blood.*

"You know the one thing I regret?" I whispered. "Not killing the selfish men like you who destroyed everything I loved. That will always be my biggest regret. You, however, are nothing but a selfish man who feeds his fantasies by fucking little girls before selling their lives to the devils down under. Valuable? You weren't valuable here, and you surely won't be in the depths of the darkness you'll be in until your beating heart finally stops," I seethed.

With a cynical smile on my lips, I rose up, seeing the defeat in his eyes.

*He knew his end was here.*

Not a single sound left him as I turned around, knowing in three seconds, he'd be engulfed by my dark element.

A full minute passed, and the first roar of thunder thrummed through the dark sky.

"Right on time. Though, I'll be rained on by the time I can get an Uber."

Pulling out my phone, I pulled up the app. "Shadow? Are you done? I thought you were going to sing the rest of the way home?"

Another ten seconds went by before she finally replied.

***"All done!"*** Her voice had returned within my mind, telling me the task was complete. Looking back, the man was nowhere in sight. Not a speck of evidence on the ground he once laid upon.

"You're getting really good at this whole 'vanquishing into the darkness' thing," I complimented out loud. "The target's in the questioning room?"

***"Yes! Didn't kill,"*** Shadow Jade replied.

"They always believe us when we say that. I feel it's because you make me look crazy."

**"Me? Kill!"** she cheered, not really understanding what I was getting at.

"Yeah...you can sing now," I encouraged.

"*Kill. Kill. Kill,*" she began to sing happily.

As long as my dark element was pleased, the others stayed just as content within my body.

*Thank goodness they all don't have forms like my Shadow. That would be an identity crisis.*

Staring at my phone, I opened the Tracker app, quickly typing in my code, followed by a quick update.

"Professor is in custody. Confirmed Leonardo prime target," I mumbled. "How long will it take them to get that mafia guy, I wonder?"

"He's already caught."

A smirk formed on my lips as I looked up from my phone. "I better not be in trouble for missing curfew."

Alaric walked out from the shadows, his golden cane in his grasp. He wore another perfect suit, this time in maroon. His hair was slicked back, and today he wore silver glasses.

Even though he looked the same as he had ten years ago, his vision was beginning to fail him tremendously.

"Headquarters warned me that they sent you out late, which is annoying because I remember telling them not to send you."

"You're correct." I locked my phone and put it in my pocket. "Until three of our other agents showed up dead four hours ago."

He blinked at my statement and I shrugged. "You should know your beloved daughter doesn't take cases anymore unless they excite me or my Shadow."

"DAD!"

I rolled my eyes at my Shadow, who was back in the flesh, running to Alaric and hugging him. "Me! Did good! Kill!"

"Good evening, Shadow Jade. I was watching. You did very well capturing the target and sending him to the depths of the questioning room." Alaric smirked, giving me a mocking look while he hugged my Shadow back.

"Sometimes I wonder if you acknowledge that you're my dad or as competition seeing as you have a competitive side to yourself."

"I wasn't the slightest bit competitive with my comment."

"'Very well' by your standards means I had a flaw somewhere. That results in me thinking our tactic wasn't perfect, and I want to know why." I narrowed my eyes at him.

My shadow skipped back to me, wrapping her arms around my neck. "Not good?"

"Yes, Shadow. Alaric's praise is missing something," I replied.

"I wonder who taught you to be so perceptive," he muttered more to himself.

He tapped his cane to the ground, the wall next to us creating a portal of some sort. My eyes widened when ten men fell out of it onto the ground, all of them dead.

"These are the ten individuals who were ready to ambush you throughout your leisurely walk after your club inspection," he declared.

"Jade, look! Ugly!" Shadow Jade pointed to one of the guys we'd noticed at the club. I'm sure Shadow Jade only recalled him because he had far too many piercings to count and he was interested in buying us a drink.

I crossed my arms and tapped my chin. "See. I could have totally handled all of that. Except for that pierced guy. He freaks me out."

Alaric gave me a bored look.

"Ten missed guys is a slight oversight. We caught our stalker and I'm assuming you were the one who caught Leonardo. Problem solved, right before the storm," I pointed out.

"Bianca has to stop training you."

"No," I whined. "She's badass and understands my dark humor,"

"She's teaching you how to harness that tunnel vision of yours. What if I hadn't been told you were sent out without my confirmation?"

"Jade would have gotten it."

He arched an eyebrow at me. "Jade. Meaning you."

"Ah, no. Shadow Jade." I pointed to her as she rested her chin on my shoulder.

"Me?! Kill!" She beamed at our attention.

"See? She was more than ready."

"I really should ground you."

"Alaric! I'm eighteen. You can't ground me!"

"You could be twenty-seven and I'd still ground you," he noted. "And it's past curfew."

"You said it wouldn't count!" I gasped in horror.

"Curfew? Bad." Shadow Jade shook her head. "Kill!" She began to skip around us, singing the Kill song.

Alaric and I watched her, just as the droplets of rain began to fall from the dark, grey sky.

"Aww. I like this outfit," I mumbled, realizing in a minute we'd be soaked.

Shadow Jade stopped skipping, moving to stand next to Alaric. "Dad! Home?"

I returned my gaze to see Alaric's smile as he lifted his cane and shifted it into an umbrella large enough to fit the three of us.

"Yes, Shadow Jade. We should head home."

"What about the bodies?" I asked, pointing to the pile.

"Right. Forgot about those," he said. He flicked his free hand to the side, the pile of dead men flying right back into the wall. "They'll dispose of them later."

Shadow Jade looked my way. "Home!"

"I love how excited you are." I shook my head, but walked up to where they stood. "Why can't we just teleport back or something?" I asked Alaric, who offered his arm to my Shadow. She hugged it like she always had since the day we officially became Alaric's daughter.

"It's not family time if we just teleport home. Walking in the rain is more of a bonding experience," he replied, offering his other arm.

Hooking mine in his, I gave him a curious look. "As long as you don't lecture us, which is basically just me since Shadow Jade won't listen to you."

"Why is that?" Alaric curiously asked.

"She's gonna sing the Kill song until we get home," I admitted. "I promised."

"Ah." He nodded his head in understanding, like my words truly made sense. "Well, then. I'll lecture you two when we get home."

I rolled my eyes but smirked. "Gives me enough time to figure out a way to escape such a punishment."

"Kill. Kill. Kill!" Shadow Jade began to sing, her appearance shifting to match mine once again. "Kill?"

"Yes, my Shadow. You can sing all you want now. We're going home."

"Kill. Kill. Kill," she sang happily through her eerie giggles.

Alaric began to walk and we both followed his lead in unison, the three of us walking in the rain, under Alaric's golden umbrella.

*What a weird family we are, but...I'd never regret accepting Alaric's love.*

## ❧  4  ❧

### ACADEMY WHO?

"Y ou want me to do what?!"

"Shhhh."

I deliberately took my time as I turned my gaze to the tall, pink-haired woman to my left. She blinked her pink eyes while giving me an innocent smile.

"Keep your voice down." She pointed to the chair next to me. I looked to my Shadow, who was curled up hugging one of our many dolls and was fast asleep.

"Really, Bianca?" I muttered, looking back at her. She shrugged.

"What? You don't want to wake up your adorable Shadow," Bianca reasoned, walking from her spot near Alaric's desk to stand in front of the chair my Shadow was curled up in.

With a flick of her hands, a light pink blanket appeared out of nowhere, floating down to drape over my Shadow, who didn't even stir at its light weight.

"You tuck her in, but always kick me out off the couch when I fall asleep by accident," I voiced, crossing my arms as I narrowed my eyes accusingly at the woman.

"That's because you're either having a nightmare or causing everything else in the room to float but yourself," Bianca argued. "Besides, you're nowhere as cute as her. Look. So adorable."

"She looks exactly like me right now. Down to the damn cells," I argued.

Bianca thought about it. "Nah. She looks less likely to kill me than you do."

"Now you're making me want to change your mind about that."

"If you did, I'd be dead. It wouldn't prove your point to me."

"It would when your soul goes down to hell," I huffed.

"Now, Jade. How can you say such a thing?" she said dramatically, flipping her pink curls. "I wouldn't go straight to hell. I'd have a pit stop in purgatory to see if I can get some Christian Louboutins for the trip.

You know I must be all fashionable before meeting the devil himself. If I have no choice but to burn from my sins, I'll do it in a fashionable manner." She checked her fingernails. "And make sure I get rid of these hideous nails. Who encouraged me to get white nails?"

"Dad did," I reminded.

"Horrible decision. I'm nothing close to the holy color," Bianca admitted.

Alaric cleared his throat, catching our attention once more.

"Right." Bianca bobbed her head. "Going back to Jade attending the academy."

"Dad. I'm eighteen. Why do I need to attend an academy when I'm already a Tracker?" I questioned Alaric, who sat at his desk.

This was the lecture he'd been talking about. When we'd walked in and I saw Bianca, I knew something was up. I just never would have expected him to bring up this need for me to attend school for four years.

*FOUR YEARS!*

Just the start of his explanation put Shadow Jade straight to sleep. It worked better than all the lullabies he'd sing to us when we were younger and woke up from nightmares.

"Jade. I understand your shock with all of this,

but the Tracker Hive Academy would assist you in many ways. Think of it as a learning opportunity."

"A learning opportunity is being trained how to do that cool portal thing you do all the time," I offered. "That's a learning opportunity. Sending me off to some school for four years is slavery."

"It's not that bad," Bianca said, walking over to sit on the left side of Alaric's desk. "I'm one of the professors!"

"I guess that's not *so* bad," I huffed with an eye roll.

"But so is Tanner," she revealed with a sheepish smile.

"UGH!" I groaned at the name.

Bianca and Tanner were Alaric's "friends."

He liked to refer to them as the individuals who were forced to accompany him on missions if he wasn't approved to go solo. He'd tackle the assignment by himself while Bianca got Starbucks or Tanner read a book.

*It was basically babysitting, except for adults.*

Personally, I was fine with Bianca.

She'd taught me how to use each element, from the basics to the more difficult combination spells that required two or more elements at once.

I wasn't perfect at it, but the reason I loved Bianca was her unique way of teaching. She was supportive, almost like a mother would be to her daughter, and didn't mind my Shadow self joining in the training when she felt like it.

Tanner, on the other hand, was a complete jerk.

He was a cocky martial arts genius who trained me when he felt like it. He always followed rules down to the very detail and especially despised when people didn't follow the rules. He also hated my guts.

*Don't blame him. I hate following rules, after all.*

"See? I can't possibly attend now. Tanner would fail me for breathing."

Alaric arched an eyebrow at me. "I told him he can't fail you for being your usual self."

"Then I'm totally safe," I declared. "Since he can't fail me for being a little cynical. Does that give Shadow Jade a pass, too? Because he hates her as well."

Alaric took his glasses off, putting them on the desk. "Tanner has to abide by the regular grading rules of Tracker Hive Academy. He can't fail you because of a personal bias."

"Still doesn't explain why I have to attend." I sat down and crossed my right leg over my left. "Alaric. I'm already one of your top Trackers. Why do I need to attend an academy?"

"Jade. Everyone can learn and grow by taking a

few extra lessons. You may be one of our top Track-ers, but you're lacking in a few areas," he disclosed.

"No one is perfect. I think I do pretty well," I argued.

"Aside from your miscalculation from earlier," he offered.

"Aside from that. " I brushed away the ten-guy mishap. "I've been an amazing daughter."

Bianca laughed. "Oh, really? So can you explain why there's a Ferris Wheel in the backyard?"

My cheeks began to grow red as I looked back at Alaric, who looked confused.

"What?"

"Uh..." I began, watching Alaric push back his chair. I braced myself when he got up and moved to the window, pushing the curtains to the side to peer into the vast backyard of his mansion, which was on the same property as the school.

"Jade," Alaric groaned, letting go of the curtains to peer at me. "Why is there an actual Ferris Wheel in our backyard?"

"See, what happened was I'd just gotten back from an assignment, and the asshole I had to catch really did a Kung-Fu number on me, so I decided to drink that sweet stuff in the fridge. You know, the one in our other office that you tell me not to go into?" I began.

"Oh! Did you drink my strawberry Bailey's?" Bianca gasped.

"Is that what it is?" I pondered. "It did have strawberries on the bottle. It was super sweet but with some ice, it's not bad."

"Right! A bit of ice goes a long way. I knew you'd like something like that once you were allowed to drink," Bianca praised, looking excited that I'd tried it out.

Alaric cleared his throat, reminding us that I was technically in trouble.

"And?"

"I was getting to that. Anyway, I drank about two glasses of the strawberry stuff and I felt so much better. I had a really hot bath with my Shadow and we were thinking about how cool it would be to have our own Ferris Wheel! It would be like having our own carnival in the backyard. We could make some popcorn and go on the Ferris Wheel during the sunset and watch the view. We found that one online with the light-up function and free delivery and installation. We used your credit card, by the way, since you hid mine after that last shopping spree in London during the sale."

"Aerie was having a sale in London? When?" Bianca questioned, fully intrigued by that small detail.

"Three weeks ago. Everything was on sale. Shoes, clothes. Thongs! Can you believe their rhinestone thongs were 80% off?!"

"Shut up. Don't you dare tell me you didn't pick some up for me!"

"I did." I sat up with pride. "It's in Alaric's custody right now, but once he forgives me, I'll hand over the goods."

Bianca turned to Alaric, who looked completely annoyed. "Give the goods, Alaric."

"Did you completely ignore her explanation about buying a Ferris Wheel after getting drunk on alcohol that you stash in *my* fridge because you're too lazy to get your own?"

"I did," Bianca said with confidence. "Admit it. The backyard looks a little livelier. You know what? We should add a Merry-Go-Round, but instead of white horses, it should have black ones to empha-size the darkness in all of us." She said it so sweetly, it didn't sound depressing whatsoever.

"Bianca," Alaric groaned. "Do you mind giving me a moment with Jade, please?"

Bianca sighed. "All right." She got off the desk and gave me a wink. "I'll make sure your uniform is crisp for the morning."

*Aw, no.*

That meant there was no way out of this.

"Thanks, Bianca," I mumbled. She patted me on the shoulder when she walked past, heading out of Alaric's office and giving us the privacy I was sure he thought he needed to convince me.

When the door closed, Alaric didn't speak until Bianca's heels faded down the hall.

"Jade, the academy would be good for you," Alaric reasoned, walking back to his desk to sit down. I bit my lip and rose up, walking up to his desk.

"Alaric. I understand that the academy means a lot to you. You are the headmaster, after all," I began. "But you can't expect me to attend and not make everything go horribly wrong."

"You're making it sound as though you are cursed."

"You know I don't get along with anyone. We've gone through that multiple times over the years when you've tried to put me in one of those horrendous groups."

"Teams, Jade. Teams."

"Torturous groups filled with a bunch of incompetent individuals who are forced to come together and attempt to get along in a short, allotted time, all without killing one another, EVEN if you want to."

When Alaric simply stared at me in response, I

rolled my eyes. "They were never fond of Shadow Jade. That's basically rejecting me."

"Even though Shadow Jade tried to take them into the depths of darkness for fun?"

"They were all wimps trying to get out of the mission. It was a scare tactic," I defended. "Besides, that guy called her crazy. It hurt her feelings."

"Your feelings."

"No."

"You always say you two are the same person."

"Well, not in this case. We were two different people then."

"You love contradicting yourself."

"If it gets me out of going to your school. Which, let me guess, is filled with magic-hungry delinquents who all want to become elite Trackers like me."

"You sound like a cocky teenager." Alaric smirked, leaning back into his chair.

"Yes, but maybe that will help me fit in since you're forcing me to attend this school even though I've been a Tracker for ten years and trained by the best of the best. Going to school will be a walk in the park for four years. All for a piece of paper." I picked up a paper from his desk and waved it around.

"I want my diploma in a pink and gold frame," I said sarcastically.

"Jade, I need you to attend."

"Why?" I questioned, crossing my arms and inspecting him. "You never force me to do anything I don't want to without an underlying reason that you think I, of all people, can't handle."

He closed his eyes, pinching his nose as he took a deep inhale.

"They are forcing me to make you attend. I can't officially upgrade you to full Tracker status unless you do."

"Who?"

"The magic council."

"Those geezers who can't even shoot a fireball from their hands are telling you, Alaric Masters, well-known extraordinaire of all things wizardly in this entire city — not to mention the international deeds that you've done to save millions of people — to have your adopted daughter attend the very school where you are the headmaster," I summarized in one breath.

"Yes," he replied. "And how do you do that?"

"State the obvious? It's quite easy, I start by—"

"No. Say all of that in one breath," he interrupted.

"Oh. I do that when the words just flow

through my mind and out my mouth when points A, B, and C don't add up," I explained. "There MUST be a reason that they aren't telling you."

"I'm aware." He opened his eyes to look into mine.

"But you haven't figured it out yet...OR...you're trying to find who's pushing them to get me into school," I concluded.

"At least you absorbed my observation skills," he joked, trying to lighten the mood.

"Awww. Now you feel my dark humor." I grinned. Turning my attention to my shadow, I stared at her peaceful expression.

"Dad," I whispered. I shifted my gaze back to him, noticing his focus was solely on me. "I won't get along. You know I don't fit in." My voice was a whisper.

"I know, Jade," Alaric replied.

"You don't partner with anyone. Why do I have to go to an academy with other students?"

I knew his school was for the overly gifted. It was also filled with a bunch of stuck-up, rude, preppy individuals who preferred to fight one another instead of focusing on becoming a Tracker.

"I don't partner with anyone because I lost my teammates in one of my many international assignments and still deal with the after-effects from such a loss." His statement was filled with raw emotion, a mixture of sadness and regret that tugged at my heart.

The light element within me surged to help, to ease the pain it sensed within his beating heart, but I tamed it. I wasn't going to be the one to help him. That was a wound I couldn't heal with a touch of light magic.

*At least, that's what my mind concluded.*

"Sorry." I could at least apologize. That's what a real daughter would do. I had no intention of bringing something like that up.

He shook his head, pulling out from his chair to rise up. Walking around his desk, he moved to face me. I looked up to him, wishing there was a way out of this.

"Do I really have to go?"

"You know if I had a way of making you an official Tracker of the adult division, I would. You're overqualified to attend the school, but gaining more knowledge and interacting with your peers could be helpful, Jade."

"I won't make any friends."

"You don't know that."

"I'm weird, don't play well with others, always break the rules, and if a bitch calls me Jude instead of Jade I'm kicking some ass."

He raised an eyebrow at me, but I copied his look with my own.

"That's non-negotiable."

"Fine," he replied. "The students there aren't all from the best upbringing. They come from all over this city and range from rich to poor. Yes, they love to rank one another based off of power and skill, but those are qualities and traits you already carry."

"I only had a decent upbringing because a certain someone was willing to take my homeless ass in and didn't blow a fuse when my Shadow destroyed the bedroom," I reminded. "Not to mention the other twenty times I almost got arrested after being blamed for Shadow Jade's actions."

"Minor details." Alaric winked.

"Hah." I shook my head. "Again, my dark humor is way better."

"Jade." His voice was so low I almost missed it. Meeting his stern gaze, I realized he had something important to say. "I need you to be my eyes within the school walls until I can figure out what's going on or if my school has been infiltrated somehow."

I grinned. "See? If you asked like that I would have donned the ugly uniform and waltzed right in there."

"Why are you so complicated?"

"I think it's in my DNA," I cheered. "What am I looking for?"

"Suspicious activity."

"That's hard to pinpoint when half the students are crazy."

"You don't know that."

"Our house is five minutes from the main building, and some of the activity buildings are a minute from our gate. I've seen a few crazy students while you're away."

"Does that mean you're willing to attend?" he questioned.

Tapping my chin in thought, I pondered it. "With a few conditions."

"And she resorts to blackmail," he complained.

"You wouldn't want it any other way, admit it," I chimed.

He didn't agree, but I could see it in his eyes. "What are your demands?"

"First, you have to enroll my Shadow as my twin," I announced.

"Why?" he asked.

"This may be a school for the crazy gifted to become Trackers one day if they so choose, but I won't put a target on my head by showing off. Shadow Jade proves my dark element is the strongest. You know dark element users are hard to find and are twice as likely to be wanted in the Black Market," I acknowledged. "Someone like me combined with another dark magic user. The end result? Lethal destruction. Well...unless we kill each other first."

He looked displeased with my comment.

"Back to the point. Having Shadow Jade register makes it seem like she can harvest only the dark element and if she acts a little crazy, no one will question it. They'll look at her and say, 'Oh, she's a dark user? They're all a little cuckoo up there. Hahahaha.' See? Works out brilliantly."

"Fine," Alaric approved. "Next?"

"Can I have my credit card back?"

He crossed his arms over his chest. "Are you paying me back for that atrocity in the backyard?"

"It's not that bad," I gasped. "You have to at least try it with the flashing lights on," I encouraged.

"I can't believe I actually have a Ferris Wheel. Unbelievable," he mumbled. "All right. I'll give you your credit card back, but no online shopping unless it's an emergency. You have two wardrobes of clothes. You don't need more."

"Bu—"

"You wear a uniform for school."

"No casual days?" I exclaimed.

Another stern look.

"Fine. I'll be a good girl," I agreed with a pout.

"Anything else?" he asked.

I glanced over to Shadow Jade. "Shadow Jade wants a dark unicorn plushie doll."

"A...what?"

"Dark unicorn plushie doll. We saw it on a TV commercial. I think they only sell it in Denmark," I explained.

"Why Denmark?"

"It's where dark unicorns live," I bluntly replied. When I didn't add a humorous remark, he titled his head. "You're actually serious."

"Yup." I nodded once. "She wants one."

"Sure," Alaric gave in. "Not like she doesn't have two rooms full of dolls."

"Actually, one is filled with limited edition Beanie Babies. The OTHER room is for her stuffed dolls and animals. All color coordinated and stacked based on future value."

"Those things do not increase in value."

"You say that now, but in fifty years, those Beanie Babies are going to be worth thousands, if not millions. Don't ask for a bit of our fortune in the future," I proudly stated.

"Alright." He gave me a kind smile. "Does that mean you'll attend?"

"I agree to your terms and conditions. I'll sign the dotted line in the morning," I concluded.

Walking over to where Shadow Jade was sleeping, I knelt down and stroked her head a few times.

Those identical eyes opened up, their black orbs focused on me at first. "Sleep?"

"Yes. Time to sleep," I encouraged with a loving smile.

Shadow Jade rubbed her eyes and slowly nodded. "Sleep. Night."

Her body began to lose its corporeality, shifting to her dark form before fading completely, back into the depths of myself.

Rising up, I stretched out, feeling tired from the whole assignment from earlier. "I'm heading to bed."

"All right," Alaric replied.

Heading to the door, I stopped when a thought came to my mind.

"One more thing." I looked back at him. "The uniform needs to have red in it."

"What's with you and red?"

"It reminds me of the blood of my enemies," I said dramatically, followed by an evil laugh. He frowned and shook his head.

"God, you're going to be suspended before you're there a week."

"Maybe seventy-two hours. Give or take." I reached for the doorknob and took a deep breath. "I'll try," I whispered. "Just don't get mad if I can't get it right the first time around. I'm not going to go by the typical rule book."

"Thank you, Jade," Alaric said, knowing well that I was only agreeing to this because of him. He knew I'd be creating my own rules to whatever underlying game was happening here. "Your attendance means a lot to me."

I gave a little nod and slipped into the hall, closing the door lightly. With another sigh, I began to walk away, stopping when I reached one of the tall windows.

Peering up at the full moon, I bit my lip. Who would have thought I'd be attending Tracker Hive Academy?

*This is going to be a pain the ass.*

## 5

# TANNER THE ASSHOLE

"**OOF!**" I crashed into the blue mat, trying not to make another snarky remark.

*Or slur a bunch of swear words like it was a romantic language. The language of insults.*

"No snarky response this time?"

I responded with a long groan, looking at the upside-down image of Tanner, who was in full combat gear. "You're a jackass."

"Shouldn't be saying that to your future Professor." He looked beyond pleased that I was going to be at his mercy in the academic department.

*As if being at his mercy five days a week at four in the morning wasn't torture enough.*

"Dad said you can't fail me based on your bias!" I announced, sitting up seconds before his foot slammed into me.

Without skipping a beat, I was up in the air and landing on one of the ceiling lights. Looking down at Tanner, I stuck my tongue out. "So there!"

He ran his hand through his short silver hair before crossing his arms and giving me a tilt of his head.

"I'm seriously debating whether or not your immaturity is a disguise," he muttered. "Where's your Shadow?"

"She's organizing her Beanie Baby collection," I announced. "Dad's getting her a dark unicorn plush doll."

"She has two rooms full of dolls," Tanner argued, rolling his black eyes.

"Actually, it's—"

"Never mind," Tanner interrupted. "I don't want to hear your explanation of why Beanie Babies and dolls are different. I promise not to ask for any bit of your future fortune."

"Good. We're on the same page."

"I'm still failing you."

"Oh c'mon! You're not allowed to fail me out of hate!"

"You're correct," he replied and vanished.

I cursed, quickly hopping off the light I'd been balancing on, flipping my body to face the ceiling mid-fall, and raising my hands to create a fire shield a second before Tanner attacked me with a rock hammer.

"But I *can* fail you for being slow as fuck."

"You're not allowed to swear either!" I argued, stopping myself from being smashed into the ground with a wind spell that stopped him in the nick of time.

"Says who?" Tanner grunted, his hammer still attempting to squash me.

"Says the school policy!" I exclaimed, fighting his resistance. "And...ugh! Stop trying to Thor me to the ground!"

"Use your magic and not your running mouth!" he shouted, lifting his hammer up. I squeaked as his hammer swung into my side, sending me flying into the opposing wall.

I crashed into the wall, but managed to plant my feet against the cement, giving me the leverage as I pushed off it and aimed straight for Tanner.

He lifted his hammer in time for my attack; my flaming red fists created a sword out of solid rock, the two weapons colliding.

"My running mouth is what gets me out of the best jams!" I argued.

"It won't when you have to deal with the real world."

With a grunt, I added a burst of magic to my

defense, giving me the upper hand as I pushed him back. His feet skidded across the matted surface beneath us, and he stood his ground as I charged toward him.

"The real world? I think I've seen enough of this world's true colors," I voiced, my flaming rock sword crashing into his hammer.

It cracked but didn't break entirely, not that Tanner cared. He could easily make another one.

*He had a thing for hammers. All he needed was to learn how to use thunder and grow out his hair.*

"You've seen a portion of how cruel this world can be," he growled.

I grinned in return, feeling the trickling darkness begin to flood through me.

"The world I see is black and white. The only reason I acknowledge the colors are for the few individuals in my life who care for me," I whispered. "And the one who always makes it a living hell."

I pushed him back with ease, and he cursed when my shadow's scythe almost cut his arm off. He pushed off the ground to create some distance, but my Shadow and I jumped after him, ready to execute a tandem blow.

"JADE?!"

My wind magic kicked in, pausing my assault as

I floated in the air. Shadow Jade stalled as well, her shadow body beginning to fade as she assumed a form identical to mine, including my black combat gear.

Glancing down, I saw Bianca waving at us. "I made you and Shadow Jade cookies."

The three of us just stared down at her.

"What? Was I interrupting something important?" she asked with a wide smile.

"Cookies!" Shadow Jade cheered, flying down to where Bianca stood with the tray of freshly made cookies.

"Your Shadow is weak," Tanner grumbled, crossing his arms over his chest.

"She likes sweets. That doesn't make her weak," I argued, side-eyeing him. "Besides, you stopped, too."

"I wasn't referring to me stopping. I'm your enemy. You shouldn't be distracted."

"Even for cookies? Hm. That seems flawed," I countered. "Everyone likes cookies, including evil people."

"You realize how stupid that sounds?"

"Nope. Not in the slightest." The wind beneath me began to lessen, my wind element acknowlededging that I wasn't in danger anymore.

Lowering to the ground, I began to stretch

while Tanner hovered over me with a displeased expression. "You're going to get hurt at Tracker Hive if you fall for something as simple as cookies."

"I think I'll be just fine, but if I do find a man who can make an excellent batch of double chocolate cookies, I'll happily let you know."

"I don't care."

"I know," I replied. "But you'll still keep a watchful eye on me." I winked.

"Alaric spoils you."

"I've never disagreed with that in the ten years I've lived here," I called out, walking over to Bianca. My Shadow was sitting cross-legged on the floor, a cookie already in her grasp as she nibbled on it.

"Isn't it too early to be baking cookies, Bianca?" I questioned. "And good morning."

"Morning, Jade." Bianca offered the tray to me. "It's never too early for cookies. To be honest, Alaric was craving some yesterday."

I picked up two cookies before I reached out with my free hand to pat Shadow Jade's head.

"Did you finish organizing? You didn't need to appear," I acknowledged.

"Want to help! Yes, yes!"

"What does that even mean?" Tanner mumbled.

I looked over my shoulder to see him walking toward us.

"It means she did finish organizing and came to help me kick your ass since that's our prime goal in life at this moment," I explained, lowering to the floor.

Crossing my legs, I began to nibble on my cookie, a smile forming on my lips.

"Chocolate."

"Chocolate!" Shadow Jade copied.

"You two are hopeless," Tanner concluded.

We both stopped to look at him. "Hater," we said in unison.

"Tanner. Stop picking on them and have a cookie," Bianca encouraged.

"You spoil them," Tanner countered but took a cookie. "They're going to be shocked when they see how you act as a Professor."

"I doubt it." She shrugged. "Jade's reactions are the complete opposite of the norm. Knowing her, she'll simply nod and be excited to be tortured with work and assignments."

"Correct," I replied. "Are there a lot of assignments in your class, Bianca?" I asked.

"Not really. It's all about magic study with a few surprises. Think of it more like gym most of the time, but with elements in the mix," Bianca explained.

"Cookie?" Shadow Jade looked at Bianca, showing her empty hands. Bianca grinned and offered her the last two cookies.

She took both, offering one to me. "Cookie Me. Cookie You."

"Thanks, Shadow Jade," I replied sweetly, accepting her generous offer.

"How is your Shadow tagging along?" Tanner inquired. "You'll be a target automatically."

"She's my twin," I muttered, quickly chewing my piece of cookie delight before continuing. "I asked Dad to register her as a twin."

"She would have to attend all your classes," he pointed out.

"Ah," Bianca interrupted. "Not necessarily."

"Hmm?" I glanced in her direction. "What do you mean?"

"I have a pair of twins in my class. They don't always need to be there. As long as one twin is there, the other doesn't have to attend. Unless there's a scheduled exam involved."

"Why?" Tanner and I asked together before I diverted my gaze to him.

"Shouldn't you know this?"

"I don't teach twins," he grumbled. "Don't question me."

"Questioning your authenticity as a professor is a consequence for having me as your student."

Tanner muttered something under his breath, but I ignored it and focused on Bianca, who was smiling.

"Some twins are connected to the point that they share each other's thoughts. A rare quality, but more common to those with magic traits. Seeing as the students attending Tracker Hive are powerhouses in and of themselves, we don't require both twins to come to class unless they feel like it," Bianca concluded.

"See?" I said to Tanner. "We're cool."

"You don't have a twin," he pointed out.

"Thank goodness." I shrugged. "Imagine having two of me with the common mission of pissing you off. You'd wake us up at three in the morning to extend the torture."

"You're a Tracker but hate waking up early."

"Early to my biological clock is nine in the morning, and that's with with an added bonus of coffee," I said, standing up to stretch some more.

Shadow Jade was still nibbling on her cookie, her mind elsewhere.

*Or at least, that's what I felt within our connection.*

"Technically I can classify us as twins because she can read my emotions and thoughts. She's not entirely her own, because she's definitely a part of me. But she does have her own personality and some autonomy. Which is how twins are...kinda," I offered.

"It's too early to explain the details regarding twin anatomy," Tanner concluded.

"Asshole," I replied.

"I dare you to call me that in class."

"You don't need to. I will, but seeing as you challenged me to do so, I'll make it my daily mission to refer to you as Professor Asshole with every opportunity that arises," I declared.

Bianca sighed, shaking her head. "You out of all people should know Jade doesn't back out of challenges," she warned Tanner, who shrugged.

"Maybe if she says it enough times I can fail her."

"Your mission to fail me seems to be more important than training me to be a brilliant Tracker. I guess I'll remain at my excelled state until you change your mind."

"You are nowhere near excelled," Tanner argued.

"Compared to my peers, I'm rather confident in my Tracker skills. Particularly given the addition of my elemental advantage," I reasoned. "I'm sure Tracker Hive students are nowhere near as qualified."

"They're not nearly as cynical, depressing, and downright dangerous as you," he said.

"Your compliments will make me blush." I sweetly smiled.

"All you're doing is adding to her dark ego, Tanner," Bianca said. "Now you wonder why she does so well as a Tracker? Negatives are only turned to positives in her mind."

"Bingo," I replied with a shrug. "What am I supposed to expect from this school anyway? From my takeaway of all the times I've observed from afar, I can conclude that the students are either from super rich families, are actually power whores, or are just cocky as fuck. I'm an exception though, since I'm technically being forced to attend this school thanks to Papa Dearest," I elaborated.

Bianca and Tanner shared a look.

"Tracker Hive accepts individuals whose power levels or talents would be frowned upon at a typical school," Bianca revealed.

"Some don't know how to control their powers. Others are too calculative for common schools to handle their powers and properly train them," Tanner added.

"Therefore, Tracker Hive is filled with a bunch of rejected delinquents," I concluded.

When they didn't answer, my Shadow peered up at me.

"Fit in!" she cheered, lifting her hands up.

"Essentially," I replied to her with a pleased grin.

"God, you're weird," Tanner huffed. "Where did Alaric find you again?"

"In an alley." I winked, flicking my hair with pride. "Or, if you want the more glamorous story of how Alaric found my eight-year-old self: it was in a grimy alleyway that smelled and had blood spattered on the walls. Oh, and it was raining. Perfect movie effect if you ask me. I should have my own documentary. Jade Storm, Tracker Hive's only hope."

"This is why Alaric says not to feed her sugar." Tanner looked annoyed, walking over to his gym bag while he pulled off his drenched shirt.

"She's optimistic," Bianca complimented.

"I'm amazingly confident in my weird, conflicted personality and overflowing talent," I summarized. "But I still feel insulted for being forced to attend."

"It's not that bad," Bianca comforted.

"Why do rich people go there?" I asked. "Is it

one of those 'I'm rich but don't study so I bought myself admission with my parent's credit card' situations?"

"When she gets things right like that, it actually impresses me," Tanner admitted, putting on a dry white shirt.

"It's not like that," Bianca groaned, giving Tanner the side-eye. "They want to graduate from Tracker Hive."

"Ah," I replied with a nod. "And they found a loophole that allows them to simply pay to become a Tracker."

"You know Alaric wouldn't allow that," Bianca answered.

"Dad wouldn't fall for the petty machinations of the rich, but alas, we live in a society where money makes the world go round— not the power blessed to us from the person up high," I dramatically replied, raising my hands up in praise. "If Dad truly had a choice in the decision-making process of who would be accepted as a Tracker, I wouldn't being going to school."

Tanner walked back to us. "And he'd totally ignore the fact that she's almost gotten her partners killed due to her recklessness, or the reality that she ignores their very existence like they're a walking brick wall."

I kicked him in the back of his left calf, but he didn't budge. "Your kicks need more oomph in them," he whispered with a taunting grin. "Make sure you're on time for my class."

"Alright, Mr. Asshole," I replied, blinking my eyes innocently. "I'll be late every day."

"You never learn," Bianca sang while Tanner rolled his eyes and began to walk away.

"Training same time tomorrow. Bring your uniform. We're going straight to school after," he declared. Once he exited the room, I looked at Bianca.

"I still hate him."

"He wants the best for you." Bianca sweetly grinned. "Even if it's in a harsh, trainer kind of way."

"I still hate this idea of going to school. Does that mean I can't take assignments?" I inquired, walking over to my training bag to get my red water bottle.

"You should be able to, but your restrictions will remain. Until you officially graduate, you'll be receiving junior missions. Only when you're doing one for a school assignment will it be adult-level."

"Marvelous," I replied. "Babysitting delinquents will be fun. Maybe I'll make a friend. Or even meet a sexy hunk."

"You sound disappointed."

"The chances of me finding someone who can stand my dark-humor-crazed self is like locating another person like me or Alaric with all eight elements. Not saying it's impossible, but I'm stressing the probability of discovering such level of acceptance to be slim to non-existent," I concluded.

"There may not be someone exactly like you who carries all eight elements, but there are people who together as a team do. You'd fit in nicely somewhere there."

"Did you forget to acknowledge the level of jealousy and the dangers of students in the same competitive environment finding out I have such capabilities? Even six elements are a tough package to ignore. Me? I'll be the limited-edition candy apple on display for the world of students to fight over. If they don't try to eliminate me first."

"Your negative viewpoints are going to bring you down."

"My realistic viewpoints of how people use and abuse the power system and connections they have will ensure no one does the same thing to me. Been there, done that," I replied, taking a long gulp of my water. "Do I need to break down the child aid system and its inability to keep kids like me safe from selfish goons who want to buy kids for their own reasons?"

"Jade." Bianca's voice was soft. "I get it."

"Negativity is something to embrace. Everyone loves to be positive because that benefits them, while negativity doesn't. I'm not stupid enough to embrace one and not the other. When I did, I almost got sold on the Black Market."

Shadow Jade got up and walked over to me. She pointed to herself. "Negative?"

I stared at her for a second. "Positive," I replied, reaching out to pet her head. "Darkness is perceived as a negative trait filled with evil. If people accepted darkness as a trait like any other element, it wouldn't be perceived as something that brings an individual down," I lectured, which, in my honest opinion, felt like lecturing myself.

Shadow Jade and I had the same values. Even if she questioned herself for being a dark element that was considered bad in the outside world, she knew in our heart that I acknowledged the goodness within her.

"Positive." She smiled and hugged me. "Bath time."

"You're right, Shadow Jade. Let's go bathe," I concluded and looked at Bianca. "Anything else I need to know about this school? I think I got the rest of the welcoming vibe I'll receive."

Bianca frowned but didn't push on my comment. "You should be good. Your uniform is laid out on your bed to try on. You have to wear your blazer for your first day, but other than that and mandatory assemblies, it's not a requirement."

I nodded. "All right. Anything else?"

"Bullying is tolerated," she replied.

"Cool," I replied, beginning to make my way to the door with Shadow Jade, who stopped. I turned to her, noticing her confused look.

"Can bully?" She blinked.

Now that she mentioned it, I registered what Bianca had announced.

"What did you say?"

"Bullying is tolerated," she repeated.

"Is? As in I.S.? I can bully people?" Now *that* was something you didn't every day.

"Tracker Hive is about learning to defend yourself. I'm not saying professors won't interfere in certain things, but there's a level limit to how badly someone can bully another."

"Ah." I bobbed my head while Shadow Jade walked around me to rest her head on my shoulder.

"Kill. Kill. Kill," she began to sing.

Bianca gave her a sheepish smile. "Killing is over the bully limit, Shadow Jade."

"Oh," she replied. "Bully. Bully. Bully." She changed the word from her Kill song to Bully, but kept the same eerie tone and melody of her song.

"That's appealing," I replied. "Is there a reason aside from the self-defense angle? I feel anyone can learn how to take care of themselves without getting picked on."

"This school isn't for the faint hearted. You know the dark sides of a Tracker's role. If these students can't survive a few dirty tactics, they'll die on their first training assignment. It's necessary."

"I wasn't complaining." My amusement surrounding this new development had me smiling from ear to ear. "No problems with that at all."

"Jade," Bianca warned.

"What?"

"I know that look."

"What look?" I blinked innocently, but Shadow Jade began to giggle.

"The 'I'm about to wreck shit up in this school' look. Do not cause trouble on the first day." She had a stern look on her face.

"Dad gave me seventy-two hours."

"I give you twenty-four."

"Make it twelve." I laughed when she actually

appeared upset. "All right, all right. I'll be an immaculate student and avoid committing a single sin on my first day of school. Are you going to take pictures of me for Dad? You know he's going to make it into some huge portrait and hang it up."

"I'll make sure I take pictures. As long as you don't go all gothic on the makeup."

"A perfect black eyeshadow look does not make me gothic," I voiced.

"A pop of color, Jade." Her tone was giving me the 'no excuses' vibe.

"I'll find the perfect nude lipstick."

"Fine," she agreed. "And wear stockings."

"Why?"

"Your legs are distracting," she noted. "Don't want to be hit on."

"My legs were minding their own business when I was born into the world."

"You don't want attention."

"You're underestimating me again." I turned around to wink at her. "I LOVE attention. Especially from the opposite sex. Makes me want to—"

"Kill!" Shadow Jade interrupted.

"Sure," I replied. "At least I'd have the perfect alibi in court as to why I ended up cutting the victim's cock off."

"This is going to go horribly wrong," Bianca whined.

"Good," I giggled. "Maybe it'll make whoever suggested this in the first place regret thinking I'd be a good candidate. Tracker Hive Academy, here I come," I sang.

*This is going to be a joyous time of chaos.*

## ᔰ 6 ᔱ

## TRACKER HIVE ACADEMY

"Jade Masters. If you can sit here for a moment while we review your paperwork."

I nodded, still trying to stay awake.

*Who in heaven's name almighty decided that school should start at seven in the morning? Why? What are we possibly learning that is valuable enough to be drilled into our heads at this time?*

Even my Shadow was asleep, only proving my point of how unnecessary this was. I'd have to do this for the next four years? Eight semesters. This definitely wasn't in the fine print of the agreement.

Glancing down at my plaid skirt, I stared at the red and navy blue design, attempting to count how many white lines were placed horizontally and vertically.

I'd gotten my wish for a special uniform, because mine was the only one with red integrated with it. Bianca had been down for it in the beginning but worried it would create another target on my head.

I, on the other hand, absolutely adored it. A little color in my uniform wasn't going to make me a target.

*My last name did.*

Originally, I was going to go with my Tracker name, Jade Storm, or my true birth name, but I was positive people knew Alaric had adopted a daughter. If I was going to attend the very school my dad was running, I might as well proudly wear his name and get that on a piece of paper.

*Which he'd frame in pink and gold. Wasn't backing down with that one.*

Secretly, I knew it made Alaric really happy. I always switched between calling him Alaric and Dad, but I could see the slight smile that formed on his lips and how his eyes twinkled at my acknowledgment that he was my father.

With the new life he'd given me, I hadn't rebelled at accepting him as my parent. Even with my "weirdness," which we figured was due to my growing dark element, he never put a halt to my odd behavior or remarks.

The individual I was today had been shaped by him giving me the freedom to grow and love myself. I'm sure others wouldn't have been the same saving grace, especially with my dark element outweighing the others.

If he wanted me to attend this school as his second pair of eyes, I would take it with a grain of salt and attempt to enjoy the torture.

*But this morning nonsense was already making me have some regrets.*

Pulling my red phone out of my pocket, I began to play a random game featuring a ninja who slices through enemies while trying to climb to the top of a never-ending tower.

It was a silly game, but it always kept my mind occupied. Shadow Jade liked it because she could sing the Kill song while I sliced the opposing ninjas. With her asleep, I had a peaceful mindset, giving my other elements a break to mellow within me.

My strongest elements currently were darkness, fire, and earth. I ranked my light element the weakest, but it was more so due to me not needing it very often.

Light magic required immense energy. Like a healing mage in a video game. A few uses of it and you were out of it, like passing out after having too much to drink.

Darkness never had that type of effect. It was the opposite. The more I used it, the stronger the addiction. I craved that energy like it was my favorite treat, but I knew how to tamp it down when it got too much.

*Others aren't that lucky.*

Having my darkness morph into Shadow Jade benefited me. It allowed me to use my dark element every day without necessarily destroying anything. It also gave my other elements the space to be worked on.

On my paperwork, we only listed five elements, leaving light, thunder, and ice out of it. Those were the ones I didn't use unless a situation demanded it.

Fire loved to come out when I fought and worked well with earth in creating my usual weapon of choice, a sword. My Shadow loved her scythe. Long story short, she saw a show with a little female reaper and began copying the girl.

*I was obsessed too, but then I began to watch dragon slayer shows.*

It benefitted us either way. Harnessing the usage of more than one weapon was an advantage rather than a flaw.

I checked the time and then peered around the office. I'd only been here for five minutes and I was itching to go against the person's command of staying here.

Getting up, I walked around the room, looking around the different awards and pictures of graduated students.

Gazing over the introduction of Tracker Hive, I read it out loud.

"The Tracker Hive Academy is the state-of-the-art school dedicated to creating the highest standard of individuals who are ready to dive into the life of a Tracker. The role of a Tracker can be shaped in many ways, but all have a common goal. To protect, serve, and conquer the evil in the depths of the shadows and bring justice to the innocent. Tracker Hive Academy's mission is to create exceptional men and women who will one day lead the world to a brighter, safer future."

With a frown, I slid my phone into my blazer pocket.

"I bet Tanner wrote that bullshit." I shook my head. "If only they knew the real life of a Tracker."

"Hey, Meg. Isn't that the new student?"

I didn't turn around at the voice that distinctly acknowledged my presence.

*That's how they get you.*

"Never seen a girl with grey hair before," a higher pitched voice muttered.

*Grey hair? Are they blind? My hair is black with white strands. I even curled it today. Ah, this must be leading to bullying. What fun.*

I remained where I was, my hands in my blazer pockets as I continued to stare at the board filled with information.

"Hey, new kid."

I didn't answer, suddenly interested in a section of the board that talked about after-school activities.

*Football, Basketball, video...there's a club for video games? I wonder if they play RPG ones? Actually, do they have a dance class? Oh...they do! Heel dance...pole dancing. Hmm. They should combine those two together. Maybe I'll join a club. I'll let Shadow Jade join the videogame one. Beat all the students' butts at Mario Kart!*

"Hey!" the demanding voice shouted. It was loud enough to make me realize whoever it was stood behind me now, rather than in the hall.

Turning around, my eyes locked onto two girls. One was tall and very plump. I'd say she was chubby, but she had the height to carry it. I wasn't into her red hair and tan skin. They clashed.

She wore an angry expression on her face, unlike her friend. The other girl also had red hair, but it was curled and definitely went well with her overall look. She had pale skin, not a pimple or imperfection in sight. She was super skinny, about half of my slim, curvy size.

Arching an eyebrow, I waited for them to speak.

"Are you deaf or something?" the tanned girl mocked.

"She must be mute." The pale girl laughed.

"I'm neither," I replied. "I just hate replying to people who expect me to."

They both grimaced, but I cut to the chase. "What do you want?"

That must have thrown them off because they didn't answer right away. With a dramatic sigh, I tilted my head. "Nothing to say? You just shout at people and then go silent? Yet I'm the deaf-mute one."

Walking around them, I sat in one of the waiting chairs, crossing my legs as I leaned my head back against the wall.

"It's seven in the morning. If you guys have nothing to say, don't waste my time."

"Who the hell do you—" the tanned girl started, but I interrupted, opening my eyes that I figured were shifting in color.

"Jade Masters, that's who. You got a problem with me, keep it to yourself. Unless you want my brand new black heels up your ass."

They were both stunned by my combative

response, and I stood back up, walking to stand before them.

"I'll warn you now. I don't follow the rules, and if you need clarification of exactly who I am, do some research on your headmaster. Now, you two can scurry along to class and hope I'm not a part of it." I smiled, glancing between the two of them.

"Kill, Kill, Kill."

The three of us looked to the door, hearing the melodic sound. In seconds, Shadow Jade arrived. She glanced my way, slowly taking in the two girls before she skipped over to me, wrapping her arms around my neck.

"Kill?" she asked innocently.

"Morning...Spade, my adorable twin. Nope. You can't kill them. I think it's against the school policy. Maybe?"

"Not kill?" She looked at the two of them, and I noticed their confusion but also the hint of fear. It didn't take a genius to sense that.

"You're right, Ms. Masters."

I looked back to the door to see Bianca leaning against the door frame, her arms crossed over her chest. She was in a tight black dress with a black and blue blazer that rested on her shoulders. Her pink hair was up in the perfect bun and she wore black glasses. Aside from her hair and eyes, the only pop of color was her dark red lips.

"There is a section on when you can and can't kill a student. Since you've just arrived, those do not apply until I read them to you in a few short minutes. Do you have some business to take care of? I can always come back."

Turning my attention back to the two girls, I noticed how pale their faces became, realizing their very poor mistake.

*So tempting.*

"Kill?" Shadow Jade asked. I giggled and lifted my hand to pet Shadow Jade's head. "No, Spade. We'll be good students today. I mean, we're not good at following rules anyway, but seeing as they don't apply to us as of now, it seems pretty pointless to commit the deed and not enjoy the thrill of doing something wrong. Maybe tomorrow?"

"Boo," she pouted her lips but returned to singing as her attention moved from the girls to notice board. "Kill tomorrow. Kill tomorrow."

I loved watching the girls visibly gulp.

"All right. Emma? Heather? Do you need something from the office?"

"No, Professor Sky," they said quickly, shaking their heads to prove their point.

"Then get to class," Bianca stressed.

They rushed out of the room and Bianca walked in just as the secretary came out from an office with my papers.

"Oh. Professor Sky. Glad you're here. Do you mind admitting Ms. Masters? I have to cover Office B for a moment," she asked.

"Certainly." Bianca smiled.

The secretary noticed Shadow Jade, who was still singing quietly to herself.

"Um..." She glanced at both of us. I giggled. "That's my twin, Spade Shadow Masters. It was in the box beneath my info. Everyone assumes it's my birth name since I'm adopted," I explained.

"Right, my apologies." She bowed her head slightly.

"No hurt feelings. It happens," I assured her. She gave the papers to Bianca and with one last smile, she headed out. Bianca closed the door and then turned her attention to me.

"Spade?"

"Just be proud I handled the situation without killing anyone. I think this calls for a celebration," I complimented my own actions. "And the name was all I could think of. Shadow Jade likes it."

Shadow Jade looked to us, responding to my call. "Me? Spade!" She grinned happily.

"See?"

"You could call her a tree and she'd be happy," Bianca countered.

"Not wrong, but Spade's cooler."

Bianca sighed, pulling off her glasses. "It's too early."

"You're telling me. Maybe I'll get a coffee."

"Please don't," Bianca muttered. "You have more than enough energy. I don't need Shadow... Spade to be bouncing off the walls. I already had to stop her from hugging Alaric in the hall."

"Oops." I tried to imagine how that unfolded. "Did she squeal Daddy before or after you stopped her?"

"Neither. I was able to divert her attention with a cookie."

"Where's mine?" I pouted.

Bianca smirked. "Let's go inside the office and finalize your acceptance, Ms. Masters. Then you'll earn a cookie."

"No fair," I whined. "I was good already."

"It hasn't been twelve hours yet."

"At least fifteen minutes have gone by. What's another eleven and a half hours?"

Bianca gave me a pleased smile, walking over to one of the empty offices and gesturing for me and Shadow Jade to enter.

"Let's get this over with," she declared.

*Why do I have a feeling this ain't ending well?*

"Can't I just call you Bianca?" I questioned.

"Not during school hours. I have to keep up my image or people will think I'm someone they can walk over," Bianca noted.

"Spade," I called out. Shadow Jade paused in her skipping movement, waiting for us to catch up.

"She learns quickly," Bianca admitted.

"Yes, but now I don't know if I like Spade," I admitted. "I kinda prefer her Shadow Jade name."

"You're so indecisive." Bianca shook her head. "You're lucky Tanner isn't giving you a tour."

"He would have signed the papers to my acceptance and then expelled me," I concluded.

"He would not."

"You know he would if Alaric didn't have a say," I argued.

We looked at my Shadow as she stood there patiently. "Let's go back to Shadow Jade. It's easier."

She nodded her head once. "Okay."

I reached out and stroked her head. It was a habit we'd kept up with for many years, and to my Shadow, it was a form of praise.

Spinning around, she went back to skipping along the stone path, and we carried on with my school tour.

"There are four main topics the curriculum focuses on during each semester. There's the basic knowledge component, one that I see you having no problem with. The second is based on elemental mastery. The third is element manipulation, and finally, the fourth is based on Tracker simulation. That class is similar to gym but conducts situational assessments of assignments you would face as a Tracker," Bianca explained.

"Essentially everything I already know. Easy," I summarized, watching Shadow Jade, who stopped skipping and was currently looking at one of the many paintings hung on the cement walls.

Stopping for a moment, I turned to face Bianca. "If it's four topics, why is school five days a week?"

"Throughout the semester, each week will focus on a different class. Week one will be Tracker Knowledge Analysis, week two's focus is Elemental

Mastery. Week three is Elemental Manipulation and week four is Tracker Simulation. It will go in that order, for sixteen weeks. Then there's winter break, and similar classes but at a more advanced stage. There are four final exams."

"No midterm?"

"Only if we deem it necessary. Those who are failing or doing poorly will have to take a mandatory midterm. I'm going to assume that won't be a problem for you."

"Shouldn't. Unless all these classes start ridiculously early," I grumbled.

"You are not a morning person."

"Neither are you, but if you gave me a bit of your coffee, I wouldn't struggle."

"We both know there's more than just coffee in my morning beverage."

"I do, but that acknowledgment came from you, not me," I teased.

"You love when people fall for your word games."

"It's a habit that appeases my boredom. Or I think far too much for my own good," I confessed. "Sixteen weeks, five days of the same class per week. Not bad. Weekends off since I won't do my homework."

Bianca gave me a judgmental look, but I ignored it.

"Seems fair," I determined. "Those girls from earlier. Is that what you consider bullying, because it was pathetic. A disappointment, actually."

"I'm not even surprised that you'd see it that way."

"Aw. I love when I don't surprise you." I laughed.

"To answer your question, yup. That was an early attempt to make you cave to their demands. Others fall prey to it, but most bullying isn't so boring and childish," Bianca disclosed. "Fights break out often."

"Fights, huh?" The word had me excited.

Shadow Jade caught my attention as she pointed to the painting she'd been staring at. "Like!"

"You like the painting?" I questioned. Shadow Jade was picky like me, but once she liked something, she really loved it.

Walking toward her, I slipped my hand into my pocket to take my phone out. "Want a picture with it?"

"Picture!" Shadow Jade jumped up and down.

"Seeing you so excited in this form makes me see how I look when I'm overly excited," I muttered. "Another weird sight."

We took a quick selfie, and I took a solo of Shadow Jade. I was sure she'd want it in her beanie room somewhere. Nodding silently to myself, I locked my phone and slipped it back into my pocket.

"All right. Let's finish thi—" I stopped, only for Shadow Jade to raise her hand before us protectively; the wall in front of us exploded and sent large and small rocks everywhere.

"Oh, my," Bianca voiced, but from her tone that somehow managed to reach us over the rumbling, she wasn't surprised.

When Shadow Jade deemed us safe, her body dissipated, forming into dark energy that wrapped around me protectively. I didn't feel threatened in the slightest, my eyes trailing the commotion that was happening.

"You fucking wimp. No one likes your nerd ass who thinks he's the smartest in the room. It's about time someone ripped those eyes out of your sockets and showed you what being a Tracker is all about!"

Peering over to the boy on the ground, I took in his nerdy appearance. He definitely gave off those vibes, with curly ginger hair, freckles, big circular glasses, and a mini computer tucked protectively under his arm. He was curled on the ground and at the mercy of this 6'7" guy.

"I-I'm not afraid of you! Go ahead." His voice trembled, not in the least convincing as he shook uncontrollably. I could immediately tell his tall, buff opponent could control the earth element; the rocks and debris began to rise and gather behind him like bullets ready to fire at their target.

*"Picture gone..."*

I grimaced at Shadow Jade's sad voice. That was the one problem with her getting strong attachments quickly. If they got destroyed, she wasn't pleased.

*You want me to do something, don't you?*

*"Kill!"* she declared, beginning to sing.

The sound wasn't merry at all. It was like she was singing for revenge for her picture that was gone too soon.

*Thank goodness we don't have a boyfriend. I wouldn't want to deal with the consequences if we broke up.*

With my resolve clear, I glanced at Bianca, who was currently checking out her nails.

"Aren't you going to interfere?"

She looked at me, but I noticed the change in her attitude as a wide, mischievous smile cloaked her lips. "They're adults. Let them get at it. We'll finish your tour once the cleaners come fix the mess."

Not waiting for my reply, she turned around and

walked away, the sound of her heels fading away as she turned the corner.

"Polar opposite of her usual self. Cool," I admitted out loud, bobbing my head in approval. "Guess she won't mind me interfering," I concluded.

Paying attention to the crumbled wall, I noticed the students all peering in excitement at what was about to happen. I also noticed that the teacher was Tanner.

When our eyes locked, I couldn't help but grin, noticing the irritation flood his eyes. I bet he was mentally cursing to himself, knowing I was about to intervene.

*Time to help the nerd boy and gain some enemies.*

***"Picture! Kill!"***

*Right, right. Get revenge for your picture.*

With my hands in my pockets, I practically skipped over to the nerd, whose orange eyes met mine. He appeared surprised to see me, having not noticed me prior to this moment.

Standing between him and the oversized dude, I crouched down to get a better look at him.

"Have to admit, you do look pretty smart," I noted. "What's your main element?"

"Uh..." He stared at me for two blinks. "Fire."

"You're pretty weak for a fire user," I confessed,

quickly assessing him. My fire element could barely pick up a spark in him. He'd be squished by this dude in a second.

"I-I'm working on it. That's why I'm here," he stuttered.

"Oh." I rose back up. "In that case, guess you can't die. How disappointing."

"Who are you?" the guy asked.

"Jade. What's up?" I lifted my head in greeting.

"Shouldn't you get out of the way?"

"What's your name?" I asked, ignoring his question. I wasn't stupid. I was fully aware of and purposely ignoring the giant behind me.

"C-Calvin," he replied nervously, his eyes darting back and forth.

"Nerdy name, but decent enough. Calvin, today's your lucky day. I'm in an energy spending mood. Plus, I'm exacting revenge at the moment."

"Revenge? For what?"

"The painting," I answered, turning to face the tall guy. I leaned over to one side, pointing to the exact place where the picture was. "There was a picture right there. I really liked it. Now it's destroyed."

"Uh. That's the third time it has been destroyed," Calvin admitted. "They have a few spares. This happens commonly."

"Oh," I replied.

***"Oh,"*** Shadow Jade copied. ***"No kill."***

*You changed your mind quickly this time.*

"Is that so? Then I don't have anything to take revenge for. All right, see ya." I waved goodbye and began to walk in the direction that Bianca had gone, which I assumed was back to the office.

"W-wait! Where are you going?!"

I stopped and looked back at Calvin, who rushed over and hid behind me. "Y-You have to protect me!"

"Why?" I bluntly asked. "You're a guy. Do it yourself."

"Weren't you going to be all heroic and save me?"

"No," I honestly replied. "I was just getting revenge for the painting. Who cares about you?"

He looked stunned by my response, but I was being honest here. He was no use to me now that Shadow Jade didn't care what happened.

Lifting my hand up, I stopped the rock that was aimed to slam into my head, slowly looking over to the guy who'd shot it at me.

"Who's this bitch?! You fucking interrupt me, grab all the spotlight, and now want to run away like a coward?!"

I twirled around on one leg and slipped my

hands back into my pockets, the rock falling to the ground.

"I already introduced myself. Are you deaf or do you have a non-existent attention span?" I questioned.

"Fucking cunt! I'll teach you a lesson for even interrupting me!"

I cracked my neck. "Professor Asshole," I called out to Tanner. Everyone turned their attention to him, causing his whole face to burn a bright red.

"Don't call me that, Ms. Masters," he snarled.

"But you responded," I acknowledged. "Aside from that minor detail, is that your classroom for today?"

"Yes," he replied.

"From my view, I don't think you can teach for the rest of the day," I concluded.

"Why not? I've taught with a broken wall before, Ms. Masters," he grumbled.

"That's not what I was referring to," I replied.

With one step I was standing next to the giant's left side, surprising him with my sudden movement.

"Wh—"

I personally felt bad for the guy, but the sudden spike of enjoyment that came from seeing his and the rest of the students' shock was enough for me to hip check him.

Half a second later he was crashing through the wall of the other side of the classroom, along with whomever was in his pathway. Only three students had fast enough reflexes to move out of the way on time.

"Oops? Guess class can't possibly continue under these conditions," I announced. "Anyone else have an issue with the nerd named Calvin?"

The crickets from the courtyard down the hall could be heard from here.

"That's a no? Cool." Looking at Tanner, I grinned. "It's too early for class, anyway."

Tanner groaned. "Ms. Masters. To the office. Now," he growled and looked at Calvin. "You as well, Calvin."

"B-But sure. I'm the victim here. Jade saved me!"

"I had no intention of saving you," I admitted, sliding my hands in my pockets yet again. "I just wanted to piss Professor Asshole off."

A few people snickered, while Calvin gawked at me. "Do you have some loose screws up there? He's the professor! He can fail you! Expel you!"

"I'm not sure. I've had a brain scan and it appeared pretty good to me. As for him being a professor, I couldn't care less. His job title means nothing to me. In fact, I've done a good deed. We can all go home." I complimented my own actions. "And he can't fail me."

I looked back into his raging eyes when I said it, twirling around to face the opposite direction.

With that, I began to walk away. "I'll be taking a nap in the office. See you, Professor Asshole."

**"Forty-five minutes!"** Shadow Jade cheered.

*Oh right. We were supposed to last twelve hours before causing trouble. Well...that failed. Maybe we can say it's that giant guy's fault.*

**"Broke picture! Kill."**

*Yup. Let's use that as an excuse.*

Turning the corner, I began to skip back, a little excited for what was to come.

*All eyes on me? Check. Time to start tracking down our button pusher.*

## THE TROUBLED FOUR

"Tanner is pissed off," Bianca concluded after she closed the office door.

I had to fight not to giggle, feeling complete accomplishment.

"Did you see the look on his face?" I emphasized. "I'm so glad Alaric's my dad. I swear, if it were Tanner he would have beat me right there and then."

Bianca walked over to the desk, sitting down in the black chair and crossing her legs. "You did that on purpose."

"I'm glad you're catching on and using your enhanced intelligence, unlike Tanner, who's spending all his hot air on whining to Alaric. I'm sure Dad knows what my intentions are," I voiced, relaxing in the seat. "Besides, that giant guy was a blockhead. If he hadn't tried to hit me with a rock, I wouldn't have ruined my "be good" streak."

"You have no intention of trying to fit in, do you?"

"I apparently have grey hair instead of black hair with white streaks. You really think I can fit in?" I presented. Bianca sighed and sat up, a firm look on her face.

I waited for her to lecture me, but there was a knock on the door a second later. "Professor Sky?"

"Yes?" Bianca answered in a monotone voice.

The secretary was the one to open the door, poking her head to look between us. "Sorry to interrupt, but the newly enrolled students are here. The Maxwells."

"Ah. I forgot they were arriving today. All right. Let me wrap this up. Can you retrieve Alaric for me? I might as well combine the rest of the tour with the new students and Ms. Masters. He'll only have to give his speech once."

"Certainly." The secretary bowed her head in understanding, closing the door once more. We both waited to hear another door close before we carried on with our conversation.

"More new students?" I questioned.

"It was a special request from Alaric," Bianca whispered.

"Why?"

"You'll see when you meet them. They'll like you."

I laughed. "Bianca. No one likes me."

"I like you."

"You're technically like a mom to me. That doesn't count," I whispered with a tiny smile. She rose up and walked over to sit on the desk, her gaze softening as she stared at me.

"I know this is going to be a weird change for you, and though you hide it well, I can tell you're worried."

"I'm that easy to read? Tanner never sees it," I huffed.

Bianca giggled. "Tanner notices. It just takes him a little longer to figure it out."

"The school itself isn't weird, but the students surely are. I did spot a few powerful ones, but Tanner's class was generally soft. What's with the nerd?"

"Calvin? He's a special case."

"How is he a fire user? The amount of magic in him is almost non-existent," I commented.

"It's hard to explain with so little time. We'll get into the details later, or I'm sure you'll find out soon enough." Bianca reached out and stroked my cheek. "I'm not sure what exactly you're thinking about when it comes to attending this school, but be careful. Alaric, Tanner, and I can't do as much in our roles here as we would at home."

"All right," I replied. "I'll try not to break too many rules at once."

"It's sad that your answer actually brings me relief." Bianca shook her head but looked extremely happy. "Let's get this tour over with so I can have another cup of coffee."

"Me too," I hinted.

"No."

"I tried," I voiced with amusement. "At least get more of that sweet stuff in Alaric's fridge? Please?"

"He'll kill me if you go on a drunk spending spree again."

"I'll be good!" I voiced. "Please?"

She sighed. "I spoil you."

"Because deep down you love my craziness," I hummed, rising up.

She opened her arms up and I smirked, giving her a quick hug. "Be careful and don't get into too much trouble."

"Yes, Mom," I playfully replied, but deep down I was happy to get a hug from her. Since I rarely showed these type of emotions, getting a hug or comforting gesture seemed rare to me.

"Let's go meet the other new students. Hopefully you'll avoid a lecture from Papa Dearest."

"Ugh. Not a lecture," I whined but headed for the door. Opening it first, I walked out and straight into someone. "Ow."

Opening my eyes, I noticed the muscled chest at my eye level. I slowly looked up into a pair of red eyes. They reminded me of mine when they shifted, an attribute common to my dark element.

Speaking of darkness, the very element within me flickered with desire. I was impressed Shadow Jade hadn't made a dramatic appearance due to how the element pounded within me. It wasn't the only one yearning for release; my light element that rarely surfaced began to creep into my limbs.

It left me confused, and I didn't attempt to hide it as I narrowed my eyes at the individual.

His eyes slowly returned to a solid black with a silver rim around the iris, reminding me of a ring of light shining in his eyes.

Both dark and light elements began to calm, but I immediately took in the male's features.

He was 6'4", clearly taller than my 5'9" height. His shoulder-length black hair, pale white skin, and smooth, light pink lips had me intrigued. His harsh jawline only accented his oval, clean-shaven face. He smiled just slightly, obviously enjoying my extended analysis of him, which everyone else would consider checking him out.

I mean, it wasn't like his hot appearance didn't deserve it. He had buff muscles, his biceps pushing against his white uniform shirt.

He had broad shoulders that made me want to delicately wrap my arms around his neck and pull him close. His chest was wide, and as I lowered my gaze I checked out his slim waist and built legs.

There was no way he was eighteen, and if he was, he looked nowhere near it, even in a school uniform.

*I wasn't complaining.*

He was someone I'd jump and fuck without a second thought. I was pretty sure that was my dark energy talking, but I wouldn't fight back too hard.

That's at least what I thought when his smile widened and showed me a dimple.

*White flag! Retreat! Retreat!*

I'd never been turned on like this by anyone. I've had my share of one-night stands, but those were spur-of-the-moment interludes to experience the hype regarding sex. They weren't with people I'd commit to, especially with the whole relationship emotion factor.

I struggled to sort out my emotions. I'd feel bad

for anyone attempting to deal with whatever went on with me on a daily basis.

"Like what you see?" His voice was as smooth as chocolate and there was something deeper there that was pushing all the right buttons.

*If I jump the new student, would that give Tanner a good excuse to get me expelled? It may be worth it.*

"Yup, but I'd like to avoid getting expelled for jumping a student," I responded.

I waited for him to be thrown off by my response like anyone else, but his smirk widened into a full smile.

Now that could make my heart stop and my panties wet all at once.

"Don't have to tell," he replied.

"True, but Professor Sky can hear us," I reminded, nudging my head slightly to the left. If it wasn't for Bianca's light sweet perfume, I would have surely forgotten she was even observing it all.

*I'm acting like I've never seen a guy in my life. Get your act together, Jade.*

"Too bad." He licked his bottom lip. "Would have enjoyed the ride. "

**"Jump him,"** Shadow Jade concluded.

*Oh no, you don't. Stay down.*

My grin widened to hide my true shock. "Maybe

next time." I walked around him, heading to the door.

"Jade, hold on," Bianca called out.

"Hmm?" I turned back while taking another step forward, instantly crashing into another person. "Why am I crashing into everyone?"

Looking up, I had to do a double take. The same guy I'd bumped into was now in front of me. "Either you're really good at using the wind element, or you just did a magic trick," I determined, but bit my lip when my wind and ice elements began to react.

*What the hell is going on?*

The guy was giving me a strange look. "Four elements?"

His voice was different, a slightly higher tone, though it wasn't so dissimilar that the average person would pick up on it.

"Excuse me?" I asked.

"Zackery," Bianca announced.

*His name is Zackery? Hmm. That doesn't match the dark mood from a second ago.*

"What? She's hot and tugging at my elements. I'm intrigued." Zackery smirked, a playfulness shooting through his eyes. That's when I noticed they went from black to an icy blue.

*Wait.*

"Hold on. You're not the hottie with the sexy voice." I pointed to him accusingly, and turned around to bump into someone else. "Who keeps entering my path?"

"I didn't think she'd turn around that fast," an extremely calm voice stated, the sound so soothingly rich I had to open my eyes and stare at the same guy again.

My water and earth elements were tugged forward, feeling the similar energy pulsing off this guy.

"Triplets?" I concluded, not having to look past him or behind me to realize all six of my elements were reacting.

"Six elements," the calm guy declared, and for a second his eyes flashed a teal blue.

"Eight."

I turned to my left and literally gawked, something I rarely got caught doing. My fire and thunder elements were now up and ready to fight for first in line.

*No fucking way. This can't be real.*

The guy I'd bumped into three other times stood there with his hands in his pockets. His eyes were shining orange-gold.

Taking a look in all four cardinal directions, I realized I was surrounded by hot, sexy quadruplets.

My body felt like it was on fire, all of my elements fighting to manifest. Biting my lip, I tried not to show how strongly this was affecting me, but I began to struggle, trying to calm my elements from their little power war.

"Zackery, Zion, Zeus, and Zeke." Bianca's voice was ice cold. "Turn it off, now."

The four of them frowned in unison, but the tugging sensation finally began to abate.

I took a deep inhale, letting it out slowly. My dark element took the longest, Shadow Jade still hyped up, but I knew where it was coming from, turning my attention to the guy I'd bumped into first.

"You're Zeke, aren't you?" I questioned.

"What makes you think that?" His smooth voice had that seductive, taunting tone to it.

"It's a sexy name. So is Zeus, but he looks scary over there," I answered.

I caught the calm one smirking, giving me the impression he was Zion.

There was a hearty laugh from behind me, pulling my attention to Zackery.

"Jeez, Zeus. If you laid off on the scowl, we'd be able to blend in a lot better. Meet a random girl and she's able to identify us like we're wearing name tags."

"Fuck off," Zeus grumbled. "Only because she apparently carries all the elements."

"Isn't that rare?" Zackery questioned, walking around me. "My elements never react like that. I almost forgot we were at school."

"It would be nice if I knew who the hell you four are before you start asking twenty-one questions while checking me out," I disclosed.

"From the girl who was checking Zeke out for a full two minutes."

"It was a minute and twenty-six seconds," I corrected, giving him a snarky smile. "And I'm allowed to check him out."

"You're allowed but we aren't?"

"Of course you aren't. It would be narcissism if you started checking out your quadruplet over there. Do that with yourself in the mirror."

Zackery covered his mouth, but his snickers were clearly audible.

Zion cleared his throat, hiding his amusement with his hand. Zeke was grinning, giving me a full display of his dimples.

*I have to jump this man. I need five minutes alone with him. I hope he's good in the bedroom with all that sexiness. Jeez, I'm falling hard for a stranger. Or, well...strangers? It's clearly only my elements acting up. Why am I reacting to them?*

Bianca cleared her throat. "Seeing as the five of you are new, you might as well introduce yourselves before we go on this tour. Maxwell quadruplets, you go first."

"They don't need to introduce themselves anymore. I got it. They can be called The Trouble Four," I declared.

"The Trouble Four?" Zion wondered. "Why?"

"I just met you and I can smell trouble around all four of you. Definitely off limits," I elaborated. "To be nice, Jade Masters. My twin is skipping around here somewhere," I introduced, making an excuse for Shadow Jade's absence.

She was present but was now acting shy as she secretly analyzed all of them slowly. If we were having weird reactions, we were most definitely going to figure out why.

"Twin?" Zeke sounded intrigued, but from the dark flicker in his eyes, I felt he'd already caught on to our secret somehow.

"Yup. You'll see her around," I announced. Turning my attention to Bianca, I gave her an innocent smile. "Can we finish this tour now?"

"Sure. Let's get started. You all can talk and walk." she clapped her hands. "Boys," her voice was stern again. "Keep your elements in check or I'll force you to."

"Yes, ma'am," they said in unison.

***"Trouble,"*** Shadow Jade mumbled.

*You're totally right, Shadow Jade. The four of them are trouble central, and I think we're caught right in the middle.*

## ❧ 9 ☙

## INVESTIGATE THE TROUBLED
## FOUR

"*Lick, Lick, Lick.*"

*Please don't tell me you're actually thinking of licking one of these men, and I know which one you're referring to.*

**"Intriguing."**

*That's your power talking. You're making me acknowledge I have hormones and emotions. Not the time to be doing it.*

I tuned back into Alaric's speech to the five of us. We stood before the gates of the school, getting an overview of the massive mansion-like structure.

It was all familiar to me, so I was far more focused on trying to figure out where these guys came from. Did they always exist? How could four identically perfect men just exist like this?

I'd been doing my best not to show my uneasiness around these guys, but I was mentally wishing for this to be done so I could go back home and try to find out every single detail about them.

*Which basically meant questioning Alaric myself.*

I'd managed to turn the spotlight on myself for one brief moment, but with the introduction of these four power-loaded beasts, I wasn't sure if I'd be the apple of everyone's eye anymore.

*And if I was, it would be out of jealousy that I was the only girl in our fivesome.*

Taking the tour together had lumped us up as a group within the minds of the students. If I actually knew more about these guys and their real purpose for being at this school, this opportunity could be a huge advantage.

However, I knew nothing but their names, how they made me admit that I was a female with feelings, and that they were making me imagine irrational, unrealistic situations in the bedroom rather than focusing on my purpose for being here.

They could be the very reason Alaric wanted me to attend and I was falling for whatever charm spell they had going on.

"Do you have any questions?" Alaric asked.

"Are you and Jade related?" Zackery asked.

We all looked at him as he shrugged. "What? It's a good question to ask."

"Yes, we're related," I answered for Alaric.

"You two look nothing alike," Zackery replied. Zion, who stood next to him, elbowed his arm.

"Ow!"

"Zackery's wondering which parent you got your good looks from," Zion said sweetly.

"Bold thoughts to have when my dad is right there." I winked.

"You definitely don't act like the average girl," Zackery mumbled.

"I'm not average." I crossed my arms. "See? My uniform has red in it. That makes me extra special."

"Why does it have red in it anyway?" Zackery asked. "I want red in our uniforms, too."

"Red is an ugly color," Zeus commented with a scowl.

"That's color prejudice," Zackery accused.

Zion and Zeke just watched their brothers argue, turning their attention to me.

"We like our element colors," Zion said with a tender smile.

"Makes sense to promote your respective shades," Zeke encouraged. "Makes me wonder if red is your favorite then."

"Red and pink. Gold isn't bad either. It depends on how I feel." I was trying to divert them from bringing up my element situation again.

They shouldn't have known about that from the get-go.

My mission to investigate the Trouble Four. *Maybe I'll threaten them later.*

"I have a question," Zeus announced, pulling our attention to him. "Do we need to attend all the classes? Our thought processes are connected. I don't see the need for all four of us to attend the same classes each week."

"Zeus has a point," Zeke supported, looking at Alaric and Bianca. "We can transfer information to one another. I don't see the need for us to go to each class unless it's a mandatory session."

"We did that at our high school. I went on Monday, Zeke Tuesday, Zion Wednesday, Zeus Thursday, and Friday was usually assemblies or other group sessions. Those were the only days we all attended," Zackery explained.

"Can you guys communicate with one another through thought?" I asked.

"Yes," the four of them announced.

"Doesn't that remove the privacy factor?" I questioned.

"We can decide what to share with one another," Zion replied.

"Do you share feelings as well?" I questioned.

"What do you mean?" Zackery asked.

I looked at him, thinking of what to do. *Or how to prove my train of thought.*

Zackery suddenly flinched, quickly taking two steps forward and looking behind him. "What the?!"

"Boo."

Shadow Jade had a wide grin on her face as she blinked innocently from where she stood. Her hands were in her pockets, replicating my current stance.

The only difference was her wide smile versus my bored expression.

"Who is that?" Zackery asked. "And did you just bite me?"

She giggled and skipped over to me, wrapping her arms around my neck as usual. "Me!"

"This is my twin. Just call her Shadow Jade," I introduced. "And she proved my point."

"You wanted to know if our connection includes pain," Zeus said as a fact.

"Correct," I replied. "Didn't think Shadow Jade would bite you though," I admitted.

"Lick!"

"No," I immediately replied, noticing Zeke's grin.

"You can lick me whenever."

"My dad is right there!" I groaned, but secretly I

liked the idea.

Shadow Jade giggled in reply, resting her head on my shoulder. "Daddy home?"

Alaric smiled in our direction. "Yes, you all can go home now. The tour is over. To answer whether the four of you can alternate in attendance, I have no objection to that idea. One individual can be assigned to a class. You've already been informed of the class schedule. You all must attend the final exam. Any other questions?"

"No," they replied. "Thank you."

"Weird," Shadow Jade announced, creeped out by their unison. She unlatched from me and walked over to Alaric. "Home!"

"Yes. We can go home." He gave her a tender smile. Shadow Jade looked back at me. "Home?"

"I'll go home in a little bit. You can go with Dad," I encouraged.

"Okay!" She wrapped her arm around Alaric's. "Kill. Kill. Kill."

"Is that your theme song, Shadow Jade?" Bianca questioned, giving her a concerned look.

"Kill song!" she cheered happily, tugging Alaric's arm.

"Have a pleasant evening, everyone," Alaric bid us farewell.

"Thank you, Headmaster," the brothers replied.

"Bye, Dad. See you later, Shadow Jade." They began to walk away, and Bianca clapped her hands. "You guys will all officially start tomorrow. I suggest you go check where your lockers and the locker rooms are to make sure your assigned numbers are correct. Jade? Can you show them where the change rooms are? I believe that's the only thing we missed."

"Sure," I replied, but mentally groaned.

*I don't want to be alone with these dudes.*

She grinned and fixed her glasses. "Perfect. Welcome to Tracker Hive Academy. I hope you all enjoy this semester and excel in your knowledge and magic potential."

We thanked her and watched her leave as well.

Once she was gone, I looked at the four men before me.

"Let's get this over with. I'm hungry," I announced. With my hands in my pockets, I began to walk away from the group.

Zackery was the first to catch up to my swift strides. "You walk fast."

"Thanks," I replied.

"That was my way of trying to make conversation," Zackery countered.

"I know," I replied. "Predictable and boring." I began to skip, wondering if he'd keep up.

He actually did, skipping to match my pace. I stopped and began to snicker. He raised an eyebrow at me.

"What?"

"I've never seen a guy skip before," I admitted. "You look funny."

"I thought you'd say I looked attractive," he mumbled in disappointment.

Someone laughed, and I looked back to see it was Zeus, which was unexpected. "You looked like a fucking llama," he roared.

"Attractive, my ass," Zeke chuckled.

Zion smiled at me, reaching where I currently stood. "In his mind, he thought he was all majestic looking and would sweep you off your feet. In reality, he looked like a big-ass guy trying to skip."

"That's why it was so funny." I giggled. "Are the rest of you going to skip?"

"Nah," they said together. "Seeing Zackery do it is enough torture for the day," Zeke replied.

"You guys suck!" Zackery huffed. "Picking the girl's side doesn't land you the girl."

"Figured." Zeus shrugged.

"From the guy who began to skip like we were on the brick road of Oz," Zion chuckled.

"Don't skip again. It only looks good when Jade does it," Zeke concluded. "Or her twin."

"Your twin seems like the polar opposite of you," Zackery commented. "No offense."

"None taken," I replied. "You don't know me well enough to confidently say that, though."

"Don't need to." Zeke winked at me. "My gut instinct tells me she's very different from you."

"Just like the persona you try to portray," Zeus added.

"Aww. Are you guys trying to figure me out?" I asked sweetly. "That's cute."

"Immune to pressure." Zion nodded. "I like her."

"I like me too," I replied and turned around, beginning to skip ahead. "Are we going to the change room or..."

My eyes narrowed as my earth magic triggered. My foot that landed on the ground was pushed back; a rock platform shot up a second before it was shattered by a ball of fire.

As I flipped in the air, my wind element activated next, wrapping around me protectively and blocking the shots of fire that tried to obliterate me.

*Who was picking a bone with me?*

My eyes began to scan the field, noticing the Troubled Four were watching from the grass. They looked confused but began to look around for the person targeting me.

Calling off the wind, I began to fall back toward the ground, but I bit my lip and swiftly turned my body to avoid the sharp shards of ice that shot past me, three of them slashing my arm.

Cursing in annoyance, I resummoned my wind element with a fierce force, creating a mini tornado in seconds that protected me.

I felt a presence behind me, but my body remained calm. Looking over my shoulder, I found Zeke chilling behind me.

Turning around to face him, I crossed my arms over my chest. "How did you get in here?"

"I jumped." He shrugged.

His eyes moved to my arm. "Didn't you just start today?"

"Yup," I replied, watching him as he reached out to take a closer look at my injured arm.

"Making enemies on your first day. Must be nice to be popular," he muttered. Lifting my arm slightly, he hovered his free hand over the injured area, which was beginning to bleed down my pale flesh and onto the ground.

"I can heal myself." I was a little irritated by his sudden affection. Light magic was the strongest but most energy-sucking element out of all eight.

*Why spend it on me, a girl he just met and who is now being targeted for no reason?*

"You're currently shielding yourself with a tornado while sending ice and fireballs out toward the three individuals who tried to take you down. I doubt you can juggle more than three elements at a time, but I will say I'm impressed with your control and perseverance." Even in his explanatory words, his voice still carried that seductiveness to it.

"Why do you talk like sex?" I questioned.

His hand began to glow a pinkish-white, but his black eyes locked onto mine, a smirk rising from the corner of his lip. "I talk like sex? Your terminology intrigues me."

"Your voice is like chocolate running over strawberries."

"I know what else would look delicious with chocolate running over it." He smirked.

"You're flirting with me," I confronted.

"Glad you notice and don't beat around the bush," he replied, his smirk widening to a smile. "Don't ignore what you're already feeling."

"Aside from the warmth your hand is producing while healing me, and the added wind happening around us, I'm unsure what you're referring to," I teased, but my body knew exactly what he was talking about.

The palpable tension between us was making me forget that someone was attacking us.

*Well...me.*

His hand moved away; the spot where I'd been scratched was healed to perfection. Taking a single step forward, he faced me. Our bodies were barely touching, but my mind was buzzing, struggling to concentrate on the elements I was wielding.

"What about now?"

*Don't fall for it...*

"Still don't know what yo—" He closed in, his face inches from mine as his eyes stared solely into mine. They were black with that silver rim, but as the seconds ticked, they began to shift to that dark blood color that matched mine when I used my dark energy.

"What about now, Jade?"

This man was going to kill me with his teasing, but I hated being the one on the receiving end.

*Doing was a lot more fun.*

That's exactly what I decided to do, closing the distance and kissing him firmly on the lips.

Neither of us closed our eyes, but he kissed me back immediately, not shocked that I'd definitely gone against the common norms and kissed him.

He brought me closer, wrapping those muscled

arms around me, and I felt like jelly in his protective embrace.

His lips were fierce, but full of passion while their softness grazed mine. He tasted delightful, and that energy between us clashed, wrapping around us like the tornado I was still managing to hold up.

Closing my eyes, I took a few seconds to enjoy the thrumming energy.

To feel the level of acceptance that engulfed my senses. His energy understood mine, and it was the weirdest but most satisfying feeling I'd experienced in all my years of intimacy.

This was far better than a one-night stand, and I was already forgetting what I'd been focused on doing a minute ago.

A moment of kissing in the middle of a chaotic battle with unknown enemies? Not something you'd see a hero in a comic book series do, but was I really a hero?

Nope. I did what I wanted, which included kissing Zeke Maxwell, whom I'd met less than three hours ago.

*Splendid. There goes the plan of investigating the Trouble Four.*

## FOUR AGAINST ONE

When our lips parted, I took advantage of the brief moment to breathe, opening my eyes to look into his playful, seductive ones.

They were a vivid red now, and on closer inspection, I could see tiny black and white orbs dancing around like sparks of energy.

"You kissed a girl you just met, yet your eyes are charged like you won the ultimate jackpot in this game called life," I purred, fully aware of the charge that single kiss had given me.

The tornado around me had grown stronger, and I was still multitasking by attacking whoever my enemy was outside of my windy protection.

*Was this why it was dangerous to put two people of darkness together?*

"Feels that way, though I can tell this connection is a tad dangerous," he quipped, but still kept me close. "I like the extra charge. Makes me wonder what would happen if we did more than just kiss."

"I'd love to test the possibilities, but I have a feeling our unidentified enemy doesn't plan to give us alone time. Also got to take into consideration we're still at school. Wouldn't want Papa Dearest to come back to find his daughter naked with a boy she just met." I winked.

"I have a feeling you don't care."

"Learning fast," I praised, leaning in to tug his bottom lip with my teeth while my eyes darkened with lust. "Maybe the change room later."

"Fine by me," he replied against my lips.

"Not fine by me!" Zackery emerged from our right, drawing our attention. His uniform had cuts in it, showing a good portion of his skin, especially his chest.

"Damn, Zackery. Can't keep your clothes on already?" I teased. "Not like I'm complaining."

"We're being ambushed by these three mega fat dudes because you embarrassed their brother in class!" Zackery pointed to me. Then he moved his accusing finger to Zeke. "And YOU! Why the hell are you making out with her while we're getting our asses kicked?!"

Zeke smirked. "If I participated, those three fat dudes would be dead by now. You know everyone likes saving the best for last. Figured I could have some enjoyable time with Jade."

"Stop making advances toward her," Zackery huffed.

"Why? You tried with your failed skipping moment. Let me have fun," Zeke mused.

Zackery rolled his eyes. "Do you want Zeus to call up a thunderbolt to strike some common sense into your lust-filled brain? Keep your cock in your pants and let's settle this combat stuff before we get into the dynamics of my rather awesome flirting game."

I lowered my gaze to Zeke's pants, noticing the bulge in them. "Hmmm. Didn't know your cock wasn't in your pants. You mean to say I missed it coming out to play?"

Zackery groaned, and Zeke began to chuckle. "God help me. I think I'm in love."

"Good." I giggled, moving out of his hold. "Let's see if you can keep my interest long enough. I'm known to get bored easily," I purred and snapped my fingers.

The tornado dissipated, revealing Zion and Zeus, who were riding a cloud platform, avoiding the incoming blasts from the three oversized men on the opposite side.

Their gazes landed on me at once, their scolding expressions growing darker with menace.

Crossing my arms, I skipped three steps forward, taking in the damage to a good portion of the grass.

"Now, now. Who do we have here? You do realize you'll have to pay for damages to this part of the school," I announced.

"From the girl who damaged the classroom earlier by sending OUR brother through the wall!" the middle dude declared. I was intrigued at how the fire element was strong enough to start tinting their skin color, reminding me of aliens.

*Was that why they were so huge? Maybe they had a lot of milk when they were young, so they could grow into 6'7" assholes. Wait...milk...isn't that for boobs? Hmm. I wonder.*

"Actually, just to correct you guys, your brother was the one who broke the wall of the classroom first. Therefore, he destroyed the property prior to me throwing him through the classroom in self-defense. He wouldn't have been a problem if he hadn't tried to throw a rock at me." I lifted my hands up to stretch, giving them an innocent look.

"You interfered!" the guy on the far right accused.

"My original thought was to exact revenge for the wonderful painting that got destroyed...again, but the nerd dude informed me that there were more replicas of its beauty in storage. I walked away after that, seconds before your brother threw a rock and declared his intention of 'picking a fight with me.'" I used my hands to make air quotes. "To make things worse, I'm an innocent new student who hasn't even started class yet. Do you think it's very smart to be fighting against me without collecting the facts?"

The three of them were shaking in anger, but they couldn't say anything.

"Ah. From your silence, I can safely assume your dumb brother came crying to you that I, a brand-new student, who just so happens to be the daughter of the headmaster, had apparently interrupted his fight, embarrassed him in front of his peers, and destroyed his honor? What a shame to be caught in a web of lies."

I lifted my hand to my side, slowly gesturing to the Maxwell brothers. "You know what's more embarrassing? Causing a fight with the other four new students who weren't even present during your brother's fuck-up. Makes him and the three of you look like douchebags, right?"

With a long sigh, I turned around. "Seeing as I've pointed out yours and your brother's flaws, why don't we go our separate ways? I'll finish off this tour by showing these guys where the change rooms and lockers are. You guys can go to the office and pay for the damages caused, and we can all pretend such madness never happened. Deal?"

Taking note of their ongoing silence, I grinned. "Awesome."

With my hands in my pockets, I began to skip away. "Let's go, Trouble Four."

"That's it?" I heard Zackery comment.

"I feel they're thrown off by Jade's personality," Zion admitted.

"Nope," Zeus grumbled.

"What do you mean, 'nope?'" Zackery asked.

I reached the entrance hall to the change rooms, stopping to wait for them to catch up while I listened to their conversation.

"They had no choice," Zeke elaborated.

"No choice?" Zion asked.

"When you have a nice, sharp ice sword pointing into your back and earth vines wrapped around your ankles, it would be rather foolish to try and pick a fight after 'talking' like civilized students," Zeke explained. "I'm impressed."

"Wait, hold on. What?" Zackery looked at me. "What did you do?"

"You think that whole tornado diversion was just for protection?" I questioned.

"Um...yes?" Zackery replied.

"You were shooting out power balls," Zion added.

"Distraction," Zeus acknowledged, moving up to stand in front of me. "With the earth element, you were tracking their every move above the surface while summoning those ice swords and keeping them hidden far up in the air where no one would look.

"When you snapped your fingers, you dispersed the tornado and powerball attacks you were sending all over the place, but you activated the vines to keep them in place and the ice swords gathered at their backs. You wouldn't see it if you were facing their fronts, but if you peered behind them, you would have noticed the ice swords embedded with light magic."

"If impaled by those swords, those guys would be on a nice light high for days," Zeke added. "And they would most likely forgive and forget about the whole ordeal in the first place."

"Wow." Zion nodded. "Smart."

"Doesn't that mean you basically used all the elements in one session?" Zackery questioned.

"Almost," I replied. "I did use the water in the air to create the ice swords at a faster pace."

"That means you really do have all eight elements and used them simultaneously!" Zackery accused.

"I never used my dark element," I noted.

"She has a point," Zion acknowledged.

"Me!"

I looked over my shoulder to see Shadow Jade skipping toward us from down the hall.

"Why is your twin back?" Zeus muttered.

"Maybe she missed her twin, Jade." Zeke grinned.

I looked at him, noticing the glint of merriment in them. He was in on my secret and was enjoying tugging his brothers along for the ride.

*Attractive quality. Bonus points.*

Shadow Jade hugged me. "Daddy and Bianca are on the field. They're helping the students out of the vine pit."

"Vine pit...oh, Jade's trap," Zackery concluded. "Wait. Did you trap them there?"

Shadow Jade and I exchanged a look, both of us

beginning to giggle. "We did no such thing," we said in unison.

"Guilty," the four of them replied. We smiled and began to walk down the hall. "Hurry up. I'm extra hungry now," I declared.

"Still think she's pretty cool," Zion determined.

"Or insane," Zackery huffed.

"At least she's powerful," Zeus concluded.

"I call dibs," Zeke determined.

"No," the other three replied.

Watching Shadow Jade skip ahead, I pondered how I would get through the first semester if these guys were attending. I'd have to take a long bath tonight with a black bath bomb to calm my mind.

*And hormones.*

*Let's get this change room tour over with.*

"THIS IS THE CHANGE ROOM. NOTHING MUCH TO see here. Showers are there. All lockers are magically enhanced. Use whichever element is your strongest to lock it. You can walk butt naked if you like, but don't drop any soap. People actually take that as a booty call," I explained, staring at my phone while I sat on the bench between two rows of lockers.

"Kill. Kill. Kill," Shadow Jade sang, inspecting the showers.

The four sexy Maxwell brothers were leaning against the lockers before me, listening to my chilled explanation.

"That's the end of this lovely tour that I humbly took you on. Any questions?"

"We should test you," Zeus declared.

I raised my head as I arched an eyebrow, glancing over to him. "Huh?"

"You've been able to tell who is who since you met us. That doesn't happen ever, but it could be due to your weird thinking process."

"Unique and talented thinking process. What exactly am I being tested for?"

The guys exchanged looks; Zeus and Zeke remained in their spots while Zion and Zackery walked behind me.

"We want you to join us."

"Join what? Is this going to be a cute cult gathering? How intriguing." I clapped my hands and raised my legs to cross them on the bench, sitting up a little taller.

"Why does she remind me of that girl from Suicide Squad?"

"The crazy one?" Zion clarified.

"Yup. Totally like that," Zackery concluded.

"Her actual name is Dr. Harleen Frances Quinzel, and I'm nowhere near her level of crazy," I elaborated. "I'm worse."

"Great," Zackery groaned.

Zeus clapped his hands, the lights switching off entirely.

"Night party!" Shadow Jade cheered. I mentally sighed but figured this was a good time for Shadow Jade to retreat. "Shadow Jade? Why don't you go check on Alaric?"

*I need you back here but can't let the others know.*

"Okay! Bye, bye." I heard her skip away. A light poked into the room when she opened the door, but it disappeared in an instant.

***"Kill time?"*** Her voice echoed in my mind, and her dark element seeped into my body while the rest began to settle in confidence, ready for whatever test these guys were trying to pull off.

*Not yet, but I'll keep you posted. You can go back to singing the Kill song.*

***"Kill. Kill. Kill!"***

"What are you guys planning?" I asked, putting my phone away. "And who said I wanted to join you?"

"We're going to test you and see if you're worth joining us on our mission here," Zeus declared.

"And we think you'd want to join us if you want answers."

"This doesn't sound like an amazing agreement. You're assuming you have the answers that I need, and I could easily find out why you're here, to begin with, if I really wanted to," I disclosed.

Looking at the ceiling, I thought about it out loud, "Four powerful brothers with the combined force of all eight elements waltz into Tracker Hive Academy out of the blue. No warning to anyone but the professors and headmaster. They join the same day that I, Jade Masters, and my twin sister do, and someone discovers my little secret on our first encounter. Why is that?"

Glancing down to stare into Zeus's eyes specifically, I gave him a playful smile.

"As a Tracker, I know things don't happen by coincidence." My voice was low and deadly. "Every decision made by a group of individuals, whether it be a team or a set of quadruplets, has a purpose. Looping me into it will either benefit you, or destroy you, but you four believe having me as an ally would aid you in your task."

He didn't answer, but I watched his Adam's apple go up and down, a sign of his nervousness.

"Did you know I hate change rooms?" I changed the subject. "I think you do, because

Alaric, Bianca, or god forbid, Tanner, would have told you," I declared. "Why would they tell you a weakness of mine, if they weren't trying to test me as well?"

With a blink, the four of them were gone from my sight, but I knew they were still in the same dark room as me. I giggled quietly.

"Did you want to know why I hate change rooms or is that a story for another day?" I asked the quiet air, knowing I wouldn't get a response immediately.

I felt the flow of hot breath tickling the right side of my neck, and a cool set of lips brushed against my skin and excited the darkness inside me.

"I'm curious," the monotone voice whispered in my ear, tugging my ear lobe lightly. I looked over my shoulder, my lips curling up as I felt one of the quad's presences.

"Hmm. Changing your speech to remove any hint of emotion. Is this game about determining who is testing me?" I inquired breathlessly, a pair of delicate lips pressed against my own.

The darkness in me felt satisfied, but there was a tug at the icy chill of my magic that caused me to smile. "If I didn't know better, I'd assume you were Zeke, but your lips are too soft, move too slowly with a hint of apprehension, and have a slight chill to them."

Even in the dark room, I could sense the person before me, not needing a speck of light to know who this was. "Zackery. I'm sure you're not as intrigued about my fear of change rooms as Zeke is, who is to my far left."

"Not bad," two voices said together.

"Is this going to continue to be a guessing game, or do I have to prove that I can take all four of you on without breaking a sweat?" I questioned.

I personally loved playing around, especially with cases like these where it was a four-against-one scenario, but my hunger was starting to make me impatient and I didn't think these guys deserved to deal with that side of me.

*Never play around with a girl who is in desperate need of some food.*

"You should be freaking out," the combined voices declared.

I sighed and snapped my fingers, a ring of floating flames wrapping around me and hovering in place. The illumination helped light the room just a little bit, revealing the guy's silhouettes, but it wasn't bright enough to allow me to see their true locations.

"Why? Did you guys think because I was in this

change room and in pure darkness that I would freak out?" I questioned. "Ah...that would make sense."

Rising to my feet, I stood on the bench, walking to the end and twirling around to walk to the other side slowly while outstretching my arms.

"Now that you gave me that information, it all makes sense," I concluded. "You four were sent by the Magic Council."

They were silent; my assumptions were right on. I could feel it.

"Considering that Bianca suggested I show you where the change rooms are, you guys must have asked prior to enrollment for a tour of those specifically. Sure, it's an important place when we need to change for physical education, but not a typical place to request a tour of. The only way to know about my weakness is to read about the incident that happened when I was twelve," I announced.

Shadow Jade appeared again, sitting on the top part of the lockers.

Locking my eyes onto hers, I could see her displeasure with the topic written all over her face, but I grinned, trying to cheer her up.

*She never was one to live in the past. You only did that if you wanted your dark energy to grow in the event of a battle.*

"I'd just finished an amazing assignment. Kicked a few older guys' butts, got them arrested, and called it a day by working out my remaining burst of energy at the gym. Alaric was fine with me doing my own thing, as long as I never caused trouble. One of my 'things' was working out at the gym in the busy city. I went really late at night, but it was a twenty-four-hour gym and had cameras. Nothing to worry about."

Looking at the ceiling, I closed my eyes. "I knew something was off the moment I walked into the change room, but I ignored it. Temporarily, of course. Even then, I was a peculiar individual who loved to be challenged. That moment was no different than facing a person in a one-on-one battle."

Lowering my head and opening my eyes, I stared at the many lines engraved into the bench.

"I got onto the bench, just as I am now, and asked the gentleman what he wanted with me. He said if I let him do whatever he wanted and didn't scream, he wouldn't hurt me. A simple threat, easy enough. It made me laugh because I found it hilarious. An older man thought I'd abide by his threats? I carried all the elements. I may have been tired, but I was ready to take him head-on before the proper authorities arrived."

I took a deep inhale, letting it out slowly.

"That's when things got interesting, to say the least. The lights flickered on and off and the air seemed non-existent. I struggled to breathe, and I had to fight the pressure that was trying to crush me. I screamed so loud, but no one could hear me. My voice was sealed into the air bubble this guy had put up. The lights went off, and the room got so cold. At one point, I actually thought I was going to die. I should have done what he wanted," I confessed.

Shadow Jade slipped off the lockers, landing on the bench and standing before me. I lifted my hand up and patted her head soothingly, assuring her that I was perfectly fine.

"It was the first time I'd experienced fear since I was eight years old. Pretty sad for a twelve-year-old girl to go through, but again, I wasn't your usual kid. The fear made me angry. I disliked being stuck in the situation with no adult to save me. It reminded me of all the other helpless situations I'd been in when I was homeless and not a single adult stopped and helped me. I was street scum, and even after Alaric adopted me, I still had that mentality drilled inside me."

Shadow Jade lifted her hand and patted my head, causing me to giggle.

"That night, in the bubble of silent chaos, I told myself I'd have to get myself out of another situation, and I did. I let my elements unleash and overcome the man who was doing his best to overpower me. Long story short, he was in a coma for six months and was arrested when he woke up. He was trying to capture me and sell me on the Black Market like many others had tried before him. It was written in my file that I had panic attacks and hallucinations. You know, the whole mental health, PTSD stuff that comes when you experience scary events that should never happen to begin with."

Shadow Jade hugged me, holding me tightly for ten seconds before she faded away, returning to her dark state inside me.

"I never updated the file when I got over my fear. After that situation happened, I forced myself to go to that very gym, at the same time, and sit on the very bench where it all happened. I'd ride through the panic attacks, silence my screams, and rock myself back and forth. I did that for about two years until it got easier. As you can see, I'm not affected by your attempt, though you're missing the wind, the pressure-sucking thing, to really get it right. Only the Council has the specifics of what happened, but I never mentioned the air pressure that silenced my screams, and that's why you guys assumed that bringing me to a change room and turning the lights off was all that would be needed to push me into a panic attack."

With a snap of my fingers, the lights fluttered back on, revealing the four guys who were so enthralled by my story they hadn't realized I'd exposed them.

"Aren't I an awesome storyteller?!" I clapped my hands in excitement.

The four of them blinked, and Zackery ruffled his hair. "That...wasn't what I expected."

"I don't think anything she does is close to the 'what to expect' department," Zion admitted.

"Hmph," Zeus muttered. Zeke walked over to the bench and jumped onto it. He faced me, his eyes scanning mine for a long moment.

"He wanted more than just to bring you in," he declared.

"You really overanalyze," I complimented.

"Jade," he whispered.

"You shouldn't show emotion for a person you barely know," I whispered. "It can get you into a tricky situation."

"You're not one to pull a tactic like that. I think I've gotten a good enough feel for you to guess that much," he defended.

I pouted my lips in disappointment. "No fun."

He grinned then, giving me a playful wink. "I'll play your game next time."

"The man in question worked with some organization. Never got the details because I was too young. Needless to say, he's dead. Got killed in jail for grabbing the soap."

"Eww," Zackery mumbled.

"How?" Zion wondered.

"Can't fit two cocks into an asshole," Zeus predicted.

"Let's NOT picture that image, thank you very much," Zeke concluded, bringing his attention back to me. "Sorry."

"Hmm? Why are you apologizing? Wasn't the purpose of this exercise to test me?" I asked, glancing at the others, who didn't hide their discomfort.

"Yes, but we weren't given the whole context of the situation. The file given to us said you froze up when in pitch black scenarios, especially in change rooms. There was no mention of panic attacks or hallucinations," Zeus explained, his usual stern tone missing.

"I figured." I bobbed my head in understanding. "Seems as though the Council is testing both of us. Or should I say a particular Council member, one who really doesn't want me attending this school."

"Why? You're Alaric's daughter," Zackery confronted.

"If you listened to my story, I did state I'd been on the streets. That meant I was homeless, and Alaric is my foster dad. He took me in when I was eight. Another important piece of information they should have told you before sending four Trackers here to pretend to be students."

"How...did you..." Zion trailed off, glancing at the others.

"I warned you guys that those with a strong dark element were perceptive. You all laughed at me," Zeke revealed.

The others glanced away, and even Zeus was staring anywhere other than where we stood on the bench.

"Adult division?" I asked.

Zeke nodded. "Yup."

"Alaric hired you?" I wasn't sure about this part, but it was the most likely possibility.

"We're Trackers from the district in the next city over. Our boss is well acquainted with Alaric and the two have noticed some fishy activity going on behind the scenes. Sending us directly to track down the culprit would be difficult, so enrolling us in the very school that was being targeted was the smartest move."

"Hmm." I slipped my hands into my pockets. "So...whose stupid idea was it to try and persuade me to join?" I inquired. "I'm positive it must have at least sounded brilliant at the time."

Everyone looked at Zackery, who began to blush. "Why is everyone looking at me?!"

"Let me guess. Your original idea was to observe me from afar during the next four weeks, see what my purpose was, and determine whether I was truly an ally or playing double agent. However, you thought it would be faster to confront me on the first day, having encouraged the others to do some research, and thus leading you to privately ask for more information on me. After reading the small bit of information, you informed Bianca before your arrival that you'd need to investigate the change rooms, thus the reason why she asked me to bring you here."

"W-well, it was smart wasn't it?! We found out the truth, even though we kind of lost our cover," Zackery argued. "Okay, maybe it was a stupid idea..."

I grinned, hopping off the bench. Zeke followed, the two of us turning to look at the others.

"Seeing as we're all technically on the same team, why don't we partner up then? You guys weren't a part of my plans, but you're fun to toy with."

"That sounds horrible," Zackery said.

"Bad idea," Zeus grumbled.

"Four Adult Trackers and a Junior Tracker," Zion summarized.

"Let's do it," Zeke approved.

"We didn't say that," the other three argued. Zeke shrugged. "You didn't say it with your lips, but I felt it." He tapped his chest.

"More like he's following his cock," Zeus snorted. "I'm going home."

"Wait for me," Zion called out. "Nice to meet you, Jade." His signature sweet grin returned, and he gave me a little wave before he followed Zeus out the door.

"Traitors! You guys sold me out like I was bait!" Zackery yelled out, then he looked back at me. "Glad we at least sorted this out. Have to admit, you're pretty cool in your own cynical way."

"Thanks." I beamed.

"Zeke, you're coming with me." Zackery gave him a look. Zeke leaned against the locker, looking as though he had no intention of moving.

"Wait for me outside."

"Tsk. I know what you're thinking."

"You wish you did. Don't worry. I'll give you

more chances to outscore me in winning Jade's attention."

"Asshole." Zackery rolled his eyes. "I'm obviously in the lead, right Jade?"

I snickered. "If it makes you sleep well at night, sure."

Zackery smiled and headed out, leaving the two of us alone.

"Seeing as we're starting fresh, I have a question."

"What's up?" I asked, resting against the locker next to him.

"Shadow Jade. She's your dark element, isn't she?"

"Wasn't it obvious?"

"To me, yes. To my brothers, no. Zeus is curious, Zion is intrigued, and Zackery has no clue."

"Serious, Smart, and Playful." I labeled his brothers in the order he'd mentioned.

"What about me?"

"Seductive," I replied, turning my head to look at him.

That palpable energy between us was back, and I slowly licked my lips.

"You're dangerous." My voice sounded haunting, even to me. Zeke pushed off the lockers, attracting my attention as I followed his movement. He faced me, placing his hands against the cool steel and closing in until our lips barely touched.

"From the girl who makes me want to follow my impulses rather than think straight," he whispered. I didn't want to ignore my need to lock our lips together, but I fought against it, trying to think rationally.

*He can't be a one-night stand. He's a Tracker. Same field, different district. If I fuck this up, it could leave a bad start to my future as a Tracker in the adult division.*

"You're going to make me wait, aren't you?" Zeke's husky voice was making me tingle all over, my dark energy racing forward to try and connect with his.

"It would be torture to not enjoy your smooth, calculative advances and fall into the darkness hidden in those pants of yours, but a little bird told me to save the best for last," I purred against his skin, as I ended up kissing his cheek, followed by his neck.

He groaned, and the low rumble that vibrated against his chest could make me lose all my resolve in trying to wait. I needed more time to analyze him. To see if this connection was a trap of some kind.

I'd never reacted like this with anyone. Was it planned, or was this truly something meant to be?

When I removed my lips from his neck and leaned back, he kissed me; the solid kiss was electrifying with pounding energy. Its steamy ferocity was making me dizzy, leaving me wondering if he was experiencing the same.

He broke the kiss, the two of us gasping for air. I leaned my head against the lockers, while Zeke rested his forehead against my left shoulder, panting quietly.

"Fuck...that was intense."

"For a kiss, too," I breathed. "Guess you're down for waiting now?"

"Not really, but Zackery's bugging me to hurry up. I'm impressed he waited this long. I'd rather deal with his nagging than Zeus's," he admitted.

I was going to move, but his lips gently pressed into the side of my neck. My moan was quiet, but it was the first time I'd actually moaned from liking something. My previous one-night stands were more for experimental purposes than sole pleasure, but this?

*This could have been something real.*

"I'll be smart and wait," he whispered against my flesh. "But I want the first date."

"If you can snag the opportunity in time, be my guest," I teased.

He pulled back and we shared a look.

"It's a pleasure to meet you, Jade Masters," he commented. "Zeke Maxwell, Tracker D of Novana District."

"A formal introduction?" I arched an eyebrow at him but smiled widely. "I feel honored."

He chuckled and offered his hand. "Let's get out of here. Remind us that we owe you dinner next time."

"Deal," I agreed, happily placing my hand in his.

The Trouble Four from Novana District. Four official Trackers sent to monitor Tracker Hive? What was really going on?

*More importantly, what's the real problem unraveling beneath our noses?*

## ❧ II ❧

### ZACKERY OF WIND AND ICE

"This should be illegal." I struggled to stay awake, yet again, wishing I had coffee.

"You really aren't a morning person," Zackery announced as we made our way to class.

"Who thought it was ethical to have class this early?" I groaned, shuffling my feet. "I should sleep in class."

"And get in trouble." Zackery grinned. "You got yelled at when the professor couldn't wake you up last class."

"Why would I stay awake during that lecture when what he was talking about was the same old stuff? It's boring. I learned all of that when I was nine years old. I might as well teach the class. I'm sure people could learn the entire thing in one session instead of an entire week dedicated to two elements."

"I love how they're my elements," Zackery mused. "Or should I say 'ours.'"

"If it makes you happy, sure." I giggled.

"Hey," Zackery whined. "What does that mean?"

"You love lumping us together." I opened my tired eyes wider to look at his puppy expression. "You look cute when you're all down."

"That hurts my feelings," Zackery replied but gave me a wide grin in return.

This week had been focused on Knowledge Analysis. It was the common basics of magic knowledge and all the written mechanics of how to use each element.

This week we were focusing on the Ice and Wind elements. It fit perfectly with Zackery because those were the very elements he carried.

If only I had his enthusiasm when it came to the general class sessions that were a bunch of chapter readings and unnecessary questions. It was like Elemental Studies for Dummies.

It was boring for people as advanced as Zackery and I, the two of us already experienced in the field. At least Zackery could stay awake.

"I'm totally going to sweep you off your feet and whisk you away first."

"I have no confidence in your claim, but again, if it makes you happy," I replied, noticing movement from the corner of my eye.

I stopped, staring down the empty hall, debating whether I'd seen someone or something dash by.

*Silver-red hair? Hmm. Someone must be running down the halls.*

"Jade?"

I looked at Zackery, who had stopped as well, his eyes analyzing me carefully. "You okay?"

"Yup!" I confidently replied. "I thought I saw something or someone. It was silly," I replied.

"Well, it's still early and people are going to rush to get to class soon," Zackery pointed out. "It could have been the nerd."

"Don't remind me," I groaned.

All this week, Calvin had been following us like a stray puppy looking for a new home. He'd sit with us in class and talk all throughout the break about how knowledgeable he was and about his intense research on Tracker Hive.

He was essentially trying to record his life at the academy and his pursuit of becoming a Tracker.

We'd been worthy enough to be mentioned in his lengthy manuscript, with me starring as his hero.

I could handle the Maxwell brothers being around thanks to our temporary alliance as we tried to figure out what was going on to get the Magic Council's attention.

*This nerdy kid was not a part of that deal.*

"Speak of the devil," Zackery sang.

I had to try to not roll my eyes, hearing the quick footsteps that came from behind us.

Looking over my shoulder, I spotted Calvin. He always carried a big backpack that held all the electronic devices needed for his giant autobiography.

You'd think in our time and age, he'd invest in a small laptop or netbook to keep himself organized, but instead, he had an array of journals, notebooks, and even a recorder in case those two options failed him.

*I wonder if it ever occurred to him that someone could take that bag off his back and soak it in water. Game over.*

"Morning, Queen Jade," Calvin breathed as he came to a stop. He was panting hard, as usual, having run from wherever he came from with his gigantic bag. His face was drenched in sweat, but it didn't stop him from looking back up and giving us a wide smile.

***"Too happy. Kill."***

*If only we could get away with murder, Shadow Jade. The deed would already be done.*

It honestly wasn't that I didn't like this dude. He was just an annoyance, and in my head, anything that annoyed me needed to be eliminated.

*Harsh? Maybe. Did I care? Nope.*

"Can you stop calling me Queen? Unless you found some documentation that determines that I'm the lost child from a royal family far away, I don't need the added title," I concluded.

"You're a Queen to me, Queen Jade. You saved me when everyone else watched. The least I can do is point out how amazing you are," Calvin defended.

Zackery just stared at him.

"We're going to be late for class if we don't get moving. Queen Jade? Should I hold onto anything for you?" Calvin offered, looking up at me with hopeful eyes. I realized how short he was, barely topping at out five feet. It was strange to have to look down at someone; I had already gotten used to staring up when I spoke to the Maxwell brothers. "I'm fine," I declared.

"Why don't you go ahead and save us our seats, Calvin," Zackery suggested, his voice a little sterner than usual.

"Sure!" Calvin cheered. "I'll get the best front

row seats!" With his declaration, he was gripping his backpack and running away. It wasn't until he was completely gone that I made a comment.

"I hate sitting in the front," I mumbled to myself. Glancing at Zackery, I noticed his frown as his eyes darted around us suddenly. I wasn't the only one who had spotted trouble.

"Guess you noticed." I slid my hands out of my blazer pockets.

"You caught onto it?"

"The moment we stopped, I did. I knew someone had passed by, but maybe that was on purpose. An illusion to make this trap."

Initially, the trap we were now in had been invisible, but now the mini-threads of magic had taken on physical form. Still, they were mostly hidden by the swift movement of wind. Someone was deliberately cloaking them.

"Wind at this speed is costly," I muttered. "The person is nearby."

"I'm on it," Zackery declared. "Don't move."

"I wasn't planning to," I commented, trying to remember any other details from the person I'd seen with the silver-red hair.

*A trap like this in the first week of school? Why?*

It definitely wasn't those fat brothers. They had

learned their lesson and none of them were in any of my classes.

Whoever set this trap knew Zackery and I had class together and took this specific route.

*An observant stalker who wants us injured. Intriguing.*

"Can you cut the threads?" Zackery asked.

"Didn't you say I shouldn't move?'"

"Yes, but I need you to cut that junction of threads," he declared, staring forward. I followed his gaze, narrowing my eyes and tugging at my own wind element to locate the web of strings that connected in the center.

"I could, but wouldn't that set it off and slice our body parts off? Or are you fast enough to freeze our frames without actually freezing us? When I say that out loud, it doesn't make much sense," I said, realizing that my explanation wasn't coming out the way I wanted it to.

"It makes sense. It's exactly what I'm picturing, and to answer your question, that's my plan. It would be a bonus if you can warm the environment around us real quick."

"Like a scorching hot day in summer? Easy," I announced with a devilish grin, the burning fire within me lighting up at the mere thought.

Closing my eyes, I summoned a flaming sword in my right hand, knowing it would aid the rapid increase in temperature. Droplets of sweat ran down the side of my forehead, and I was already growing uncomfortable as the heat waves were swarming us.

"Now," Zackery ordered, and I followed through, lifting my sword upward and cutting the connected threads. Bracing myself for some type of pain, I was instead treated with a mixture of hot and cold, arms holding me tightly against a solid, cold figure.

With a blink, I looked up to see that Zackery was holding me protectively while a solid wall of ice an inch thick wrapped around us.

I thought the quick trap was sprung and done, but then I noticed the scratches appearing on the outside surface of the transparent ice wall.

"It's still going," I announced.

"This is going to be annoying if it's a continuous flow," Zackery admitted. "I can do this for some time, but we'll be trapped here. If we call for help..."

"Whoever arrives will be at risk," I concluded. "Or killed."

"From your tone of voice, I feel as though you've already got a plan." Zackery sounded amused. "Tell me, Junior Tracker."

"I'm stronger than you," I pointed out. "And I'm eighteen."

He looked down at me, a wide grin on his lips. "I know, Jade. You can defend your honor after we get out of this. I'm struggling here."

Pouting my lips, I could tell the ice was becoming thinner and thinner. I focused on his concentrated facial expression.

"This may be totally random, but you're really hot when you're all concentrating and shit," I praised.

"Completely random," he groaned. "Does it at least earn me a kiss?"

"It depends. Maybe I should wait until you're at your wits' end?"

"That's just cruel."

"But exciting. I think it's a total turn-on."

"If seeing me on the brink of losing turns you on, I really don't want to be in the same bed as you," he groaned. "And knowing Zeke, he'd love the challenge."

I let out a small giggle. "You're losing at this advantage game, Zackery. You're going to be last at this point."

Leaning up on my tiptoes, I gave him a light kiss on the cheek. "But you're really hot when you're working. I'll give you some brownie points."

His cheeks grew red, and he glanced away. "Thanks?"

Paying attention to the current situation at hand, I closed my eyes and called to my inner elements. I could feel the rush of wind slashing ruthlessly against Zackery's defense, but I wasn't concerned about the current onslaught.

Getting to know Zackery during the last four days of classes had shown me that he wasn't the type to quit. It was a part of his competitive, playful nature.

My focus was on finding the root of the problem. Tracking a single thread of teal energy, I began to wonder how far away this individual was.

Even if I located the source, it wouldn't give me an image of who exactly the person was. I was following a flicker of color, and not a visual trail to the culprit behind this.

*Guess it was better than being shredded into tiny body parts.*

"Jade?" Zackery questioned. The strain in his panting voice was thick, yet he still showed immense concern in the simple call of my name.

"A bit more. They're...farther than I expected," I admitted. "Oh fuck!"

I had to curse because the source was now on the move.

*They caught on.*

"What?"

"They're getting farther away. They shouldn't have sensed me," I huffed, beginning to feel the exertion of it all. "If he gets too far away, I'll lose the trail."

Wind magic definitely wasn't an element I could perfect in seconds. Just the pressure of trying to catch up to the vanishing trail of the dark vision within my mind was slowing me down.

"Jade?"

"What?"

"I'm going to try something, but that means doing something a little touchy."

"Touchy? We're already intimately hugging one another while I'm keeping my eyes closed and trying not to lose this damn tra—"

A jolt of energy pulsed through me suddenly, and I felt the slow movement of Zackery's hand slipping beneath my uniform dress shirt.

His chilled hand sliding upward along the left side of my rib sent cold shivers through me, ones that were exciting my ice magic immensely.

"Zackery," I panted, but it sounded like a light moan to my ears.

"Shh," he hushed me. "Focus on the trail. Don't lose it."

His lips brushed along my neck, electrifying my skin and tugging at my wind element. The tug at the two energies somehow rejuvenated them, resetting their strengths and giving me a huge boost.

Just like that, I wasn't weak anymore, and my breathing began to level out as my mind cleared. Zackery didn't stop teasing my neck, kissing me lightly, which was personally distracting but providing a lot more energy.

*Is he using that connection we had in the office to give me a boost? Doesn't that mean I could do the same in return?*

Realizing what he was doing, I decided to multitask. As I tried to balance tracking the energy with my eyes closed, I slipped my hands beneath Zackery's dress shirt, moving slightly up his back.

"Jade," Zackery warned, but it wasn't like he was in pain. His warning was low and ignited parts of me that hadn't reacted to him prior to this.

My ice element was reacting, flooding my physical senses and directing itself to my hands, transferring into Zackery like I was now his battery source.

Refocusing, I noticed the sudden growth of my wind element, aiding in my mission to catch this person. Not only did I spot their energy, but the surrounding environment also seemed to light up in turquoise.

Whoever this person was, they were definitely tall, with a thin frame. Closing the distance with a pushed boost, I was finally able to strike the source, the connection slicing in half like a sharp blade had cut it.

Snapping my eyes open, I looked up to meet Zackery's. They were intense, suddenly a mixture of almost-white, blue, and teal. The silver surrounding his iris was still prominent, his expression was cloaked with such an intense level of lust that I had to blink a few times to make sure I wasn't seeing things.

We stood in place, my hands still pressed against the middle of his back and his on the sides of my waist, just at the waistline of my red and blue skirt.

I was struggling to think, my ice and wind elements fighting to return to their proper places when deep down, they now wanted to explore and intertwine with the man who had ignited a hidden power within us.

*What is this power? Where is it coming from? Is it due to our connection? Our closeness? What the hell is going on?*

I thought the intense connection I'd experienced with Zeke was only due to our strong dark elements, but now in this silent moment, I was feeling that vibrating energy between Zackery and me, too.

*If I don't pull away now...I may not want to later.*

"Kill. Kill. Kill!"

We both flinched at the close sound, both of us moving apart from one another and looking to our left where Shadow Jade stood.

She stared at Zackery for five seconds, analyzing him carefully before she disregarded him and gave me her full focus.

"Jade!" She wrapped her arms around me. I hugged her back but was silent, still riding an energy high while I tried to wrap my mind around what had just happened.

"There you are!"

Tanner emerged from down the hall, only looking confused when his eyes landed on the three of us. "What are you two doing here when class started ten minutes ago?" he questioned.

*Ten minutes ago? We'd been fifteen minutes early to class. You're telling me twenty-five minutes went by? It felt like minutes. Not THAT many minutes.*

"Me!" Shadow Jade looked at Tanner, who groaned. "And you too, Shadow Jade."

"Tanner." My voice was serious. "Did you pass

by anyone down that hall?" I questioned, narrowing my eyes at him.

"What? No. I've been chasing Shadow Jade, who's been running all over the place saying she was chasing something,"

"Bad. Kill. Kill. Kill!" Shadow Jade declared vehemently.

The three of us looked at her. "Looks like your twin noticed the person who set this trap," Zackery announced.

"What trap?" Tanner looked between us.

"Do you mind if we take this conversation to the office? I hate to admit it, but I need to sit down," I confessed.

It wasn't that I was tired, but I was a tad light headed. It happened with individuals who had multiple elements. They needed a balance, or all sorts of things happened.

"Let's go to the office," Zackery declared.

I took a few steps forward but was swept off my feet by a wind spell, the gentle cool breeze wrapping around me and carrying me.

Zackery's playful grin was back, and he took two steps forward; the wind lowered my body into his hold.

"I'll be a gentleman and carry you."

"I never asked for your help," I clarified.

"I'm aware. I'm doing the chivalrous thing," he stated proudly.

Tanner looked disgusted. "Shouldn't you be carrying her twin, too," he said in a bored voice.

Zackery slowly looked at Shadow Jade, who blinked innocently. She lifted her hands up. "Piggyback!"

She ran around us, while Zackery groaned. "Hold on! That's not fair. I was trying to be cool and seduct-OW! Shadow Jade....you're going to choke me."

"'I could have just walked," I concluded.

"He's carrying you for a reason," Tanner whispered.

I looked at him, noticing his frown as he looked behind us. I wasn't sure what he was staring at, but from his comment, I knew someone was watching.

*Someone's trying to eliminate me. Ugh...this should be an easy cat-and-mouse game. Yet they were powerful enough to spring this intense trap from far away. Whoever is targeting us is not an inexperienced person.*

"Mr. Maxwell, call your brothers and ask them to join us in the office. We need to talk."

"Understood," Zackery replied.

He began to carry both of us, me in his arms and Shadow Jade on his back.

I looked up at him, noticing his eyes were scanning the area, a darkened seriousness to them. He looked upset, as if something bad had happened, but we both were okay.

No one had gotten hurt. Yet, he looked as though we'd lost a challenge.

"Zackery?"

"Hmm?" He looked down at me, and I stared up into his eyes.

"Are you okay?"

"I'm fine." He smiled slightly, but it didn't reach his eyes. "I'm just annoyed we were in that tight jam. Sorry about...uh..." He took a peek at Tanner, who was walking ahead.

"It was nice." I knew he was referring to our rather intimate touching, which was a lot more pleasurable than I'd expected.

It made me wish I had been able to focus on his actions rather than deal with chasing the mysterious enemy who tried to annihilate us.

That made Zackery truly smile. "Do I get a brownie point for trying to be cool?"

"You do." I winked. "We'll have to reserve that for another quiet opportunity," I whispered.

"Hope there's more to come," he hummed.

*Me too, Zackery Maxwell, Tracker of Wind and Ice.*

# 12

# ZION OF WATER AND EARTH

"This feels like a family meeting," I declared. "Except with the boys."

"You make it seem like you don't want us here." Zackery sighed. "I'm tired."

"I don't even want to be here," Zeus groaned.

"You guys can leave. I don't mind the alone time," Zeke drawled.

"Always taking advantage." Zion shook his head. "Brother, you're a player."

"How?" Zeke questioned but chuckled. "Honesty gets you far, you know."

"That's bullshit. I'm honest and yet I'm last in line. How did Zeus beat me?"

"In?" Zeus questioned.

"The path to Jade's heart, that's what!" Zackery argued.

"Acting like you're not attracted to a person goes a long way," Zion determined, pulling out a pair of glasses from his uniform pocket. "Better than you begging, anyway."

"When was I begging?!" Zackery gasped.

Tuning out their bickering, I looked out of the clear window to see Alaric, Bianca, and Tanner talking outside of the office.

By the time Zackery and I had reached the main office, the others had arrived. Tanner had then gone off to get Alaric and Bianca to discuss what had just happened to us.

Under normal circumstances, I wouldn't have cared about the trap. In a school like this, with competitive students all trying to prove a point, I assumed it wouldn't be smooth sailing.

The problem was the source of the trap. A student with that level of control shouldn't be in this part of the school, which was mostly for first year students.

The school grounds were basically divided into four sections based on our year of attendance. It helped maintain balance and routine, instead of forcing the students to struggle getting from one class to the another on the other side of the ginormous campus.

With eight semesters, it meant we'd spend two semesters in each section.

I felt a lot better now that I was sitting. The meeting room was more of a lounge, with couches and comfy chairs. I was sitting on the couch in between Zion and Zeke.

Zeus was sitting in a chair on our right while Zackery sat on the left. Zackery looked tired, but he assured us that he'd leave school early and take a nap.

The trap was uncalled for, but Trackers always had to be prepared for these things. School wasn't going to change that.

Tanner and Alaric walked in the room, while Bianca left.

"Where's Bianca going?" I asked once the door was closed.

"She's going to check the surveillance cameras to see if she can spot the individual you said you saw," Alaric answered, walking over to sit on the couch opposite ours.

Tanner followed but remained standing, crossing his arms over his chest. Looking my way, he questioned, "Are you sure about what you saw, Jade?"

His tone annoyed me, but I held my tongue, not

wanting to get into an unnecessary conversation that tugged at my past issues.

"Positive," I replied.

"I trust that Jade really saw someone," Zackery added.

He was looking between Tanner and me. "Also take the intensity of the trap into consideration. Unless we're dealing with a veteran magic-user, there's no way that was a long-range combo."

"They had to be super close to activate it," Zeus agreed.

"You guys were stuck for twenty-five minutes and it must have taken time to track their energy before they went fleeing away. This person's intentions had to be planned out. I doubt Ms. Sky will find anything. They would have made sure they were magically cloaked from video surveillance if they were able to hide their actual presence from Jade and Zackery," Zion explained.

"Do you two always go that route?" Zeus inquired.

"Yup," Zackery replied. "It's the easiest to get to class."

"Why would someone be trying to get rid of both of us?" I wondered out loud.

"Me!"

Everyone else flinched as Shadow Jade appeared

literally out of nowhere. She'd "left" after the piggy-back ride, saying she was going to nap, but here she was, behind the couch and circling her arms around my neck.

"Kill Jade?"

Turning my head slightly to see her curious eyes, I realized that was her opinion of the situation and not a simple playful taunt.

"You think they're after us?"

"Us!" she emphasized with a smile.

"Why?" Zackery questioned. "Up till now, things have gone smoothly. Since that whole incident with the brothers, no one wants to pick a fight with Jade. Not when I'm around anyway."

"And since he follows her around everywhere, his words are valid," Zion affirmed.

"Hey!" Zackery looked insulted but didn't push it.

"I don't care if someone has a vendetta against me, but why? Also, they wouldn't go attacking Zackery as well. Stupid move, in my opinion. They must have not researched which elements he carries, or they would have set up a different trap."

"Or they could have known and wanted to see if he'd get the two of you out on his own," Zion reasoned. "Or whether you two would have to work together."

Tanner and Alaric exchanged a look, the action drawing my attention.

"You two know something," I announced. The five us looked at them, and Alaric cleared his throat.

"We think whoever they are don't want the five of you near one another."

"Why?" I questioned. "Last time I checked, we'd only just met. We had no connection prior to this school. The culprit must have found out we're all attending, but even that doesn't explain why they attacked only Zackery and me. Why not wait for a mandatory class and go for all of us at one? We're missing the primary motive."

Zion laid his hand on mine, catching my attention. I glanced over to him as he analyzed me carefully, only now realizing he'd put on those glasses he'd pulled out beforehand.

"Jade. Can you try something real quick?"

I stared at him for ten seconds. "You look innocent enough. Better than when Zackery asks the question," I muttered.

"Jade," Zackery whined. "You're hurting my pride."

"I'm impressed you still have some," Zeus concluded.

Zeke chuckled. "What are you thinking, Zion? Your thought process just went into overdrive."

"Overdrive?" I interrupted.

"That's the term we use to label Zion's more extreme thought processes. He's the smartest out of the four of us, and once he starts putting the clues together, he gets all scientific with it and basically forgets we exist for a few minutes," Zeke explained.

"I don't forget," Zion grumbled, but he lifted my hand. "Shadow Jade? Can you go sit with Alaric for a moment?"

"Me?" Shadow Jade blinked and looked over to Alaric. "Daddy!"

She let go of me without another question, skipping over to him.

"Do you and your twin have different levels of intellect?" Zeus questioned.

"Are you calling Shadow Jade stupid?" I questioned back.

"If he did, might as well dig his grave now. We'll miss you, brother," Zeke teased.

"Right. Zeus, apologize. You don't say that to a girl!" Zackery stressed.

"That was mean, brother," Zion mumbled, adjusting his glasses on his nose.

"Seriously? It's just a question," Zeus grumbled.

"A mean question," Zackery corrected.

"Shadow Jade doesn't care," Tanner barged in.

I smirked. "Shadow Jade," I sweetly declared. "Tanner just called you stupid."

"Hey!" Tanner exclaimed. "I did not!"

He then looked at Shadow Jade, who was sitting next to Alaric.

"Me?" Shadow Jade pointed to herself. "No stupid." She blinked her eyes.

"I know, Shadow Jade. Tanner is just a big bully. You should kill him," I suggested. "We need less of him in the world."

"Dammit! Shut up, Jade." Tanner was off the couch and near the door. "Alaric! Interfere."

Alaric was calmly cleaning his glasses. "Hmm?"

"I love how your dad doesn't even care," Zeke praised.

"I know. Isn't he awesome? No wonder I never get in trouble with Tanner," I concluded.

"Kill!" Shadow Jade stood up, a large scythe forming in her hands. She grinned happily. "Shadow Jade hurt! Kill!"

She was right in Tanner's face in less than a blink; Tanner was already summoning his sword and blocking the attack.

"Alaric!" Tanner said through gritted teeth. "Really?"

"Did you want me to do something?" Alaric questioned. The four of us snickered while Zeus shook his head.

"I don't understand the logistics of all this. Just apologize."

"You're the one who insulted her!" Tanner declared.

There was a knock on the glass, and all of us turned our gazes to see Bianca holding a tray of cookies. "I brought cookies."

"Cookie?" Shadow Jade paused in her quest to kill Tanner, looking over to me. "Jade! Cookie! Me?"

"Yes, Shadow Jade. You can move Tanner out of the way and get some cookies from Bianca," I instructed with an evil smile.

"Yeah!" Shadow Jade cheered, literally picking Tanner up like he weighed nothing and throwing him over to Alaric's couch.

Alaric rose and moved out of the way a second before Tanner crashed into the couch, which fell over. We all burst into laughter while Shadow Jade opened the door and gestured for Bianca to come in.

"That was the best shit I've ever seen." Zackery laughed.

"Why didn't we record it?" Zeke whined. "It was a golden moment."

"Blackmail at its finest," Zeus chuckled.

"Whenever we see Tanner in class, that's what we'll envision." Zion grinned.

"We went far off topic, but for that Kodak moment, I'd ask Shadow Jade to do it all over again," I concluded, using my free hand to wipe newly formed tears from my eyes.

"Seems I arrived at a good time," Bianca concluded, walking into the room. She offered Shadow Jade the tray, and she took two cookies, skipping over to me.

Offering me one, she smiled. "Cookie?"

"Thank you, Shadow Jade. You can...uh...well, when the couch is back up, you can sit with Alaric again," I concluded.

She nodded but lowered to sit in front of my feet, crossing her legs and focusing on her cookie as she began to nibble it.

Tanner groaned and finally got up. "I hate you."

"That's old news. Next," I replied, returning to my own cookie.

"Bianca?" Alaric turned his attention to her. "Anything on the surveillance?"

She frowned, beginning to walk around and offer the others a double chocolate cookie. "Nothing, which makes no sense. It took a bit of concentration, but I confirmed there is a trail of energy going down the hallway, out the school, and into the woods. Jade was right with her explanation of her needing to chase the source. Whatever happened was definitely caused by someone, and NOT an illusion," she stressed, giving me a small smile.

I smiled back, feeling relieved by her emphasis. I hadn't experienced my hallucinations for more than a year.

Even if Tanner had meant well in some weird way by mentioning it, I personally didn't want the guys knowing about it.

*But they may have already picked up on it.*

They had read my file. They may have very well found out that I'd been taking medication for my hallucinations for years until recently. Deep inside, I felt there was always a stigma when it came to mental health.

Add my rather abnormal personality to it, and I was the person everyone loved to call crazy when they simply didn't understand me.

*I didn't want to be misjudged by these guys. Awkward to admit such truth...even to myself.*

"Zion? You were up to something," I reminded, turning my focus back to him.

"Yes," he replied, lifting my hand and turning it

so my palm faced up. "Can you make a bubble with a floating rock inside?"

"Sure." It was easy enough, the action taking barely any concentration to accomplish.

Finishing up my cookie, I did as he asked and formed a bubble with a pebble in the middle.

"Bubble!" Shadow Jade had maneuvered herself around and was watching closely while finishing off her cookie. The other guys had risen up to get a closer look, just as Alaric, Bianca, and Tanner moved to stand on the sidelines; everyone's attention on the floating bubble carrying the rock.

Zion smiled. "Now, I'm gonna do something weird, but I need your other hand."

"Define weird," I said, but offered my other hand. "If it's painful, I don't care."

Zeke was standing the closest to me. "Are you thinking of testing out what happened when we first met Jade?"

Zion grinned, giving Zeke a bob of his head. "Yup."

"What happened when you guys met?" Alaric questioned. When no one replied, Zion stepped in. "You'll see in a second, and maybe you'll have answers for us instead."

I thought he'd pinch my hand or squeeze it, but

he lifted it up to his lips, pressing them tenderly against my palm.

My shock was having a delayed response, but two elements rushed forward at his touch, the bubble beginning to grow rapidly as the pebble inside started morphing into odd shapes.

I bit my lip hard, hoping the pain would minimize the heat pulsing through me, as well as my sudden desire for Zion, whose eyes were locked on mine. They were changing in color, dancing from a strong blue to a grey.

His lips moved gently along my skin, my eyes fluttering closed as I sighed. "Zion," I warned, my breath but a whisper. I was struggling with keeping my water and earth elements intact.

"If that bubble bursts, are we all going to get soaked?" Zackery pondered.

"The tree inside is pretty cool," Zeke pointed out.

"Are you two ignoring what the hell is happening on purpose?" Zeus sighed. "And Zion. Quit it already. You proved your point. It's getting hard to ignore you."

I opened my eyes slightly, seeing Zion's amusement as he gave my hand one last kiss and pulled away. "That was the reason for Jade and Zackery being targeted," he declared.

"You weren't there kissing her hand," Zackery pointed out.

"Are you stupid?" Zeke, Zeus, and Zion said in unison.

Shadow Jade and I focused on the bubble that had tripled in size, harboring a beautiful tree inside it.

"Nature!" Shadow Jade declared. "Mine?"

I gave her a smile and nodded. "If you want the tree, you can have it, Shadow Jade. Just make sure you water it," I encouraged. "How did an apple tree grow from a pebble?"

"I imagined the pebble would morph into soil and would grow something manageable to feed a person. The increase in water heightened the speed of growth, using it as a substitute source of light with that added boost. I also like apples."

"Impressive," I replied, using my finger to pop the bubble.

It didn't splash out like a normal bubble would when popped, the tiny droplets instead remaining in the air and floating around.

Shadow Jade giggled, taking on a new challenge: popping them all with her fingers.

I looked at Alaric, Bianca, and Tanner. "Why does this happen? Since the day I met these guys, their elements tug at mine like they want to connect."

"I feel offended that she used 'these guys,'" Zackery mumbled.

"We haven't been upgraded to friend status yet." Zion had a sad expression on his face.

"Don't care," Zeus shrugged.

"I'll just slide into the more-than-friends department." Zeke winked.

"Cheater!" Zackery accused.

"You had every opportunity to make that situation yours," Zion suggested.

"And failed," Zeus concluded.

"Zackery makes this too easy," Zeke determined.

I waited for them to end their debate. "Yeah. These guys," I emphasized with a teasing grin.

They all sighed, but Bianca took the opportunity to speak. "We're going to have to look into it..." she trailed off, glancing at Alaric, who appeared deep in thought.

"You're not thinking what I think you're thinking," Tanner spoke up. "They can't be a match."

"It's possible," Bianca replied. "Quadruplets and Jade. Makes sense."

"Me!" Shadow Jade declared.

"And Shadow Jade," Bianca acknowledged with a smile.

"What are you guys talking about?" I questioned, unsure what they were referring to. "What match, and where do we," I pointed to Shadow Jade and myself, "belong in this apparent equation?"

Alaric sighed, crossing his arms over his chest.

"You five may be a Hive."

"A what?" the four brothers asked in unison.

I glanced around them. "That's totally weird."

"From the girl who'd rather experience pain than pleasure," Zeus sighed.

"I never said that," I pointed out. "I like both."

"Kill!" Shadow Jade added.

"I feel as though exacting pain on others outweighs any chances of pleasure," Zeke noted. "Sign me up."

"Someone cock-block him," Zackery complained.

"Admit you hate losing," Zion replied.

"Can we get back on topic? This thing is interrupting my nap."

"Aww. Zeus is a big baby who needs nap time," I squealed in delight. "Can I come and cuddle?"

"No," he grumbled.

Zion leaned in. "That means yes. You can't feel it, but his heart is beating really fast."

I giggled, noticing Zeus's face growing redder by the second.

Bianca shook her head and Tanner rolled his eyes. "Focus, Trackers," Tanner declared.

We all returned our attention to Alaric, and I took the lead to ask the question again.

"What's a Hive?"

"The reason we go by Tracker Hive Academy. Being a Tracker is normally a group effort that brings people together to resolve evil that happens, for example, in the Black Market," Alaric recapped.

We intently listened as he continued.

"Hive is a term used for bringing people together as a cluster. It demonstrates that such unions can work as a group to complete one unified goal. However, there is a uniqueness that comes with the term Tracker Hive."

He lifted his right hand out to the side, placing it in front of Bianca. A tiny flame emerged in the palm of his hand.

"On rare occasions, individuals are connected to one another, and that connection heightens when they find one another. Think of it like a bond with one or more individuals that can complement your element."

Bianca placed her hand beneath Alaric's, the small flame growing dramatically and shifting in colors from red to a gorgeous pink that matched Bianca's hair.

"These connections are, again, rare, but they occur between individuals with immense power or various elements. That is why Tracker Hive Academy was created: to gather those individuals who either struggle at pulling out those potentials, or those who have too much and are rejected by the standard schools."

"But...it's only with one person? Not multiples, right?" I questioned. "It's based off intimacy, correct?"

"It can be," Alaric noted. "Touch is the primary base for it, but the more intimate you are, the stronger the connection," he declared, placing his left hand to his other side where Tanner stood; a tiny ice shard formed and hovered above his hand.

"The more intimate one is, the stronger their connections?" Zion questioned. "Doesn't that mean for Hives with three or more members that there has to be a connector? Like a king or queen of the Hive who anchors the whole cluster?"

"You're correct." Alaric nodded. Tanner's scowl was as strong as ever, but he reluctantly placed his hand under Alaric's, the ice shard multiplying in size and shifting into an ice flower that blossomed outward.

"Hold on," Zackery commented. "I know I'm the slowest here, but does that mean if we label Mr. Masters as the Hive leader — the king or whatever — does that mean with that demonstration just now, Ms. Sky and Mr. Asshole are connected to him?"

"Hey!" Tanner growled. The rest of us ignored his response, piecing together Zackery's question.

"Alaric is the Hive Leader. Bianca and Tanner are connected. The more connected the three of them are, the stronger the overall Hive is. Does that mean with you guys being a team, together you're a triple threat?" I concluded.

"Correct," Alaric replied.

We were quiet for a full minute, soaking in this new information. I looked at Tanner.

"Does that mean you're gay?"

"What is it to you?" he huffed. "Don't go using that against me or I'll surely fail you."

"Nothing wrong with being gay." I shrugged. "I just wanted to state that I knew that already."

"You did?" the four guys asked.

"I live with the three of them. I'm not stupid," I noted.

Tanner began to blush while Bianca snickered. "I told you she was observant."

"Hmm. Her acceptance of things makes life a lot easier," Alaric complimented.

"Us, too!" Shadow Jade announced, skipping over to get a closer look at the ice flower.

"Us, too?" Zeus questioned.

"Hmm? Oh, we don't have a preference," I answered.

"Meaning?" Zackery inquired.

"You like boys and girls," Zeke concluded.

"Yup!' I replied with a nod. "I can date either."

"Interesting," Zeke smirked.

Zeus groaned. "Stop fantasizing about the possibilities. It's seeping into our minds and we don't want it."

Zion smiled sweetly. "Zeke has an intriguing imagination. It excites him to know he has possibilities."

"Can we change the subject before this guy starts making the rest of us horny?" Zackery reached out to try and slap Zeke's head, but he ducked.

"Last time I checked, I was entitled to my own fantasy. No one said to announce it in front of Jade's guardians, but cool. I'll be able to ask them first to take her out for some fun," Zeke said with confidence.

I actually blushed at his declaration, looking at

Tanner, Bianca, and Alaric, who were staring blankly at us.

"For once, I'm unsure whether to be excited or to wonder if I'll get banned from dating you four." I shook my head.

Bianca leaned over to Alaric. "We should buy her an apartment. I don't want to interrupt them."

"I guess," Alaric replied.

"Are you two listening to yourselves?" Tanner glared at them.

"Me!" Shadow Jade declared, picking up the ice sculpted flower. She walked back to me. "Ours with the tree!"

"Sure," I approved, not minding the fact she just stole the flower.

"Guess I better make that permanent, or Shadow Jade may destroy the office if it melts," Zackery concluded.

"Good idea," the three others replied.

"So...let me get this straight. The reason why my elements got all crazy on our first encounter was because we are potentially a Hive, and I'm the connector? Does that mean they're my only Hive...members?" I inquired.

"They should be since together they harness all the elements to match yours. In our case, we're lucky to be able to balance Alaric out. Both Tanner and I have four elements that together make up the eight. This is still something relatively new. However, we have noticed a recent uptick in those with Hive potential being murdered or sold on the Black Market," Bianca explained.

"That would make sense," Zion declared. "Gathering those with the potential of being a part of a Hive or a connector. Those with more elements have higher probability, making them the perfect targets. If they aren't one, they can use them for other things or kill them."

"You're thinking that someone in this school suspected that we're a Hive and wants to eliminate us," Zackery declared.

"They don't want to eliminate us," Zeus pointed out. "That was a trial."

"Confirming whether we have a reaction to Jade." Zeke bit his lip. "There was no other way for you guys to get out of the trap without using that connection. It was the perfect demonstration, and now our hidden enemy knows."

"So?" I asked. "What does that mean, then?"

"They're going to come after Jade," Zackery confirmed.

"Or kill her," Zion muttered.

We glanced at him, noticing his dark eyes were deep in concentration.

"Think about it. Look how powerful Alaric, the headmaster of Tracker Hive, is. Someone on the council clearly doesn't like that. I don't know what circumstance led to Jade being under his care, but that made it more dangerous because Jade has eight elements and is being taught by someone who also has all eight elements. That's powerful. When Jade gets upgraded to official Tracker status in the adult division, she'll be one of the top Trackers in the ranks. Someone, or a group of people, don't want that. Now add in that she's a connector to us, four high-ranking Trackers from another district, and what does that look like?"

"We'll want to join this district's Tracker agency," Zackery whispered.

"Which makes us a bigger threat for those in this city because there's Alaric, who already has his Hive, and now Jade," Zeus determined.

"Thus, the reason why they may be after Jade," Zeke said.

"Alaric?" I looked up at him. "I know you mentioned strange things have been happening here, but how strange are we talking?"

Alaric grimaced as he called off his magic. Tanner and Bianca still kept their hands under his as he spoke.

"Students have been winding up dead. It's happened three times so far."

"Death happens all the time," I admitted with a shrug. "Students die from fights and challenges. What makes these three deaths different?"

"They killed themselves," Bianca answered.

Tanner frowned but slowly nodded. "No signs. No warning. These are students with no history of bad behavior or mental illness. They all excelled and were promising Trackers with three or more elements. All three deaths have been random and totally unexpected. It was decided by the Council that it would be good for Jade to attend after the third death."

"As bait," the four brothers said in unison, all of them sounding irritated.

"Bait?" Shadow Jade pouted her lips. "No bait," she huffed.

"Figures." I wasn't in the least bothered. "I already knew that was a possibility, but this just confirms it." I rose up and began to stretch. "That means we just have to keep playing the game."

"What?" Everyone looked at me like I was mad.

*Normal reaction.*

"Whoever made that trap either thinks we have no clue about this Hive stuff or thinks we only have a very broad understanding of it. I think the former option is more likely. If we'd known about it, it wouldn't have taken us twenty-five minutes to get out of that situation. They're going to believe we're newbies and certainly, under normal circumstances, you guys wouldn't be as open to telling us."

"That's true," Bianca admitted.

"I'm a Junior Tracker by rank but I'm still a part of this district. They're not expecting us to all chill in a meeting room and discuss this with the guys who are from another district. It's a common assumption. Predictable. The advantage we have, as of now, is that we don't follow the rules."

With a clap of my hands, I looked around. "We keep playing this game. I continue going to class, each week with a different guy, but with a plan."

"I can create something that can detect strange, hidden activity, using the magic that should still be lingering in the hall atmosphere. I'll create a tracker that connects with Jade's phone, and it'll alert us whenever that energy resurfaces. Whoever is closest to her will check on her while the rest are on standby. I bet we have a few weeks before they try something again. More than enough time for me to work my magic," Zion explained with a wide grin.

"Zion, you're so smart," I praised.

"I can do more than play with a few droplets of water and rocks." He winked.

"Exciting." I licked my lips.

"Please don't tell me that's Zion's way of flirting," Zackery whined.

"He's doing better than you." Zeus chuckled.

"Definitely ahead of you," Zeke added.

"Then we're set," I confirmed, and leaned down and gave Zion a kiss on his cheek. He began to blush.

"W-what was that for?"

"For being smart and giving Shadow Jade a new plant," I concluded.

"You demonstrate affection so easily," Tanner grumbled.

"You're just jealous." I stuck my tongue out at him. "Professor Asshole."

"I can't wait until morning so I can kick your ass in training," he scolded.

"Dad!" I immediately looked at Alaric. "Your lover is abusing me."

Bianca snickered, beginning to laugh while Tanner and Alaric both blushed.

"Child abuse!" Bianca accused through her giggles.

They tugged their hands away, and Alaric cleared his throat.

"You are all dismissed. Zion, please keep us updated on the device you're making."

"All right," Zion replied.

I looked at him and we shared a smile, a little excitement bubbling inside me. It was weird to think of this as an assignment, but it seemed like my school life was going to be more eventful than I'd anticipated.

*Zion, Tracker of Water and Earth. Smart but intriguing. This is going to be an interesting connection for all of us.*

## 13

# ZEUS OF FIRE AND THUNDER

"If that stupid asshole asks me if I'm Zeke one more time, I'll—"

"Are you going to snipe his ass with thunder?" I asked with an elated grin.

Zeus gave me a blank expression.

"Kill?!" Shadow Jade rested her chin on my shoulder, adding to my happy stare, the two of us waiting for his agreement.

"You actually want me to, don't you?"

"It'd be more exciting than class," I admitted.

"No kill?" Shadow Jade blinked, sounding disappointed.

"No. I guess Zeus can't kill anyone yet unless they threaten his patience." I sighed dramatically, feeling just as disappointed. "It's okay, Shadow Jade.

Next week is all combat. We can kill someone there," I vowed.

"Kill!" Shadow Jade cheered, and a few of the students sitting at the nearby tables turned to look at us nervously.

Zeus reached for his orange juice, not bothered by the stares. "You're far too happy to declare your desire to spill blood."

"It's a lot more fun than studying. Where's the drama? Or school fights?" I sighed.

Shadow Jade was staring at Zeus's orange juice. "Me?"

Zeus paused in drinking the bottle that was half done, glancing at Shadow Jade's tray of food. "You have one."

"All done." She picked it up and turned it over; not even a drop of orange juice remained. Zeus looked my way, noticing I had a carton of milk today.

"Why didn't you get orange juice?"

"Bianca said my left boob is slightly bigger than the right and milk helps your boobs grow," I declared.

Zeus looked speechless.

"What?" I shrugged. "It's true. Well...that and bones, but anyway. I'm adding milk to my diet to ensure my boobs even out."

"You can't be serious."

"Very serious." I nodded my head. "I'd show you the difference, but I'm wearing a bland cotton bra and not a bedazzled lace one."

"Shouldn't you be more concerned that we're in the cafeteria with students and teachers?"

"So? They're just boobs. They're nice during playtime and are a food source for babies. Nothing so shocking about them. Even if mine are slightly uneven."

"I really don't know what to expect when having conversations with you," he grumbled, offering his remaining drink to Shadow Jade, who squealed and accepted it.

"Mine! Thank you." She got her straw from her previous bottle and plopped it in this one, beginning to drink it and stare at her burger wrapper.

"You barely ate," Zeus acknowledged, his eyes on my tuna wrap that had no more than two bites missing.

"It wasn't made right," I replied. "Far too much mayo, and it's clearly not fresh, making the wrap soggy. I don't like wasting food, but soggy anything...it just bugs me."

"Bugs you?" Zeus stared at me, his eyes looking deeply into mine.

He must have been attempting to figure me out.

It wasn't as though I had anything to hide now that I knew him and his brothers.

"When you live on the streets, people like to throw food at you. If it was still in decent condition I'd be fine with eating it, but most of the time they would throw leftover sandwiches and those healthy wraps no one likes. Sometimes one of the staff members from the restaurant I'd always sit in front of would feel bad for me. She'd bring me some of the expired wraps that they couldn't sell anymore. They're not supposed to, obviously. If it's expired, they throw it out, which is such a waste and merely feeds raccoons instead of those who may not be able to find a place to call home."

Shadow Jade's head moved in front of my line of vision, and she offered the bottle of orange juice that had a little bit left.

"Juice."

"I don't need any, Shadow Jade." I smiled at her.

She stared at me for a long moment. "Juice," she said again.

I figured this may end up as one of those back-and-forth non-negotiables Shadow Jade sometimes had. I reached for the juice and accepted it, offering a light pat on her head in return. "Thanks, Shadow Jade."

"Kill!" she declared in reply, beginning to sing

the Kill song quietly, the tune a little perkier than normal. Must have been her way of trying to cheer me up, which I did need.

I personally disliked talking about my year on the streets.

"Anyway. The food was always soggy. Especially the next day. I can smell the odor of the tuna which tells me it's not fresh. That's why I'm struggling to eat it."

"Why don't you get a burger? It'll be freshly made," Zeus offered.

"I don't want to waste food." I gave him a conflicted look, trying to stay positive. "I'll eat it. Just need a few more minutes, that's all."

Food was precious. When you've gone days without it, even wasting a crumb due to the five-second rule could make your heart ache. I remembered all the times I scrounged in garbage cans for hours to find leftover food that wasn't drenched with liquids and other unidentifiable nastiness.

The thought made me grimace, only giving me a harder time of trying to accept that I'd have to eat the tuna wrap.

*I'll surely have nightmares tonight after eating this.*

My tray slid forward, and I lifted my gaze to see Zeus pick up the wrap. "If I go get you a burger, will you eat it?"

"Yes, but my wrap..." I trailed off when he got off the bench of our table and took the wrap. He began to eat it in front of me, covering his mouth for a moment to speak. "I'll be back."

I stared at his back as he walked away munching on the wrap, feeling a little warmth deep inside me. The flicker of my fire element acknowledging what he'd just done.

"Nice. No Kill," Shadow Jade declared and looked at me. "Juice?"

"Right," I replied, and worked on finishing the remainder of the orange juice.

*Zeus is always gruff but he's also really nice deep down on the inside...somewhere. Probably buried under all that irritation. Kinda hot.*

Once I was finished with my juice, Shadow Jade gathered our trays, stacking them up and beginning to go through what was actual trash and what could be recycled.

That was another pet peeve of ours. Our world was dying from all the trash and plastic lying around on the ground, in the sewers, and even in the ocean. It was really troubling and always made me wish I could use my magic to aid in the global effort of making our world a better place.

When I was homeless and searching through garbage cans and dumps, the vast number of items I found that could be reused or created for other things was unreal. Yet, they were piled in the garbage.

I tried to recycle as much as I could or reuse old clothes by creating something else with them.

Shadow Jade petted my head, catching my attention. "Hmm?"

"Nap!" she declared.

"Okay. Are you going to the washroom to do your magic trick?"

"Yes," she replied.

"All right. Goodnight," I encouraged.

She got up with the trays, walking over to the three bins that were labeled with what went where for proper disposal. Once she finished, I watched her disappear out of the cafeteria and head to the washrooms down the hall.

It was moments like these where I felt more like a mom to Shadow Jade. My other elements were calm or kept to themselves until it was their time to shine, but I liked the connectedness I had with her.

She'd been who I needed to cheer me up during the rough, snowy nights in winter or the drizzling rainstorms in spring. Her affection, even in its peculiar, kill-like way, always left me feeling happy to be alive and have her as my strongest element.

I raised an eyebrow when my view was impeded by a female who sat right in front of me, taking Zeus's seat.

Her appearance gave off Barbie vibes. Perfect blonde hair, not a curl misplaced, with pretty red lips and the perfect shade of blush to compliment her mannequin skin. Even her uniform was neatly pressed, not a wrinkle in sight even though it was lunchtime.

She had a peppy smile on her face, waiting for me to acknowledge her sudden, unwelcome presence, but I was never one to be predictable, so I just stared back at her.

When I didn't ask her what she wanted or greet her, the once-perfect expression morphed into irritation.

"Hello?" The greeting that sounded more like a question was full of annoyance. It didn't bother me in the least. How can you be annoyed with someone when you're interrupting them?

When I didn't reply, she groaned and rolled her eyes.

"Hey, I'm Sallie Williams."

"Cool," I replied.

When I didn't continue to appease her, she continued. "Pretty emo for a girl who hangs with the Trouble Four."

"Trouble Four? Who are they?" I questioned, playing it off. Obviously, I knew who they were. I made up their group name.

*It does feel cool to hear it being used by others. I wonder if the guys mentioned it and someone picked it up?*

"The Quad," she replied.

The silence continued between us.

"The Maxwell brothers," she huffed.

"Ah!" I emphasized with a little bob of my head. "Nice name for them. They are pretty troublesome to tell apart."

I leaned back into my seat, pulling my phone out to check my messages. I'm sure Zeus was taking some time since they made the burgers fresh and they were eight-ounce patties.

"Whatever," the girl brushed off my comment. "Where's your twin?"

"Hmm?" I questioned, looking up from my phone.

"Your twin. The weird one."

"We're both weird," I replied.

"Jeez, I know that. The one that sings that stupid kill song like a lunatic."

"She sings it as a theme song to hype herself up before slicing the throats of people she doesn't like," I said in a deadpan tone.

Sallie's eyes went wide for a moment, and I

smirked in return, loving how her skin slightly paled by my statement.

"I'm joking," I said with a cheery voice. "Can't take a joke?"

I bet Sallie wanted to groan in response, but she held her tongue. "Do you know where your twin is, or not?"

"Of course I know where she is," I replied, lifting my hand to tap my right temple. "Right up here."

***"Me? Need?"*** Shadow Jade asked.

Her voice was thick with sleep, as though she'd already begun her nap.

*No, Shadow Jade. Go sleep. We can kill people later.*

***"Kill. Sleep,"*** she mumbled in return, her presence fading.

Sallie crossed her arms over her chest and glared at me. "Where did she go?"

"Somewhere over the rainbow where the valley of 'none of your business' lies in wait," I replied. "I'll happily forward a message to her."

Sallie looked unsatisfied but sat up and smoothed out her white uniform dress shirt.

"We'd like to invite her to a party that's happening next week, on Friday night."

"Next week?" I thought about it, realizing it would be the week I was taking classes with Zeke.

*Having a little play time at a party would be fun.*

"She should be free." I shrugged. "I'll let her know."

"You can't come though," Sallie said with triumph.

"Why?" I arched an eyebrow at her. I wasn't offended. I found this extremely amusing and couldn't wait for Shadow Jade to wake up for me to recap the situation to her.

"We want the cool twin. Not the slutty one who's tailing the Trouble Four."

"Tailing?" I ignored her slut comment.

It was a common assumption jealous girls made, when they saw one girl around a group of sexy, smart guys who they knew weren't looking in their direction. "Is that one of those new terms? Or are you referring to chasing, because I don't chase."

I could see her eye twitch again, making my grin widen before I sighed.

"Anyway. I'll let her know. I have a date that night," I declared.

"D-date?!" Sallie almost choked on her own saliva. "With who?"

Her eyes were glaring venomously at me, but I merely shrugged, returning to my phone.

"With me," a soothing voice announced.

Someone rested their chin on my shoulder, and

I could automatically guess from the way my dark magic spiked that it was Zeke.

"Uh...aren't you Zeus?" Sallie questioned.

"Hmm? Could be." I felt a soft kiss to my right cheek. When I turned to look to my right, it was indeed Zeke with a playful grin that was all too similar to Zackery's.

From the glint in his eye, he was playing a game and wanted me to follow along.

"Who could you be, hmm?" I hummed in delight, loving how Zeke's lips curled up higher. He leaned up to stand at his full height, his hands in his pockets.

"Where did my bro go?" Zeke wasn't asking me but Sallie, who was fidgeting in her seat.

"Um. I think I saw Zeke walking away eating a wrap earlier. I don't know where he went." Sallie answered nervously, trying to fix her hair even though it hadn't changed a bit. "I was going to invite you guys to a party."

"Party, huh? I'm not really the party type, but Zeke loves parties. I'll let him know. I, however, have a date with Jade next Friday."

"Y-you two are dating?" she shrieked.

"Maybe. I like testing the waters. Jade is the same, though her sister isn't into anyone yet." Zeke continued to play. "Right, Jade?"

"Yup," I replied with a confident bob of my head.

Sallie's face was so red. She rose up and tried to play it off. "Well, I'm sure all it will be is testing. Not to be rude, but the Maxwells deserve better." She flicked her hair and stood a little taller, puffing her chest.

"Better what? Boobs?" I questioned trying to determine what bra size she was. "Even with you puffing your chest like that, I have bigger breasts."

I few students snickered to our left, and Sallie's face was so red, I wondered if she was holding her breath.

"If we're talking about Jade's chest and ass, she scores an A-plus in my book."

Sallie turned her head over her shoulder, just as Zeke and I exchanged a look, noticing that Zeus was back with a tray holding my freshly made burger.

He looked even more annoyed that Sallie was in his seat, arching an eyebrow at her and looking down to the chair she sat in.

She quickly got out of his seat, offering for him to sit. "H-here you go, Zeke. Welcome back."

Zeus just stared at her, glancing over to the two of us. He paused his gaze on the real Zeke, who had the biggest smirk on his face.

With an eye roll, Zeus walked forward and slid the chair to his right, the move graceful but strong enough for it to slide right into the group of individuals sitting at the table next to us.

More than a few people looked our way, but Zeus didn't care as he placed the tray down and slid it in front of me.

"Sorry it took so long. The cafeteria lady wanted my autograph."

"Thank you." I beamed at his compassion, staring at the burger like it was one of a kind. "I'll be quick. We need to pass by the lockers."

"Cool," he replied, still ignoring Sallie, who at this point must have been so embarrassed it wasn't processing at all.

"Z-Zeke." Sallie's voice was squeakier, which only made it louder and more attention-grabbing. Poor Zeus was going to pop a vein with how angry he looked.

"Why can't anyone tell us apart?" he grumbled under his breath and looked to Sallie.

"Yes?"

"Um. I-I was wondering if maybe—"

"Get to the point," Zeus huffed. "What dumb event are you trying to invite me to?"

I hid my smirk by taking a bite of my burger. Zeke was having the time of his life, taking the seat next to me and casually leaning back to watch the show while his right hand lightly rested on my leg.

*Man, his touch alone makes me excited. Imagine hugging. Or dancing. Hmm. I'm gonna convince Shadow Jade to let me go to this party. If Zeus follows the plan.*

"It's a party. At my three-story mansion on Boulevard. We're only inviting a few chosen individuals and were wondering if you and your brothers would want to come?"

Zeus sighed. "When?"

Sallie clapped her hands and her face lit up like a puppy. "Next Friday! It would be awesome if you can come with your brothers," she offered.

Zeus looked at Zeke, whose finger was running circles along my skin while I multitasked at eating, listening, and attempting to breathe at a normal rate with how Zeke was teasing me.

"Zeus hates parties," Zeus declared, making me smile.

*They must be exchanging thoughts.*

"Zackery has a basketball game that night and Zion has a video game tournament. I can come, though," he explained.

"It would be amazing if you did." Sallie blinked her eyes, trying to pull off some form of seduction.

Zeus looked at me. "Are you going?"

"I wasn—"

"Of course, Jade's going," Sallie laughed, giving me a wide smile. "I was just telling her that she and her twin are both invited, but she was saying she has a date with Zeus."

Another arched eyebrow headed my way, but I'd already finished my burger and was patting my mouth with a napkin.

"Correct. I have a date with Zeus," I purred, leaning a little closer to Zeke for added emphasis. "We're testing the waters."

"Yup," Zeke agreed. "However, you should go. Parties are your thing and the rest of us will be out and about doing our own things. Jade's twin is going. Keep her company."

Sallie didn't look pleased with that comment, but she quickly hid her displeasure.

"Fine," Zeus sighed. "I'll come. Next Friday. The three-story mansion," he clarified.

"Yes, that one. You know all the rich kids live on that block," she bragged.

"I know." Zeus shrugged. "One of our homes is at the end of the block. Should only take five minutes to get there."

Sallie's jaw dropped open, and I could already hear the whispers from the tables around us. "Y-you mean the huge, four-story house with the pool, golf course, lake, and runway for that private jet?"

"Yup. That one. Since we're attending here, we decided to go back to our old home to stay for the year. We'll head to our second home in the next district during the summer," Zeus explained.

"Ah. Wow." That was all Sallie could say, looking shocked with the new information.

"Jade?" Zeke's warm voice had goosebumps running up my arms. I looked over to him, a second before he lightly kissed my lips, earning a few gasps from our audience.

"I'm heading back home. Only came to tell my bro something real quick. I'll see you later?"

"Yes. Text me when you get back," I replied. He rubbed his hand lightly up my thigh again, slipping under my skirt and gripping it slightly before he rose up.

My heart was racing, and I didn't want to focus on the spot between my legs or I'd bail out on the lockers and head straight to the girl's washroom.

*Wasn't going to go into my next class with an ache like that.*

"Okay. Bye, Jade. See ya, bro." Zeke waved, giving me a wink for added measure, and began to walk away, many of the other students watching his exit before turning their attention back to our table.

"Are you done?" Zeus asked, looking down at my tray.

"Yup." I nodded, pushing my chair back. "Can we pass the lockers? I need my tie."

He nodded his head in a silent reply, reaching for my tray and picking it up.

"So, Zeke," Sallie squeaked. "You're coming for sure?"

Zeus gave her a look, and she quickly put her hands in defense like he was about to attack her.

"I-I need it for the guest list."

"Yes, I'll be there. Is that all?" he questioned, his voice deeper and lacking emotion, making Sallie tremble.

*Not in a good way.*

"Yes, that's it. Thank you so much. I can't wait to se—"

Zeus turned away, heading to the three bins to separate the recycling from the trash and placing the tray on the already stacked ones.

Slipping my hands into my blazer pockets, I walked over to Sallie and winked.

"My twin will see you at the party. Have fun." With a proud smirk, I skipped over to where Zeus was waiting for me, hooking my arm around his.

He didn't seem to mind me playing along, the

two of us heading to the exit, knowing well that all the students were watching us.

We reached the hall and began to make our way to our lockers.

"Are you going to pop a vein?" I happily asked, leaning over to look at him.

He gave me side-eye, but his anger calmed down a notch. "I feel that would only excite you."

"It would. Blood everywhere." I used my free hand to demonstrate how it would pop. "However, I wouldn't want to clean it up."

"Doesn't even care about the chance of me dying." Zeus shook his head.

"Hmm. I'd be worried," I admitted, feeling the fire and thunder elements doing their thing inside me. Having a simple arm interlocked with his was already making it difficult to think.

"Just a little," I concluded.

Zeus looked at me, our eyes locking. I wondered what was running through his head when Zeke arrived, or what they were even talking about.

"Why did Zeke show up?" I inquired, trying to divert my attention from the pulsing energy between us.

"He's testing out Zion's prototype device. Trying to see if he can detect the same energy that was lurking around when you and Zackery were stuck in that trap," Zeus replied, looking away as we continued forward.

We turned down the empty hallway, heading for my locker, which upon arrival looked different than the rest.

Zeus grimaced, while I turned my head to the side to view the graffiti. "Hmm. The person misspelled slut," I pointed out, using my right index finger to point to the black paint that slashed against the red of my locker.

"That's what caught your attention?" Zeus sounded irritated.

"I don't care if they vandalize my locker. It's temporary. I only keep my tie in there because I hate wearing it all day long and I'll lose it if I keep it with me. Zeke puts his tie in his locker. Just makes sense," I voiced. "However. If they're going to try to call me an insulting term, they could at least spell it correctly."

Zeus sighed. "What's your code?"

"Why would I tell you?"

Zeus moved to face me, inching his face so close our lips were nearly touching. He stared into my eyes first, lowering his gaze to my lips and then back up. My gut told me he'd almost forgotten his train of thought.

"Because a, you trust me, and b, I want to make

sure nothing's inside ready to pop out at you."

"Aww. Are you trying to make my heart flutter in affection?" I teased. "It's not working, but okay."

*He is making something else flutter in need.*

I would have bet that he was one second from popping a vein, but he surprised me by closing the distance between our lips. I was ready to step back by instinct, but his arm hooked around my waist, pulling me against him as he deepened the kiss.

*Goddess, I can't ignore this.*

To say Zeus didn't turn me on as much as his three identical brothers would be the biggest lie of the school year. My flames burned for his, my body temperature spiking up with the bits of sparks fluttering down my arms and legs.

Zeus groaned when I kissed him right back, both his arms wrapping around my waist and holding me close. I could feel the drumming heat that pushed off his skin while tiny currents of electricity began to spark around us.

In the back of my mind, I knew we had to stop, but fuck. He tasted so fucking good, and I wasn't ashamed to want more. I was against the red lockers before I knew it, his body pressed against mine and his tongue tangling with mine as we fought for control.

My hands moved along his back, fingertips

digging into his blazer, as we continued to kiss. The energy building between us was getting to a dangerous high, but we kept going.

The consequences of this would have to take a back seat while we simply enjoyed how amazing this felt.

When his groin pressed against me, I almost came from the mere touch.

There was a huge popping sound as all the lights in the hallway went out at once, leaving us in pitch darkness.

We broke the kiss and I could see his eyes were now a vivid glow of gold, red, and orange. I wondered if my eyes were doing the same, but I couldn't tell.

While we both focused on catching our breath, we could hear the commotion farther down the hall, the two of us moving our gazes to see that our hallway wasn't the only one blacked out.

Zeus let out a groan. "Stop bothering me. It wasn't me," he grumbled.

I looked back at him, arching an eyebrow for him to enlighten me with what his comment was referring to.

"Zeke thinks I caused the blackout," he muttered. I grinned, hooking my arms around his neck and bringing his face closer.

"Before I get to that, why did you kiss me?"

He slowly bit his lip, his eyes scanning mine. "Blame Zeke," he grumbled.

"Zeke is walking around the school. You, on the other hand, are right here," I purred. Zeus swallowed, our energies dying to be reunited once again.

I was fighting the urge, but it was a difficult match to win. That connection was what I would consider an addiction.

*An addiction I would indulge in over and over again if it didn't cause blackouts.*

"I'm intrigued," I whispered, brushing my lips lightly against his, a light spark jolting there. He bit his bottom lip in return but tightened his hold around my waist and held me even closer to him.

I had to hide how our proximity was affecting me. I was waiting patiently with an amused expression on my face, but my mind was racing, trying to calm my hormones and tell my lady bits to settle the fuck down.

"Zeke seriously likes you," he admitted.

"Do you like me?" I questioned.

I wasn't brushing away the fact he revealed Zeke liked me as more than just a Tracker-class-mate-friend working together in one common goal. But I needed to know.

"Not sure," he admitted. "But you're dangerous

to be around."

"Because?"

"You make me want more," he whispered. "And that's a far too dangerous want to have."

"Does it imbalance you four?" I pondered.

"Somewhat," he replied. "If only Zeke could follow the rules."

"If Zeke is anything like me, he doesn't do rules."

"That's exactly the problem and why we are both standing in the dark," Zeus replied.

"Not bad." I shrugged. "Could always take advantage."

"I'd love to, but we're going to be late for class," he whispered. Moving away from me, he eased over to my locker.

"Number."

"12345," I concluded, needing the space to think straight.

"That's stupid," he mumbled but began putting the code in. "Anyone can figure that out."

"And yet you asked," I reminded, leaning against the lockers and slipping my hands back into my blazer pockets.

I was expecting his side-eye, and he merely groaned when he saw my enjoyment. "You love when I'm angry."

"It's kind of hot," I admitted. "Aside from me worrying you'll pop a vein, muscle, or your brain cells, I'd be perfectly fine seeing you upset."

"You wouldn't say that in bed," he casually replied, opening my locker and searching it with his eyes. When nothing popped out, he took my tie and closed my locker. He offered me my tie, staring into my eyes once more.

"I actually would." I surprised him with my answer, the shock flooding his eyes.

Or enlightening them with the possibilities.

Taking my tie from his hold, I hooked it around my neck. "Angry sex is hot. It means steamy, dominating stuff. All we'd be missing are some candles and whips. You can do a lot with those and a bit of imagination."

"I can't handle you." Zeus shook his head. "No wonder you connect with Zeke the most."

"Does that mean he likes whips and candles?" I clapped my hands.

"No," Zeus argued.

"That's no fun." I pouted my lips.

Zeus pinched his nose. "I don't know what he likes in that department."

"Do you like it?" I asked.

When he didn't reply, I actually squealed. "It's going to be so fun with you in bed. When you have sex, does lightning strike through the sky? No. A better question. If you have sex in the forest, does it cause fires? Are you the reason why there was that huge fire after this party a year ago in the other district and—?"

"No, that wasn't me," he groaned. "Fix your tie."

"You're avoiding my question!" I argued.

"No, I wasn't at a party last year."

"So you do start fires and shoot lightning in the sky when you orga—" He slammed his lips against mine to shut me up, his hands working overtime by fixing my tie all at the same time.

I was in no way fazed this time when he kissed me suddenly, pressing my lips firmly against his and struggling not to fall in the depths of our emotions.

He released me when he finished fixing my tie, but I didn't mind tugging on his bottom lip lightly with my teeth.

"Dangerous," he huffed.

"A lot of people say that. I wonder why." I giggled. Twirling on one foot, I slipped my hands in my pockets. "We should go before the professors come down here. Don't wanna explain that we were the cause of the blackout."

"Jade," Zeus whispered.

His arm managed to hook around my waist, even with my hands in my pockets. He pressed his body against my back and lips lightly brushed my neck.

"You really don't want anything to do with us. We're trouble." His voice held a hint of hurt, leaving me to wonder what he and his brothers had gone through in the past.

Turning just slightly, I kissed him, not with urgency or a determination to outdo him, but as a simple connection that held a hint of comfort.

"If I didn't know that, I wouldn't have called you guys the Trouble Four."

He let go of my waist and I began to skip away. "We're going to be late if you don't start skipping."

He was silent, and I wondered if he heard me, but I noticed his presence was close, and with a slight look over my shoulder, I realized he was now walking only a step behind.

"Boo," I commented. "I wanted to see you skip."

"That's Zackery's job. I'm not looking like a fool in love."

"But you are in love." I winked, earning me another one of his looks.

*Zeus, Tracker of Thunder and Fire. He never argued about my comment, making me wonder if I'd get the chance to enjoy his flaming thunder lips again.*

## 14

## CHEMISTRY AND DATING AGREEMENT

"**D**ate me."

"Last time I checked, we apparently were." I playfully smirked at Zeke, who was placing his tie inside his locker.

"You mean based off of Tracker Hive Gossip Blog, or the Tracker Hive Insider who loves to entertain the gossip community?" he questioned.

"Probably both, but I don't follow either," I admitted with a shrug, trying to stretch my arms and get rid of a knot in my shoulders. "Though because of our little demonstration of affection last week, the community is divided."

"Really?" Zeke appeared intrigued, closing his locker and giving me his full attention. "Which side is winning?"

"Between you and Zeus? It's at an equal rating

from this morning," I replied, giving up on my attempt to release the annoying knot. I'd take a bath when I got home and hope the relaxing waters would aid it.

"You said you don't follow either." His smirk was to die for, and if it weren't for the little restraint I'd gathered up to tackle this entire week, I would have jumped into his arms and enjoyed those lips and their taunts.

"I don't. I overheard the girls in the change room after class," I explained.

All of this week was Tracker Simulation. We'd conduct different assignments, the simulation created within the walls of our gym. It was easy enough for Zeke and me, making this week breeze by.

We'd also been very flirty this week. I was prepared for it, but damn. Zeke was that favorite snack you hid in the cabinet for those emergency days.

Our connection was so strong, Alaric, Bianca, and Tanner said Shadow Jade would have to stay home.

*Not like that was a bad thing for Shadow Jade.*

She'd been spoiled all week, having gone with Bianca on a class trip.

*Lucky darkness.*

It turned out that having two individuals with enormously strong dark elements in the same room heightened the power atmosphere. We didn't feel it during our sessions in the gym because the gym was so large, but for the brief moments we were all in a small room? At least five people passed out this week because there was a lack of oxygen.

*Who knew darkness stole oxygen for fun?*

Today was the big day of the party, and Shadow Jade wasn't up for it. She'd decided to spend the evening with Bianca painting her nails black and watching horror movies. I also figured she'd be reorganizing her collections of dolls again, since Bianca bought her another one for being cooperative all week.

"Is Shadow Jade coming along tonight?" Zeke asked.

"Physically? No," I replied. "She had a crying fit earlier before I left."

"Crying fit?" Zeke looked surprised. "She has those?"

"Sometimes. She used to have tantrums, or she'd become curious and wonder what a room would look like completely destroyed," I explained. "Just the usual stuff the dark element is known for. She did have a valid reason this time."

"What was that?" Zeke asked.

"She has a horror marathon to watch later tonight. She's obsessed with them. Also, Bianca gave her a new doll for her collection. She'll be sorting that first, which will take her a few hours, and the marathon starts at nine tonight."

"She's reorganizing the entire thing? Why doesn't she put it in the spot where it fits?" Zeke genuinely asked. He wasn't judging her. I felt he wanted to know her process.

"It doesn't feel new to her unless she takes everything down and organizes it so it reflects the true change of the new addition to the collection. Shadow Jade organizes everything by color, then by the type of doll, its rarity, and value. It's really complicated and hard to follow. It keeps her entertained and at least it's better than her destroying everything."

"Intriguing." He grinned. "Easier to maintain."

"I've always wondered. Are you able to make your darkness or light element into a physical entity?" I asked. "Or is that another 'Jade is weird' thing?"

"I like weird Jade." He winked.

"Your brother told me that," I replied.

He arched an eyebrow at me. "Who?"

"Zeus."

"Remind me to kick his balls later," he

concluded. "To answer your question, yes. I actually can make my darkness and light into a person the way you do with Shadow Jade."

"How long did it take you to realize Shadow Jade wasn't my twin?" I asked, keeping my voice a tad lower.

He slipped his hand into mine, and the two of us began to walk down the hall toward the exit of the main campus building.

"The whole time," he replied. "I just like going along with things."

"Why haven't I seen either of them?" I asked. We weren't close yet, but this wasn't an opportunity I wanted to miss.

"One is cocky and the other makes me cringe," he answered.

"Cringe as in eww, you're too holy for me?"

"Cringe as in I don't want to be near him when he goes on a purification raid."

"Purification. Isn't that supposed to heal people?"

"My light side has other plans with that."

"Kills?"

"Yup."

"How?" I asked.

"Purification as in cleansing the sins out of one

body. The problem with that? We are all born out of sin."

"That..." Pausing to think about it, I decided he did have a point. "That makes sense."

"Thus, the reason why I keep them both on the down low," he summarized. "They're bigger flirts anyway."

"The more the merrier," I hummed.

"I figured out of all the people, you'd think of this as a good thing and not a problem," Zeke mused.

"Why would it be a bad thing?" I asked. "I understand they're hard to control and they do their own thing, but I never considered that a bad thing."

"You don't think so because you have an accepting personality and are surrounded by those who see Shadow Jade as an individual as well as an asset," Zeke explained. "Our district isn't like that."

We reached outside, walking down the stairs and heading to the parking lot where Zeke's car was parked. I could easily walk home, but he insisted I let him drive me.

*It was what a boyfriend would do.*

I had nothing against us dating, but I wasn't sure it would go well. I didn't want to upset the others either. I'd joked about it numerous times since the start of the semester, but I wasn't sure if they really wanted to share one girl.

I'd be up for the challenge and fun. All I needed was the four of them to agree.

Heading to Zeke's matte black sports car, we walked over to the passenger side. Squeezing my hand slightly, he paused in his attempt to open the car door for me like he'd always done since driving me.

"You're thinking about something," he noted.

"Yes, but multiple things," I admitted, deciding to rest back against his car. Zeke grinned, clearly checking me out.

He slid his hands into his pockets and waited for me to carry on. I personally loved that. It showed he was intrigued by what I had to say and took it seriously.

"Back to your first statement. Do you actually want to date me?"

"I wouldn't have asked if I didn't," he replied.

"What if your brothers like me, too?" I inquired, observing his entire persona. I wanted to catch even the slightest switch in behavior with my flood of questions.

"It wouldn't matter. I'd still want to date you."

"Would you seriously be fine with me dating all

four of you? If that was 'allowed' and the four of you agreed."

"Perfectly fine," he confirmed.

Staring at him for a few seconds, I determined he was speaking the full truth.

*He's really okay with it. Very intriguing.*

I knew he'd pick up on why I was being extra cautious about this, even if it wasn't my normal behavior. Another common attribute of those who carried darkness was their possessiveness.

They hated sharing with others, but it happened in spurts for either short or long periods. I'd seen it plenty of times with Shadow Jade, and that possessiveness had influenced me a few times.

It wasn't necessarily a bad thing, but it was a characteristic that could be bad in a relationship with three other individuals.

"If you're worried about me being possessive, I'm not that bad."

"Define 'not that bad'," I encouraged with a tiny smirk on my face.

"When we were kids, we each got teddy bears for our fifth birthday. I loved my black bear, but Zeus had a white one with gold eyes and I liked that one too. It reminded me of my light element. So I took it."

"That's horrible," I said, struggling not to laugh. "Please tell me you gave it back to him."

"I did." He nodded with pride. "After a year."

I gawked at him. "That is NOT what you consider 'not too bad!' Did Zeus cry?"

"In the beginning, yeah. Zackery gave him his bear and I think my mom bought him another one or something. I did give it back to him."

"My gut tells me he didn't want it anymore and you kept it," I sighed.

"Accurate," he replied.

"That proved absolutely nothing. It doesn't even lean in your favor." I smirked.

"True, but it was honest. That gives me some points." He winked, taking two steps forward. He leaned down to press his forehead against mine.

"Yes, I'm possessive. I like to protect what is mine and hate sharing. However, with my brothers, I can make a small exception and try to fight against that strong craving to keep what I love all to myself."

My ears were listening to everything he said, but his husky voice was having that lovely hypnotic effect on me, making it hard for me to follow along.

*Or it could be his closeness, or his gentle cologne that wrapped around me, or even just me enjoying the tingles that were teasing my body.*

"You're not listening."

"Listening, yes. Absorbing the information? Give me an extra minute," I whispered.

"I really do want to date you, Jade Storm."

"There's a lot of layers of me, Zeke. Do you really want to attempt to peel each one?"

I was weird, that was obvious, but did he or the others want to dive into knowing me? The true me under the layers of protection built from a single year of devastation?

*Would they really be okay with that? And was I okay with letting them in?*

"I'd be more than happy to peel back every single layer and learn all the shades of our Junior Tracker," he whispered against my lips before sealing them completely.

I made a mental note to return to the 'Junior' mention, but I allowed myself to let go and revel in this sweet and gradual kiss. I wasn't worried about people seeing us, or the fact we were kissing in public for anyone to see.

All I wanted was to enjoy Zeke's lips and allow myself to accept how serious his statement was.

*He wants me. Would the others be down for all of this?*

The thought made a bubble of emotions boil inside me; my elements felt just as thrilled at the idea. Their reaction to my feelings was only making this into something I wanted to happen.

Zeke smirked against my lips, prompting me to open my eyes.

"What?"

"Slow kissing with you makes me feel really calm," he admitted.

"And not-so-slow kissing?"

"Makes me want to pin you against the wall and do a lot more than kissing. My energy spikes up to the 'let's not think' level."

"Fun." I licked my lips. "And I'll be a regular Tracker before you know it."

"I never doubted that." He chuckled. "And you're clearly down for either."

"If it means more kissing, yes," I replied.

"Do you want me to answer more questions?" he asked. I grinned and gently wrapped my arms around his waist, giving him a soft hug.

"No," I whispered, resting my head against his chest. I listened to his swift heart rate, the sound only making my grin widen.

"When would our first date be?"

"Tonight," he suggested.

"Since you missed what little Sallie Walker said before your arrival," I teased, using the song lyric to add to the amusement, "I wasn't originally invited. Only Shadow Jade."

"Why?" Zeke asked, his hand possessively wrapping around my waist as he returned the hug, the two of us staying in that embrace while we continued our conversation.

"She's cooler than me, I think? Who knows."

"Silly," Zeke mumbled. "Come with me tonight."

"What about my supposed date with Zeus?" I teased, knowing that was merely a cover.

"That isn't valid when you're not regular Jade." He leaned back to look down at me, giving me a playful smirk. "You'll be Shadow Jade at the party."

"I'll do my best to act the part," I assured.

"That means you're going?"

"I do like a good party. As long as they have sweet alcohol."

"Do you drink?"

"Not often. I like whatever Bianca hides in my dad's fridge in his office."

"You sneak in there and drink some, huh?"

"Guilty as charged."

"What are you going to wear tonight?"

"I'm not sure," I confessed. "Whatever I wear won't matter since the girls call me a slut anyway."

"Which you aren't," Zeke grumbled. "You get a new locker?"

"Not yet. Zeus won't let me use my old one until it's changed. Now that you mention it, I wonder where I put my tie?"

I didn't have it around my neck, and I didn't remember the last time I had it aside from this morning.

"You lose stuff a lot?"

"I lose my tie at the same rate as hair ties. It just falls in the category of lost and never found until you don't need it." I rested my chin on his chest, continuing to look up at him. "I'll get a new one from Alaric."

"I'll give you one of mine," he concluded.

"Possessive," I replied. "Pretty smooth move."

He looked beyond happy with me catching onto his flirting ways. I, too, was really pleased about all of this. My conversations with each of the Maxwell brothers were simply refreshing.

I didn't need to think or worry about what I had to say around them, making the whole idea of being around them more eventful and relaxing.

"Wear something sexy tonight," Zeke stated. "You look nice in skirts."

"I feel you just want to enjoy touching my legs."

"You like it," he countered.

"I never said I didn't," I countered back.

"I wanna dance with you and feel you up," he whispered.

"Your directness really turns me on," I purred back.

"Good." He inched his head lower. "Make sure you tell your family you're not coming home tonight."

"I'm not?" Now I was really growing hot, and it wasn't because of the weather.

"Nope," he answered.

"Where?"

"Hotel. We could go to my place, but it's far and our family home won't give us the privacy I think we deserve."

"What if our elements act out?"

If Zeus and I could cause the entire school to have a blackout with our kiss, I could only imagine what my heated connection with Zeke would brew.

"There are special suites for that."

"You did your research."

We ended up kissing again, but it was short.

"No wonder Zeus was nagging me."

We turned our attention to the familiar voice, noticing Zackery's approach.

"Hey, Zackery," I greeted.

"It's always interesting to actually be identified correctly by someone," he replied. "Hey, Jade."

"Tell Zeus I don't need babysitting," Zeke replied to Zackery's main statement.

"Oh, I'm not here to babysit. I was originally here to test this prototype." Zackery lifted his wrist, showing off a device that looked similar to an Apple watch. "But then he was complaining about his gut instinct telling him a certain brother was being all touchy with our Jade."

"I love how 'we' have a claim on her yet you three haven't even told her seriously that you're into her," Zeke mumbled.

Zackery stopped in front of us, his eyes showing his moment of clarity.

"Shit, we didn't. Hmm. I thought that was an obvious conclusion." Zackery glanced to me, looking sad. "Sorry, Jade. Did you think we were leading you on?"

"Not like that," I admitted. "It was more of feeling worried about whether you all wanted to date."

"We're serious about that." Zackery looked me straight in the eye. "I can vouch for the other two, but if you want, I can text them now."

"You don't hav—"

Zackery was already pulling his phone out and

tapping his thumbs against the screen. "Zion should answer in less than fifty seconds, and Zeus will most likely ignore me."

"Why fifty seconds?" I glanced at Zeke, who chuckled. "Zion and text messages is like dropping food on the floor and giving yourself the five-second rule to pick it up."

Zackery's phone pinged, and he smirked. "Zion's perfectly fine with it," He displayed his phone to us, allowing me to scan the last message he sent and Zion's response.

### SMART BROTHER ZIZI:

"Wasn't that always the agreement? I like Jade. She's intriguing, different, and hot. We're all attracted to her. Don't see the problem. If we break it up by percentage, we're all at equal footing. As in you, Zeus, and I got 20% and Zeke got 40% because he's a selfish motherfucker. Anyway, tell Jade we're chill with dating her. As long as she doesn't mind. Whatever she wants, she'll get. Now hurry back. I have my tournament to go to."

*Zizi? A cute nickname for Zion.*

"I'm not a selfish motherfucker," Zeke grumbled next to my left ear, peering over my shoulder at the text. "I do deserve forty percent."

"Selfish as fuck." Zackery shook his head. "He's giving you that percentage because he doesn't want any more of your fantasies leaking into our heads."

"Fantasies, huh?" I repeated.

Zackery groaned. "I swear, they're detailed as fuck. Just be a writer or something and write books about all these fantasies you have. Poor Zeus can't stand them. It makes him want to do impulsive stuff."

*Was that why he couldn't help but kiss me after the confrontation last week at lunch?*

"I really doubt Zeus is going to reply to me," Zackery groaned.

"It isn't that urge..." I trailed off when Zeke pulled his phone and tapped it to speed dial. He placed it on speaker, the dial ringing twice before Zeus picked up.

"Fuck off."

"Can you pause your masturbating session for a second?" Zeke asked.

"I'm not—you know what? There's no point in wasting time on you. Why are you calling? If it isn't urgent, as in the world is ending, or about Jade, I'm hanging up."

My heart fluttered lightly at his mention of my

name, rating me on the same level as the world's end.

"Can you let Jade know that we're in agreement about all four of us dating her?"

"Wasn't that obvious or did Zackery fuck it up somehow?"

"I didn't do shit!" Zackery argued.

"Sure. You probably contributed to the miscommunication somehow," Zeus groaned. "Tell Jade we're in agreement since we agreed to work together on figuring out the school situation. Besides, if we're the bees to her Hive, we're more than happy to enjoy her loving nature in many ways."

My cheeks began to flush, finding the hidden meaning in his words.

*Something tells me all four of them are going to be interesting in the sheets.*

"We'll tell her."

"Tell Zackery to hurry up and come back. He's got his game and I have shit to do tonight."

"Aside from masturbating," Zeke mused.

"I hope you get cockblocked tonight," Zeus muttered.

"Now that's just rude," Zeke huffed.

"Whatever. I'm hanging up." He didn't let anyone reply before the line went dead.

Zeke grinned. "That's settled then."

Zackery looked at me and gave me a dazzling smile.

"Guess you're officially dating the Trouble Four, Jade," he cheered. "Now Zeke can drive me back home before I'm late."

Zeke appeared annoyed but didn't argue. "Get in the car."

Zackery laughed in joy, making his way around the car to the driver's side and opening the door. He pushed the seat down to climb into the back.

Zeke moved to open the passenger door for me and gave me a saucy gaze.

"Get in, baby," he encouraged. "We've got a date tonight."

*I was in for an electrifying night. I could feel it.*

## ❧ 15 ❧

### ZEKE OF LIGHT AND DARKNESS

"You look hot," Zeke moaned against my mouth.

"Are we going to stay in your car tonight?" I inquired, acknowledging the fact we'd just spent half an hour making out in his car.

"Maybe," he whispered. "Haven't decided if we should be good Trackers and attend this party for research or fuck it all and go to the hotel instead."

I smirked, unable to stop myself from kissing him.

Zeke had dropped me off at home first, allowing me to find an outfit, take that relaxing bath, give Shadow Jade a recap while she showed off her new doll to me and gave me her recap of the day, and tell Alaric and Bianca that I'd be going out tonight for "research."

I could tell from their grins they knew I wasn't coming home, but Alaric simply said I was an adult and as long as I didn't destroy any property, he was fine with it.

Tanner was working late grading papers and said we wouldn't be doing training tomorrow morning, giving me the sleep-in card.

To enjoy an actual date for the first time in my life was an intriguing experience. I was confident in my skin and more than capable of walking into a club, picking a man that enticed me, having a quickie, and moving on. But with this first date, I actually wanted to try.

I'd gone through my entire closet, deciding to appease Zeke's wish by wearing a short skirt. It was long enough to cover the essentials, but I knew once we started dancing, he'd easily get a glimpse of my plump ass cheeks.

I did try to make the outfit look less slutty, wearing high knee socks that were as thin as pantyhose. They even had a rip pattern going down the front, which matched my red shirt that had cuts all along the back.

*Though, slutty was kind of the look I wanted just to piss people off. I mean, if people were going to label me that way, I might as well play my role exceptionally well.*

I wore black Christian Louboutin heels and

curled my black and white hair. I took my time going through my luxurious collection of lingerie, picking out the perfect red and black set with rhinestones, lace, and even black and red beads that surprisingly hid well under my fitted top.

With my black eyeshadow, red lipstick, and very simple jewelry to complete the look, I was impressed.

When Zeke picked me up, it was clear that I'd gone above and beyond, and he was totally digging the outfit.

*With the added bonus of voicing his desire to take it off.*

He wore black fitted jeans and a white branded shirt with a bunch of symbols in black ink. He had a black Rolex watch and a few black and white beaded bracelets. His hair was up in a little pony-tail, revealing his one black stud earring.

He was extra attractive in casual clothes, and it was hard for me to keep my hands off of him. I kind of wished we could ditch the party and simply enjoy each other's company.

*However, this is the perfect opportunity to gather some information.*

"We should go," I encouraged, sliding my hand beneath his shirt, giving me a chance to feel his rock-hard abs.

His eyes darkened at my physical taunting. "Not when you're testing me like that," he whispered.

"Didn't you say Zion gave you another proto-type for the tracker device?" I reminded.

He lifted his hand to show his Rolex.

"It's in there?" I asked, peering closer to take a look at the blinged-out diamond piece.

"It's right in the middle there," Zeke replied.

"Ah." I noticed the tiny black star shape in the middle. "Blends well with the design."

"Agreed," Zeke replied. "I guess we should go. I don't want to be scolded by Zion. Once he gets into his research, he takes it all so seriously."

"That's a good thing as a Tracker, though," I admitted.

"Mhm," Zeke replied. "Still annoying."

"We don't need to stay for long," I encouraged. "Just a little viewing, talking, listening, and dancing."

"And kissing, grinding, and making sure everyone in that place knows you're mine."

"Ah. Your possessiveness is surfacing again," I flirted.

"You love it."

"I do." Kissing him quickly, I pulled away and picked up a tiny purse that held my phone.

My change of clothes was in the back and would stay there until we made it to the hotel.

I had no issues sleeping nude, but I didn't like wearing my previous night's outfit. You never knew who you touched and where their hands had been. Once the clothes were off, they went straight to dry cleaning the next day.

It was safer, especially with many reports of innocent people being accused of murder because of evidence found on their clothing.

*As a Tracker, I wasn't going to be caught in one of those situations.*

"The sooner we get this over with, the sooner we can fuck," I reminded my date.

Zeke bit his bottom lip. "You know how to motivate me."

He got out of the car, walking over to my side to open it up for me. Offering his hand, he helped me out and pressed a button to make the doors close on their own.

"Fancy," I commented.

"Do you have your license?" he inquired, the two of us making our way down the block to Sallie's mansion.

"I do. But Alaric won't let me drive unless it's for an assignment."

"Why?"

"I like to break all the rules. Driving makes me want to see just how fast I can go while swerving through traffic and disobeying traffic signs. I'm good for high-speed chases," I explained.

"Sexy," he complimented. "Drive us to the hotel."

I laughed. "You have a death wish."

"If it means getting to spend all my time with you, then let the reaper knock on my door. I'll pay for my funeral costs ahead of time."

"Flirt." I giggled, leaning into him. He let go of my hand to wrap an arm around my shoulder.

"Are you excited?" he asked quietly as we approached the mansion, more guests showing up. All their eyes were on us now, which only boosted my confidence even higher.

"I've never gone on a real date."

"Never?" Zeke sounded surprised. "Why is that?"

"I don't know. When you look at me, I don't give off the date vibe," I suggested.

"No one can look at someone's appearance and determine whether they love to date or not," he replied, his voice portraying a hint of annoyance. "Anyone who assumes such isn't into you for the right reasons."

"You think so?" I whispered.

"I asked you out. We're more than aware of our chemistry. Doesn't mean I'm fine with just taking you to bed. Your happiness and feelings matter to me, and I'd rather know what you want to do to make this experience special rather than assume all you would want is a quickie."

"If only all men thought that way," I whispered.

He didn't say anything more, the two of us reaching the invitation-only line. There was another line for those not invited but hoping for some spare space for them to get entry.

With what I knew about Sallie so far, from observing her in class and gossip, was that she loved to show off and let the world know what was going on. Then she'd limit access to really hype up the event.

It apparently made her popular, or that's what the gossip girls claimed, but I didn't see anything cool about it. If you want to have a party, do it and invite those you want. Don't say everyone can come, but secretly send invites to the ones you'd actually prefer to be there.

Seeing as I was mature in some ways, I wasn't one to get all crazy for the chance of being invited, but from the no-invite line, girls were screaming and praying to get in.

Zeke pulled out his phone from his pocket,

keeping me close as he flashed it at the security. The tall, buff man glanced at both of us, looking us up and down before he used his head to gesture for us to continue walking forward.

For security, they sure were slacking. I could have had a weapon on me, and they wouldn't have even noticed.

*Not like either of us needed one. We were the ultimate weapon when our elements unleashed.*

"Is Shadow Jade still organizing her collection?" Zeke asked as we made our way through another security checkpoint, which was just as lazy as the last.

"No, she's done. She's chilling in my head until her horror marathon," I admitted, feeling her presence.

She liked being quiet when I was being intimate with others, but I sensed her curiosity regarding the lack of security.

***"Poor Security. Kill?"*** she asked.

*Nah. I think we'll lay low tonight. If this is a huge party that everyone is fighting to attend like Sallie made it seem, we need to gather information with our eyes.*

***"Boring,"*** she admitted.

A smirked formed on my lips and I looked at Zeke, who was eyeing me.

"She's bored and says the security sucks," I summarized.

"I feel you there. I'm hoping the music is better on the second floor because the current tunes suck."

"It will be different?" I asked.

"At parties like these, there are levels. First one is the general, anyone-can-be-here floor. The second is for more of the cooler people and seniors. The third floor is usually the last and for the elite and exclusive kids on the block. All floors are sound-proof, which is why they can play different music. At home, we have four floors, so we'd add a fourth category —royal status — when we had parties."

"Royal, huh?" I asked.

"Yup. Us, and anyone we specifically wanted up there. Sallie's email said we have access to all three floors. I think all the juicy stuff will be on the third floor."

"No doubt about that," I admitted. "What's our plan? Chill and listen?"

"Yup. We can go through each floor and test out Zion's device. I do think whoever is monitoring us wouldn't miss this opportunity, especially with it being noted we'd be attending."

"You mean on the gossip blogs?" I inquired,

making sure my purse was locked before loosening the black chain and putting it over my head and across my body so it hung on the side of my hip with no issue.

"Yup. Sallie published the guest list earlier this morning."

"So you do pay attention?"

"Nah." Zeke shook his head. "Zeus told me on the way out. That, and if you somehow get hurt he'll sacrifice my blood to some cult."

"Well." I thought about it. "At least the brotherly love is strong."

"I don't know what in the sentence with sacrifice, blood, and cult shows any demonstration of brotherly love, but sure." Zeke laughed, holding me closer to him as he kissed my cheek.

That attracted the attention of the many people attending, a few individuals already pulling their phones out to take pictures. It was time for both of us to do our parts in this mini-investigation.

Wrapping my arm around Zeke's, I did my utmost best to be as flirty and lovey-dovey as I could. It wasn't super hard. In fact, it was easy when it came to Zeke.

Our conversations were casual yet complemented one another in so many ways. It was like he was meant to be with me, which made me feel even more accepting of the thought of dating him and his three brothers, because they were all connected.

We'd yet to research more about this Hive thing, but from our general understanding from Alaric, Bianca, and Tanner's demonstration, our unique connection was something people would die to have, especially in the main Tracker District.

*Or in the depths of the Black Market.*

Bobbing my head to the music, and having a few Kill song moments, we reached the second floor. I personally wanted to do a quick outfit check and listen in on any gossip in the washrooms.

There was no need to check the first floor. It was overly crowded and not the place for girls to stand and chat. However, the second and third floors would be perfect spots.

The second floor, in my mind, would be the most popular due to it being for the upper peeps who loved to gossip and gather the exclusives for their lame blogs.

Slipping my arms around Zeke's waist to get his attention, I leaned up to whisper in his ear.

"I'm gonna do a little listening in the washroom."

"Hmm." He glanced down at me for a moment. "That's all?"

"Yup." I went on my tiptoes again to whisper.

"If I needed anything else, I'd ask you to sneak in and join me." Lightly tugging his earlobe with my teeth, I heard his throat rumble at my playful taunt.

"This is why the others say you're dangerous."

"I'm merely different and not afraid to say or do what I want."

Finishing my statement with a kiss to his lips, I pulled away and waltzed over to the hall with a hanging sign that gave directions to the restroom. I could feel Zeke's eyes on me, only making me want to slow my walk to emphasize my hip movement.

*Let's be real. Every girl loved to remind their man of what they had.*

This was our first date, but there was no way I wasn't going to be fierce in my execution. I wanted this to continue, or at least last for a few dates rather then be a simple one-night fling.

*My gut told me this could actually last.*

Reaching the washroom door, I took a deep inhale, letting the air out slowly and getting into my Tracker mode. I'd been feeling a little uneasy since we'd walked in. Clubs or any type of dark atmosphere with low lights always gave me the same uncomfortable vibe.

In my homeless days, I'd been terrified of complete darkness. Now it was one of those many things I simply accepted and had to overcome. Going to clubs and parties in my teens was just another way of tackling the demon and immunizing myself to those triggers, just like I had with change rooms.

Entering the bathroom, I went into one of the free stalls and locked it. Pulling my phone out, I quickly scanned those silly blog posts, knowing how fast they would be uploading the pictures of anyone arriving at the party.

*Talk about the paparazzi, Tracker Hive Academy Edition.*

With a simple click to the most popular blog for Tracker Hive gossip, I landed on a picture of Zeke and me on the front page.

*"Us!"* Shadow Jade cheered.

*You're right about that. Hmm. Not a bad picture, honestly. We should get that developed. Looks like they can't tell if it's me or you. I guess they figured it was Zeke who attended. Good for them for getting it right, but that could have been because of that statement at lunch last week.*

I began to scroll through the images, pausing at the familiar haircut in one of them. My heart skipped a beat while my eyes narrowed on the not-so-clear image.

Taking a deep breath, I took a screenshot of it

and moved on, trying to see if I could get any other pictures of this individual.

*"Kill."* Shadow Jade's statement had a homicidal tone to it.

*We don't know if it's him, Shadow Jade. A lot of people have the same haircut.*

Scrolling back to the picture on the blog, I shivered at the reminder of the man who turned my life upside down. The one who started this all with his arrival to our home on my eighth birthday.

Closing the browser, I crossed my arms over my chest and took a minute to breathe and calm my beating heart.

*He'll eventually show himself. I have to live my life and not let him interfere like this. There's no confirmation that it is him, and I'm not the little girl who knew nothing about her elements. I can control them now, I can defend myself, and I have the resources and support to go against him and his crew of bad guys. Nothing to fear.*

*"Me! Here to Kill,"* Shadow Jade added for reinforcement.

*I know. Thank you, Shadow Jade.*

I wished she was here just for me to hug and pet her head. She knew me inside and out, and at times like these, having that sense of knowledge helped on so many levels.

The sound of four sets of heels caught my attention, and I locked my phone and slid it back into my purse.

"I swear I saw her entering this washroom."

The female voice was unrecognizable to me. With a pout of my lips, I lifted my leg to the handle of the toilet, pressing down to make it flush.

*Time to have some fun.*

Opening the door, I walked straight to the row of sinks, intentionally ignoring the four women standing to my right.

Deliberately taking my time to wash my hands, I began to sing Shadow Jade's Kill song quietly as a way to keep count of how many seconds needed to pass while rubbing my soapy hands together.

"Hey."

I rinsed my hands, ignoring whoever had simply said hey. I wasn't going to answer when I was sure they knew my name, or at least my last name.

"Masters!" the girl huffed.

It wasn't necessarily my name, but it was my adopted surname at school. It would have to do.

Turning my attention to the girls while I soaked my hands under the stream of warm water, I replied, "Hmm?"

The four girls exchanged a look, moving up until they were a step away from me. They were trying to be intimidating, but that was a little hard with them barely wearing proper clothes. I had definitely underdressed, but that was on purpose, and I still covered most of my ass and breasts.

These girls looked more like hookers with their almost see-through tops that had their nipples poking against the fabric, and their short dresses that barely covered their asses.

The main girl and two others were wearing visible thongs, only adding to their very provocative way of saying 'I want to be fucked, take me away.' Obviously, their lack of clothing didn't give anyone permission to touch them, but our society, or should I say the justice system that I'd seen with my own eyes, would work against them in this case.

To them, an outfit like this screamed trouble, but I wasn't going to be the messenger. You could say that about any outfit, but jeez. I wasn't sure I'd be bold enough to come out in public with some of these outfits.

*Just walk naked if you're going to wear a dress that practically matches your skin color, barely covers your ass when you're standing, has your breasts nearly popping out, and puts your nipples on display.*

After a good assessment of the girl in the nude dress, who so happened to be the leader of this group, I waited for them to continue.

"I said hey," the nude dress chick declared.

"You actually said Masters, but all right." I shrugged.

Her irritation had me cackling on the inside, but I was able to keep my face blank as she spoke. "Your sister didn't come after all?"

"She's around," I replied. "Jade had her date earlier." I thought it would be fun to make them think 'Jade" was at the party too, along with Zeke and me in my Shadow Jade disguise.

The main girl flicked her shoulder-length hair, standing proudly as she placed her hands on her hips.

"We need you to tell your sister to back off," she declared.

"Back off? From what?" I asked innocently, trying to match Shadow's Jade persona. She was more innocent and didn't catch on to things like I did, but these girls didn't know the difference beyond Shadow Jade's usual Kill song behavior.

*Who was I even kidding? They couldn't even tell I wasn't her.*

"Yes. Tell her to stop flirting with the rest of the Maxwell brothers," the main chick addressed. "I'm surprised you're okay with her trying to steal your man."

"My man?" I blinked my eyes and gave them what I'd deem a creepy smile.

The other girls already looked nervous by my odd behavior, but the lead chick continued. "Yes. Aren't you and Zeke dating?"

"Hmm. I think you guys got it confused again," I said to leave them second-guessing, which immediately worked as they nervously they looked at one another.

"What do you mean?" the leader questioned.

"Zeke's dating my sister. I'm not sure if I'm interested in any of them." I shrugged. "Killing and blood are a lot more fun." My smile was priceless, and the three girls standing around were beginning to turn a tad pale.

"W-well tell her the others, specifically Zeus, are off limits."

"For who?" I questioned.

The leader crossed her arms under her breasts and tried to appear taller. "I have my eyes set on Zackery, and a bunch of girls wouldn't mind a smart, handsome man like Zion, but Zeus is off limits entirely, seeing as Sallie couldn't snag Zeke before your sister made her move."

"Zeke approached my sister," I voiced, wanting to see their reaction.

The girls all exchanged looks, and the main chick cleared her throat. "That's not what we heard."

"I saw it with my own eyes. He asked her out after class this evening. Not to mention they've been flirting publicly all week. I'm sure you didn't miss the pictures of them in the parking lot kissing? That was up almost immediately on all the blogs."

The girls pulled out their phones as if this was new content being dished out onto the internet.

"T-that..."

"Marlena, look." The red-haired chick on the right quickly showed her phone screen to her friend. "She's right. I didn't see this up when we were making our way here."

"Shit," Marlena muttered under their breath.

They were doing a poor job at lowering their voices to hide their pure shock, but I stood there patiently, waiting for them to wrap this all up so I could go back to partying.

They didn't have any information for me.

"Anything else?" I asked. "I should go back before my sister starts to worry."

"Just tell her hands off. She can't have all four of the Maxwell brothers," Marlena snarled.

"What if they all want her?" I asked.

The four girls gawked at my question, but I wasn't going to linger any longer. I seriously needed to continue my investigation. I also didn't want to worry Zeke.

Tracker Protocol was to always keep time away from your partner short. The longer you were away, the more dangerous it became on a mission without a clear map of one another's location.

"Just a thought to keep in mind. Time to go kill stuff. Kill. Kill. Kill," I began to sing, turning around and heading for the door. Ending my comment with Shadow Jade's signature Kill song would ensure they didn't lob any snarky or unnecessary comments my way.

When I was able to leave without further confrontation, my assumption was proven correct. Walking down the hall back to the main chilling area, I noticed it was a lot more crowded. It didn't bother me, but it would make it a pain to find Zeke.

Deciding to head to the third floor, I turned my head in time to notice the familiar silver hairstyle. Freezing in place, I stared in that direction, wondering if my eyes were deceiving me.

Without thinking, my body moved on its own, maneuvering its way through the crowd as I kept my eyes locked onto the person. I couldn't see their exact body shape or get a true view of their height, but my heart was racing, and my elements were all pouncing for the chance to strike.

My approach was like a predator, ready to catch

its prey. Slow, but calculative, which was exactly what I needed.

A guy stepped in front of me, stopping me in my tracks. I looked up to see his seductive grin, and he quickly fixed his short hair to try and make himself look more attractive.

"Hey, baby. You want a good time?"

I returned his look with a sweet one. "I don't think you can handle me."

Walking around him to get a view of the familiar person, I frowned when his figure was nowhere to be found.

*Shit.*

**"Hmm. Unattractive boy interfered. Kill."**

That made me smile, though deep down I was fighting the bubbles of disappointment. I needed to know if he was real.

*And if he wasn't, that meant I was seeing things, which meant my hallucinations were back.*

The thought of even taking those pills again made me cringe, hating the judgment that followed with anything that labeled me as having mental issues.

Until mental health issues were deemed an acceptable illness anyone could experience and endure, I didn't want anyone finding out about that.

*Especially when this academy thing was like an assignment. These people are only here to gossip and watch. Any sign of weakness would put our cover on the line if we want to learn what's going on around here and remain as bait.*

A hand landed on my shoulder and I flicked it away without hesitation. Turning around, I was staring back at the guy who had gotten in my way.

"I could totally handle you, sexy. You'd look good riding all of this." He dramatically gestured to his buff chest, slim waist, and skinny legs. "If you know what I mean."

"From how skinny your legs are, I bet you do more upper body work than lower. If you're going to weight lift, you should even it out, or you'll really become out of proportion," I explained.

My answer threw him off his game, but I proceeded.

"Skimping on your leg workouts tells me your focus is only on specific areas that can grab attention easily rather than your entire body. That leaves me to wonder if your focus on your chest growth is to make people think you have a big cock," I theorized, the conversation only making this guy even more visibly uncomfortable.

"You won't know if you don't try," he offered, not sounding as confident as before.

"Your lack of confidence tells me I'll surely be disappointed."

My body tingled suddenly, seconds before an arm slid around my waist.

"There's my baby."

I glanced over my shoulder to see Zeke. His eyes met mine, and something flashed between us. He kept his smooth expression, but he definitely realized something was off.

Leaning down to give me a kiss, he moved his attention to the guy in front of us.

"What's up?" he questioned.

"Oh, you're um...Zeke, right? Yeah, the guest list said you were coming, along with the rest of the female population," he commented nervously.

"Do you have any business with my girlfriend, or can we move on? Some people are waiting for us on the third floor," Zeke pressed, sounding impatient.

"No, no. Not at all." The guy shook his head in denial.

"Cool." Zeke wrapped an arm securely over my shoulder. "We'll be ditching, then."

Turning around, we moved through the crowd to the stairs. Making our way to the third floor, we observed the area first, before making our way to the open bar.

Zeke ordered for the two of us, getting a beer for himself and a strawberry daiquiri for me. We were silent as we waited, but Zeke's hand was on my left leg, his finger running circles in a slow movement as if to calm me down.

I wondered if he could tell I was feeling a bit off. I also debated whether or not to tell him about what I'd seen. If it was an illusion, I was worried to admit that I was having them again.

*It could screw up this dating thing. No one wants to date a literal crazy person.*

**"Not crazy. Special,"** Shadow Jade whispered.

I was surprised she was still present and not starting her marathon.

*Thanks, Shadow Jade. You can go watch your marathon now. Zeke's here. I'll be perfectly fine.*

I felt her hesitancy, but she knew that I could handle myself and wouldn't hesitate to summon my dark power if I needed it.

**"Okay. Love you. Kill time. Bye."**

*Bye.*

She was officially gone, but a bit of the dark energy was still tingling from Zeke's touch. Our drinks came shortly after, and we moved from the bar to a quiet sitting area. There was one empty chair left that faced the balcony.

We moved to sit, Zeke settling down first and

patting his lap for me to sit. Without hesitation, I positioned myself in his lap, his arm hooking around my waist while I rested against him with my drink in hand.

Taking a sip, I needed a second to take in the mixed taste of strawberries and strong vodka.

"Sweet but strong," I acknowledged. "Not bad."

"What's wrong?" Zeke got straight to the point, not even taking a gulp of his beer. I looked into his eyes hesitantly, unsure what to say.

"What made you uncomfortable?" He reworded his question.

"Nothing, really." I tried to sound like I normally did, but Zeke wasn't buying it. His eyes darkened a shade, making the silver rings around his irises pop out even more.

"Jade." His voice was ice cold, and the presence of his magic was making me lose my train of thought. His hand slid into my hair, steadying my head as he immediately kissed me.

My body relaxed, and I let him comfort me with his affection. It intrigued me how the mere sight of those familiar silver strands of hair and tall, slim figure were enough to make me question all the hard work I'd done during those years of therapy and desensitization.

*I knew that man's dark secret, but it would all come down to whether I was strong enough to face it yet.*

"You're not ready to talk about it," he whispered.

I nodded. His eyes portrayed his understanding and he leaned back into the chair, his hand still running through my curls and making them looser.

"Whatever made you worried is gone?" he inquired.

"Yes," I whispered, taking another sip of my drink. His finger was making a circle along my thigh again.

"You want to leave?"

"Not yet," I admitted. "I want to dance a bit after this."

"Okay." Zeke grinned. "Was the washroom beneficial?"

"I got warned to stay away from your brothers," I purred. He smirked and took a chug of his beer. "Did you now?"

"Mhm. Zeus is on little Sallie Walker's radar, while Zackery's on some Marlena's watch. She was the chick confronting me in the washroom. They thought I was Shadow Jade, though. I did say we were dating."

"Really?" he smirked, looking pleased by the news.

"I did. I said that Shadow Jade wasn't interested in any of you," I elaborated.

"What about Zion?"

"He has multiple girls crushing on him." I winked. "Needless to say, they told me to back off. I can't have all four of you."

"And you answered?"

"What if you guys all wanted me?" I repeated the statement.

"Finishing blow," Zeke dramatically stated. "Fatality!"

I began to giggle, feeling more relieved than before, especially with seeing Zeke be so playful. "They were rendered speechless. I almost wondered if they understood me."

He chuckled, pressing a kiss to my forehead. "You did good, baby."

I blushed at his praise, looking into his eyes. "I like when you call me baby," I whispered.

"Then I'll keep doing just that," he confirmed. "Let's enjoy some more drinks?"

"You're promoting underage drinking," I whispered.

"True, but that's something you would have done to begin with," he acknowledged.

"One hundred percent true," I agreed. "Cheers?"

Offering my drink to his beer bottle, we clinked them together and continued to talk. He didn't bring up what happened earlier, and I was grateful for it.

I was learning a lot about Zeke and seeing sides of him I would have never expected. The darkness within him was apparent, but I wondered about the threads of light.

*Zeke, Tracker of Light and Darkness. I've yet to fully solve the mystery around him, but I feel it will be a challenge that's worth waiting for.*

## ❧ 16 ❧

## TROUBLE IN PARADISE

I f I could be lost in these lips forever, I'd have no regrets. To let our bodies have control and not think on the pounding dance floor was one of the first times in a long time where I'd felt free.

No chains to the past, present, or future. No barriers stopping me from moving my hips or kissing the man who danced with me with confidence.

This was why two of the same dark element was dangerous. Not only did we mesh together and empower our burning desires, but we also had no need to regret our decisions, feeling absolutely right with every move we made because the other was there to support.

My hands were in the air while I swayed my

hips to the beat of the music. Zeke's firm hands gripped my hips, our bodies close as we moved.

It was getting hard to control ourselves, to not let the darkness fully come out and take control. Zeke's eyes were almost pure black at this point, and I was certain mine were the same. The predator element was on the brink of surfacing, and we both knew it.

I wondered if others noticed, though if they did, neither of us cared. We were in our own little world and didn't mind if our connection brought a wave of destruction.

Zeke pulled me close, seizing my lips in a burning urgency. His hands moved possessively up my body, and I loved every bit of it.

He knew what he was doing and wasn't afraid to venture further, regardless of whether we were in public or not.

"Car?" I breathed against his lips, the two of us a sweaty mess from hours of dancing and the alcohol burning through our bodies.

I certainly was drunk, and so was he. I'd never encourage drinking and driving, but I was perfectly down for car sex.

*Any sex, really. All the sex to release the tension we built up tonight. Or was it before tonight? All week long. Yes...Zeke is so fucking dangerous. I love it.*

He sucked my lip and kissed me hard, slapping my ass before gripping it. "I don't think we'll make it to the hotel," he whispered.

"I never said I wanted to only have sex in the hotel," I purred, moving to suck his neck while grinding my hips against him.

"Tempting," he whispered.

"Please?" I probed, having little patience at this point.

The idea was embedded in my mind, and I was going to get what I wanted tonight.

"I never said no." His comebacks always reminded me of myself, and it was far too refreshing to have someone not only accept you but understand exactly what you wanted.

"Let's get out of here, baby." With those enchanting words, and one last sloppy kiss, the two of us were hand and hand, making our way off the crowded dance floor and to the exit.

I was glad we'd parked farther down the street, and when we reached the sports car, I had to grin.

"I just now realized the windows are tinted." I held his arm as we casually walked toward the car.

"Limo tint, to be precise," Zeke chuckled. "I like my privacy."

"How are we going to get to the hotel after this?"

"Autopilot." He winked and unlocked the car.

"How long does it take to get to the hotel again?"

"Ten minutes."

"Enough time." I smirked, trying not to giggle or skip ahead.

I twirled on my feet and watched his approach, licking my lips when his darkened eyes looked me up and down seductively.

"I'm going to fuck you so hard."

"You can fuck me all night long and I'd still want more," I whispered.

He pressed me against the car, kissing me deeply. "I have a better idea."

"What?"

"It requires two minutes of your precious patience."

I pouted my lips in wonder. "What's in it for me?"

"That sexy bare ass on the hood of the car with your legs spread out for me and the cool night to see and adore." His words had me grinning from ear to ear, my imagination going wild at the sheer thought.

"The hood of the car would be hot."

"A two-minute drive isn't going to make it hot. Also, the engine is at the back. The trunk is in the front." He winked and opened the passenger door for me, ushering me to get in.

"Sports cars," I mused. "Made to provide the best circumstances for outdoor sex."

"They have no choice seeing as the inside is so damn cramped. Next time we'll get a limo."

"'We' as in the four of you?" I inquired. He closed my door and walked around, opening his door and getting in. Once the door lowered to a close, he looked at me.

"You want a fivesome in a limo?"

"I want a fivesome, period," I elaborated.

"If you were any other person, I'd say you couldn't handle it, but our Hive Queen isn't like any other individual on this planet."

"Damn right." I leaned over to kiss his neck. "Wanna have some fun on the two-minute auto drive?"

His eyes met my intrigued ones as my hand circled the groin of his pants. He bit his bottom lip, his eyes telling me he was actually taking my words into consideration.

From the way they darkened as my hand reached for the button of his jeans, followed by the slow unzipping sound that seemed to echo within the quiet space of his car, I knew all reason and patience were going to be thrown out the window.

"You wanna suck me off in two minutes?"

"I wanna do lots to you in two minutes, but we can start with a blow job," I suggested. Slipping my hand into the opening of his Calvin Klein underwear, I pulled his cock out with ease.

My hand began to move up and down it, all while our eyes got lost in one another. He inched his head closer until we were kissing, and he moaned quietly into my mouth when I really started to work him.

"Start the autopilot. I'm gonna make you explode before we get there," I challenged.

His eyes flickered with hunger, my challenge the perfect motivation for him to let his car do the work as he leaned back and enjoyed the ride.

*And my performance.*

The car purred to life, and after he manually backed up and out of the spot, I got to work. Moving my hair out of the way, I moved in my seat slightly to give me the perfect amount of space and flexibility to lean down and take his cock right into my mouth.

He took a swift inhale, letting it out as a long moan as he relaxed into the black leather seat. "Just like that, baby," he breathed.

I must have been torturing him all night long,

because he was growing hard quicker than I expected, inspiring me to work harder and faster.

I let my teeth lightly skid down his throbbing length, taking a chance that the hint of pain would only bring a wave of intense pleasure.

"Fuck, yes, Jade. Do that again," he growled. I followed his command, doing that again and again, before inching his length all the way down till his head hit the back of my throat.

He gasped, and I tried not to giggle at the way his hips fought to stay still. Slowly bobbing my head up and down his hard length, I stopped playing and began to really work him up.

I was sure we were going to reach wherever he wanted us to go, and I was ready to make him cum before the car officially came to a stop.

"Jade. Yeah, baby. Like that." Zeke was enjoying every bit of this, his fingers sliding into my hair and prompting me to move even faster. If it weren't for the fact my lips were around his massive cock, I'd be smiling from the giddy excitement thrumming through me.

My own arousal was growing, impatient to feel this large cock pound into my needy pussy, but I was also patient.

*Always save the best for last. Besides, this was only the beginning of our playful night.*

Gliding my lips down to his base and using my tongue to add to the pleasure, I listened to his increased pants and moans. Hearing him say my name so effortlessly made all of this worthwhile, and I knew he was getting closer when he began to gasp, hiss, and swear.

"Shit. Fuck. Jade...ah." His cock was twitching in my tight mouth, and I knew he was super close. I circled my thumb and index finger around the base of his cock and sucked hungrily until he jerked involuntarily, his throbbing length finally releasing his hot cum into my mouth.

"Fuck," he breathed, trying to catch his breath. "Jade...you give the best fucking head."

I sucked my way up his cock, releasing it for a moment to show him my mouthful of his pooling cum. Swallowing it, I showed him my mouth again, before I smiled in triumph.

"I try." With a wink, I looked to see we were slowing down. "I win."

"Yes, you do." His intense gaze told me I was in for something good.

The car came to a stop, an automatic voice announcing that we were at the destination. I smirked, and Zeke unexpectedly kissed me.

It was a slow-paced kiss, one filled with passion

as his tongue explored my mouth. "Leave your outfit in the car," he encouraged.

"Public display of nudity." I kissed him greedily. "Does that include my heels?"

"You are far too daring," he complimented. "Yes, keep your heels on."

Stripping out of my outfit while Zeke got out of the car, I waited until he opened my door, offering his hand. He'd put his cock back into his pants which made me pout in disappointment, but from the way his grin widened, I knew it wouldn't be in the security of his briefs for long.

I shivered slightly as he helped me out. The cool breeze reminded me of how wet I was, the chill brushing against my pussy.

We were on a cliff that oversaw the city below. The trees were thick and it had to be private property.

"Aside from public sex and nudity, are we doing anything else illegal, like trespassing?" I inquired, walking to the hood of his car and lowering my ass to the sleek, cool surface.

He was right, the hood was as cool as a popsicle, but I knew it wouldn't bother me once we got moving.

I slid myself up, my feet dangling as I ran both

my hands through my hair, my eyes took in Zeke's hooded expression as he watched me.

"If we were, would you even care?"

"Nope." I let my hair down, leaning back as I pointed my finger at him and taunted him to come closer. "I just want to know all the rules we're breaking. At least then I can defend myself properly in court."

He walked up to the car, already working on lowering his pants and underwear. From my quick glance of his cock, I could tell he was already ready to enjoy my pussy, which would suck him right in and clench his hardness like no other.

"I fucking love you."

"I know." I winked. He placed his hands next to my thighs and claimed my lips. When we broke the kiss, I continued. "I really like you, Zeke. Maybe...even love you."

"What's holding you back then?" he asked. "I know it's not us."

I let my fingers run through his hair, the two of us keeping our closeness. I could feel his length between my legs, ready to slide into me with my simple permission.

"I'm weird."

"Valid. Next."

"Totally drunk."

"Your honesty carries through when you're sober or drunk. Next."

"I carry dirty laundry around."

"Everyone has secrets they never want to be revealed to the wrong people. That's any Tracker, especially people like us."

He looked into my eyes then, and for a second, his eyes brightened up, the color shifting from their usual black to almost a light grey.

My light element flickered at the shift, moving closer in longing as a connection passed between us. His energy wanted to comfort me, to ease whatever fears were in the depths of my being and envelop me in the love Zeke wanted to deliver to me.

The kiss that followed was like a balm, easing through my worries while catering to my light energy. I always felt off my game when light was involved.

It was the energy of purity and embraced the vulnerabilities we experienced in all things around life. Light revolved around openness, and that ability to tug down the emotional walls and let someone in was one of the many fears that fueled the darkness in me.

Only Zeke could make me lower my walls, to

give him a chance to feel what I felt in his addictive presence.

"Jade," he whispered. "Let me in."

"Even if it can ruin you?" I closed my eyes, breaking the contact. They would pull me in and let me act before thinking. He deserved to be warned. To be given the opportunity to walk away from all this.

*If he really wanted this to be a relationship...to be something far more than just a sexy fling, he'd have to realize just how risky this decision was. To understand that it could risk his life to be more than just fun and games.*

His hand cradled my face and his thumb ran along my bottom lip.

"Open your eyes, Jade." His husky voice sent shivers through me. I couldn't be defiant like I would have in the absence of my light element, but it was still present, thrumming through my skin and entangling with Zeke's free energy.

Our eyes met, and the level of acceptance that shone brightly in his now completely silver orbs made me take a shaky breath.

"You don't care," I mumbled, another way of acknowledging that he actually wanted this. He really did accept me.

"Life is a gamble, and I love to live on the edge.

I've yet to regret any of the risks I've taken and I always follow my gut."

"What does your gut say?"

"I want you. Ruin me, baby. Throw me in the path of trouble. I don't care about the skeletons in your closet. If they all come out, let them." He kissed me tenderly and whispered, "I love you, Jade Storm. I love every part of you. Your gentler elements and your shadow being that loves to kill. I like every shade of your essence, and if the world turns on us, I won't run. Some risks are worth fighting for, and I'm not afraid to do exactly that if it means experiencing every inch of you. I'll stay by your side, Jade, and I'm sure with my dedication, my brothers will want the same. Let me be loyal. Let me prove to you how worthy you are, Jade. Let me in."

He captured my lips, then and there, and I gave into his words and touch.

We didn't need to exchange more words. His lips gave me validation and as the light energy within us returned to its hidden vessels, the darkness surged back to full force, engulfing our senses and filling us with overflowing urgency.

By the time his cock actually slid into me, I was wet and desperate to experience every bit of his love and passion through intercourse.

"Mhmm," I moaned when he filled me up with his entire length. He slid himself in and out slowly at first, purposely slowing the pace to focus on the growing pleasure thrumming between us.

This was more than just sex. This was two people who didn't like getting into the nitty gritty of their emotions coming together, letting their walls fall and their vulnerabilities out to contribute to the overall satisfaction.

Zeke had secrets. I was confident all of the Maxwell brothers did. Yet, it didn't scare me, because they were willing to let me stick around. They didn't cringe at my oddness or push me away when the rest of the world did.

They embraced me, my circumstances, and wanted a bit of my love.

*It was the first time anyone ever wanted me for more than just what our bodies could easily provide.*

We began to move faster; the slow build of pleasure began to grow to something more. The primitive energy carved its way into our minds and urged for us to move toward the finale. I opened my eyes to stare into his, the two us of leaning until my body was pressed against the cool car surface and Zeke hovered above me. I hadn't imagined what it would feel like to have sex on the hood of a car.

Never would have thought how eccentric and

mesmerizing it would be to stare into your lover's eyes while the starry night sky beamed behind him and the cool breeze aided in keeping us from getting too hot with our sexual activity.

His eyes were now wickedly black, the darkness overtaking even the silver that normally wrapped around his irises.

"You're so fucking beautiful," he commented, his voice thick with desire. "Watching you naked beneath me and listening to your juices rub against my cock like that. Your damn hot pussy is eating me up, and god, your eyes. I love how they match mine right now."

His praise was followed by kisses and moans, the two of us straining toward the approaching orgasms. My hips were moving to meet his thrusts, and we both pulled our lips back to moan in pressing need.

"Zeke. Yes. Oh, yes. Right there." He was hitting the perfect spot, and the way his lips moved to nip the side of my neck and suck it deeply was making my eyes roll back at the intense sensitivity of it all.

Our combined energies could run free here, and I knew the darkness was working up an appetite because dark clouds came from nowhere, blocking the light of the half moon.

"Zeke." I was going to warn him, to remind him of our energies and the danger of it all, but he groaned and fucked me even faster.

"Let your energy free, baby. Don't hold back. You love this. Everything about this. Trust me, Jade," he growled into my ear.

His words were followed with a sudden shift in speed, and he began to really fuck me nice and fast.

"Zeke. Ah, yes...yes...ah!" I was approaching my climax, my pussy fluttering and tightening around his cock that was slamming into me. He drove into me, hitting the perfect spot that only tipped me closer to my exploding climax.

"That's it, baby. Moan, whimper, and cum for me! Let your power feed off of me and be free," he ordered, his voice deep like he was about to lay death to the world.

"ZEKE!" I was thrown over the edge, my orgasm throttling through me and making my body grow rigid as I shook uncontrollably.

Zeke growled and thrust into me even harder, his balls smacking against my ass, the intensity threatening to drive me into another orgasm if he didn't cum soon.

"Ze...ke, ah!" My body grew tense, another wave of intense pleasure was ready to take over me.

"Jade!" he screamed through gritted teeth as he

sank his cock deep inside me and came. His final move had me crying out in pleasure as I spiraled into another orgasm.

We both remained utterly still, our bodies rocking with the excess pleasure and dark energy that coursed around us. Zeke rested his head against my shoulder, his body shaking as he tried to breathe.

I didn't blame him, feeling just as breathless while I fought to control the dark energy. I didn't want to know what could have happened with the two of us letting go like that. Maybe nothing did happen because we were out in the open.

That was surely a lie because the almost-black clouds that had appeared out of nowhere were still in sight. I could have sworn it would rain at any moment, but the thought also excited me.

*Who wouldn't want to pull a "The Notebook" moment? Only naked with the chance of having another round of sex.*

"I'm not even going...to think...right now," Zeke breathed.

"As in...you don't want to know...what damage we caused?" I corrected in amusement.

"Hmm. Yeah. I'm secretly praying the car at least works."

"If it doesn't?"

"We'll just leave it here, call an Uber, and head to the hotel."

"For more dangerous sex." I laughed but hugged him. "Zeke. That was really good."

"Good or electrifying?"

"Life changing," I whispered.

"Good," he whispered back and kissed the side of my neck. "That's what I want. To change your life for the better, Jade baby."

I smiled at his words, closing my eyes and soaking up the intimacy our hug offered. I couldn't wait to get to the hotel and enjoy another ride on this rollercoaster of heated passion.

*This was the start of something new.*

❧

*"IT'S ONLY A MATTER OF TIME, JADE. YOU CAN RUN and hide, but I can't let you have your way. Look at what you've done. This is all because of you."*

*I could smell the blood that flooded the floor and I stared at the bodies of my mom, dad, brother, and sister.*

*"Y-you did this," my seven-year-old self yelled at the scary voice. He did this. All of this. I was innocent. I never wanted this.*

*"Jade. I pity you, child. You love to hide from the truth. Accept who you are. What you will become.*

*Whether you like it or not, you will submit to me. To us."*

*"Leave me alone!" I screamed, clenching my fists as I stared around the dark room in anger. "I'll find you! I'll kill you over and over again! YOU'LL PERISH BY MY HANDS," I screamed at the top of my lungs, knowing well that it wouldn't matter how loud or far my words reached.*

*That man always had the last laugh, the same eerie, mocking sound that flooded the room and escalated in volume, until my head was filled with his obvious amusement.*

*He was happy because he'd won. He always won, and this wasn't any different.*

**I can't let him win again. He can't take what I love the most. Never...again.**

"Jade, baby?"

I was struggling to get out of the dreadful dream that had trapped me. The dark hands that gripped my mind wanted me to return to its inviting arms and relive the scene of how my family died.

It was a cycle, and though I mentally knew it, I still whimpered quietly, wishing for a way out.

"Jade." My body was wrapped in something

warm and instead of the cold pull of darkness that always swallowed me back into the fearful land of dreams, a soft light wrapped around my subconsciousness.

Calm and clarity flooded me, and the longer it resonated with my body, the more relaxed I became. Suddenly I wasn't afraid to go back to sleep, and when I did, I was greeted with a happy dream of love and laughter.

I was with the Maxwell brothers, and we were having a picnic of sorts. It was a simple dream, one that made me smile and laugh as I listened to their bickering.

Zackery was being dramatic as he tried to persuade me to eat his version of peanut butter and jelly sandwiches.

Zion was making a contraption that would use our thoughts to control a kite. Zeus was grumbling about how annoying Zackery was being and offering me a classic sub sandwich.

Zeke was chuckling, his head lowering to my lap as he looked up to me with loving eyes.

I was happy and not afraid of losing all this. It had to be one of my best dreams in a long while.

*To dream without the fear of it being a broken illusion. A dream that was pure and one I could cherish in a box of joyful ones.*

When I turned over, I snuggled closer to the warm body next to me. I moaned quietly, wondering if it was worth trying to fall back to sleep or let the comforting dream shimmer within my mind for a little longer.

"Jade?"

Zeke's tender voice reached me. It sounded far away, but that could have been because I was on the verge of sleeping again.

"Kill!"

"Hmm? Hey, Shadow Jade."

I wondered what I was dreaming about this time, but then I felt something run through my hair and down my back.

"Jade?"

"Sleeping! Kill. Kill. Kill."

"Shadow Jade. Don't destroy that."

"Why?"

"We have to pay for it."

"But destroy."

"You can destroy the paper in the book over there."

"Not fun."

"It is if you rip the pages up into tiny pieces and throw them in the air."

"Oh."

"Yup."

"Kill!"

The thought occurred to me that we were in the hotel room, and as the conversation began to sink in, I realized Zeke was talking to Shadow Jade.

Opening my eyes, I looked up to see Zeke staring down at me. I stared back for a long moment, unsure of what to say yet.

My brain was still playing catch-up, but I wasn't sure which was more important to tackle first: The chance of Shadow Jade going on a destructive spree or confronting Zeke about why his eyes were more silver-white than their normal black.

"No more bad dreams, it seems." He moved a few strands of my hair from my face.

"You..." I wasn't sure how to respond, but it didn't matter as his lips met mine.

This kiss was comforting, healing. The sensual movement captured my attention and helped me not to panic about Zeke's knowledge of my nightmare.

It may have been a common occurrence for me, but that was my battle I faced in the comfort of my own space. Being caught having a nightmare meant I had to explain, and that only heightened my vulnerability.

Kissing him back, I enjoyed the pleasure his

kiss delivered as I braced for his flood of questions about the dream.

When he released me, he kissed my forehead and looked to the desk. Following his gaze, I realized Shadow Jade was sitting in the wooden chair, her legs crossed as she stared at blank sheets of paper in a book.

I wasn't sure where the book had come from, let alone how the room was still in one piece after my nightmare.

Shadow Jade loved to create chaos that matched the nightmares that plagued me. It was always extra tiring to wake up in terror and realize my room was destroyed, requiring me to clean sooner rather than later.

If I waited, it only got worse.

"Shadow Jade?" I quietly questioned.

She paused in her analysis, slowly looking over to us on the bed.

"Me!" She grinned happily at my attention. "Shadow Jade good!"

I blinked and looked around the room once more, wondering if this was a dream or an illusion. "You...didn't destroy anything?"

"No. Kill later. Zeke said I can rip the paper. Rip, rip, rip," she began to sing, returning to stare at the book. Though she said she was going to rip it, I didn't feel as though she had those intentions.

Glancing back at Zeke, I waited for him to ask one of many questions, but he simply stared back at me.

I was sure if I didn't say anything, he'd continue staring. "Why aren't you saying anything?"

"Am I supposed to?" Zeke countered, his eyes trailing down to my lips. "I figure kissing is easier."

I smirked, but I still didn't want to lower my guard just yet.

"You're not freaked out?"

"About?"

"Hmm." I wasn't sure how to articulate what I meant.

*Wasn't he turned off by Shadow Jade's presence?*

We were both naked under the sheets. I thought anyone else would have been bothered by her intrusion, though she was minding her own business.

She was too concerned with the blank sheets of paper to care about us.

"You think too much. It's too early," he mumbled and kissed me.

I moaned when he moved to hover over me, his hand already slipping between my legs.

"Zeke," I warned. "We still have company."

"Our company is a part of you and knows what we're doing. Besides, I feel she's more concerned with her paper than with me comforting you," he whispered, following with a sucking kiss.

I groaned at his affectionate response, though I didn't want to disturb Shadow Jade either. She did respect me and couldn't have cared less if I had sex right now, but I respected her.

"Wait," I whispered. He paused to arch an eyebrow at me.

I kissed his cheek, finding his impatience a little amusing. "Shadow Jade?"

"Kill?" She looked over to us.

"Do you mind skipping in the hall for a few minutes? I need to tell Zeke something."

"No mind. Skip away."

She got up and placed the book on the table. She walked three steps but looked back at the book.

"You can take the book, Shadow Jade," Zeke offered.

"Rip, rip, rip," she sang, walking back to grab the book. She then skipped to the door, opening it up and walking out into the hall.

I wasn't worried about her causing a commotion. She'd skip around and stare at the blank pages for entertainment until I called her back in.

Once she closed the door, Zeke looked back down to me. "The respect you show your elements is intriguing."

"You don't share the same viewpoint?" I inquired, referring to his two elements.

"We're the same. Whether in physical form or not, they know my intentions before my mind processes them. I don't see the need to tell them to give me privacy, but..." he paused. "Seeing you do it makes me wonder if I should."

"You can try and see how they respond to it?"

"Maybe." He trailed his finger along my folds, making me shiver. "Sex or talk?"

"We can't do both?"

"We could," he admitted, lowering his lips to my chest. "But the order of it depends on you."

I grinned and moved his arm from my legs, knowing if he continued lazily gliding his finger along my pussy, I wouldn't be able to concentrate.

"Talk, then sex," I determined. He smirked and nodded, resting on his side.

"Talk to me, baby." He pulled me closer and I stared into his eyes.

"What's your opinion on hallucinations?"

"Are you specifically referring to hallucinations or my opinion on mental health in general?" he inquired.

From the look on his face, he really was intrigued and I knew he could read me because he picked up the general reason for my question.

"Both."

"Hallucinations happen and shouldn't be ignored or dismissed. Sure, a lot of people can have them based off of their past alone, but you don't know if it's due to a trigger in the environment or seeing a person from your past. Regardless, there's no problem with it. If it becomes a problem and puts the person at risk, I would rather they take medication to control the severity of them, if not eliminate them, but that also depends on the side effects."

"Would...you not like me if I decided to take medication again?"

"What does me loving you have anything to do with you taking meds?"

"I don't know." I trailed my finger along his left pec as a distraction. "People look at you differently when you take meds to control your level of crazy."

"Having hallucinations doesn't make you crazy. Nor am I one of the 'people' who would judge you for wanting to control what may affect you negatively."

"At the party. I saw someone...a person from my past. I'm not sure if it was an illusion or not.

He...haunts my dreams a lot. I stopped my meds a while ago...but I may go back on them. I just..."

"Don't want us judging you?"

I bit the side of my lip and nodded. "I hate being judged. Not in the way where people judge my personality, which I can control. I despise when they judge something I have no control over. That I can't change with the snap of my fingers."

Glancing up to him, I noticed the calm in his expression, almost like he was mimicking Zion's normal behavior.

"Does this have to do with when you were homeless?" he asked.

"I hated when people called me dirty. Said that I should kill myself for taking space. A full year of constant ridicule." I poked his chest lightly at first, getting lost in the memories of all those horrible words and actions.

"Waste of space. Get a job. Go to a shelter. Trouble child. Pathetic. Useless. Jump off a bridge. Drug addict. Runaway. The list was endless. Rain or shine, it didn't matter. There was far more hate than there was kindness and sorrow. I wasn't homeless by choice. I never wanted to live on the streets. Every day was a battle to escape the people who wanted me for my power. From the man who haunts me in my dreams and follows me when I don't take my meds."

I paused in poking him, realizing I was doing it far too hard and making his skin flush red. "Sorry."

"You're not dirty." His soft tone had me looking back into his eyes. "They didn't know what you'd gone through. Your whys or hows. They knew nothing and had no right to say such bullshit."

I blinked, noticing that his anger reminded me of Zeus. "Seeing you with different emotions like your brothers is intriguing," I muttered before moving closer to him.

He sighed and wrapped an arm around me, pulling me into a hug while his hand trailed up and down my back, soothingly.

"Jade," he whispered in my ear. "I'm serious."

"It's hard not to believe them," I mumbled.

It wasn't like I was intentionally trying to move away from the topic, but it wasn't something anyone ever wanted to talk about or dive further into.

Anything negative was like that. Something no one wanted to tackle and get to the bottom of, because it left them feeling uncomfortable. Even psychologists had struggled with my attempts to understand my feelings and what I'd been through.

*Why would Zeke want to dive into those topics head-first? There was nothing in it for him.*

"Everyone always says that time heals and you'll eventually forget and move on. But the bad memories never leave. The good ones do, but the ones that hurt you most cling to every bit of your memory bank. Not to merely torment you for years to come, but to remind you that this world isn't butterflies and rainbows. Being good and following the rules doesn't achieve anything. But being bad or causing a ruckus? That gets all the attention you can ask for. Good and nasty. Fight the system of being told what to do and see how fast people will try to figure out what makes you do what you do. What makes you tick and tock, because you aren't normal otherwise. They'll give you all the meds and basic needs, but if you're good? If you follow the rules and ask for help? All that leads you to is bribery, homelessness, and the world judging you for trying to find an option not tied to someone else's bank account."

I wasn't even sure I was making sense anymore. I just let the words pour out. It didn't matter if Zeke couldn't decipher them. I didn't expect him to be able to.

"This world isn't for us," he whispered. I leaned back to peer into his eyes, but he turned us over so

I was now lying on top of him. He let go of my waist and moved his hand through my hair.

His eyes were almost pure black, the darkness at his fingertips and sending me shocks of pleasure as they ran along my scalp.

"Being normal is overrated. It's accepted and praised. Follow the laws laid upon you by selfish politicians who thrive on money and power, and you stay off the radar. They try to hide that it's a system that will take bribes to sneak people like us to the Black Market and let them silence us with torture and exploitation, all behind the mask of being good and acceptable."

He moved his hand from my hair, running it down the side of my face and along my chin. "They don't care about the pain those selfish actions cause. The torment we mentally face along with the initial physical pain. They have no clue what loss is. They sit in their power chairs and continue to make rules that favor them and their bank accounts. As for us? We're stuck and left to fend for ourselves."

He trailed his finger along my bottom lip. "That's why Tracker Hive was made. Created for people like us, who are considered 'other.'"

His eyes held heartbreak that had me wondering what hurt him.

*What embedded into his soul and left wounds in its wake to cause his eyes to reflect a need for vengeance?*

"Zeke?" I whispered. "Did the system...or this world, hurt you, too?"

He grinned then, the action cold and laced with irony.

"There's a reason we have to stay in balance, Jade. Otherwise, I would have destroyed that Black Market and every politician who hides behind their wealth as they try to kill us," he declared.

I was silent, not afraid of his words but intrigued as to whether I could do something to help.

"Would there be something for me to do if you ended up doing so?" I pondered.

It wasn't like I was encouraging him or the others to go on a killing spree, but I felt an odd desire to join in.

His smirk now reached his black eyes.

"You just need to be you for me," he whispered, pulling me down for a kiss.

"Do you think...Zion or someone you trust can make something for hallucinations?"

He thought about it as he absentmindedly stroked my cheek.

"Yes. I...used to get them," he admitted,

meeting my gaze. I didn't ask further, even though I was intrigued by the new information.

He'd share with me when he was ready, just as I was sharing bits of my past with him.

"I'll talk with Zion and we can get you on them in a few weeks. They're based on your elements. It'll take a little longer because you have all of them, but I think with the rest of my brothers' help, it shouldn't be hard."

"Just let me know how much, all right?" I urged.

I had savings and wasn't too worried about the cost, but it was good to know, just in case I wouldn't be able to afford the treatment long-term. I'd have to space out the dosage, even if it meant I had to experience a little hallucination here or there.

"You're not paying a cent."

"But—"

"No, Jade," he whispered. "I won't take money from you and neither will the others. That's non-negotiable."

"Can I pay with something else?"

"If it's sex, no. I like having it freely when we feel like it." He smirked and kissed me.

"Then..."

"Jade."

I looked up to him and he smiled, the sweetness

in his expression now reminding me of Zackery's normal cheer.

"When you shift emotions like that, it really throws me off," I mumbled, feeling my cheeks grow red.

His seductive grin was back then, and he ran his hand down my back to my ass, squeezing it lightly.

"If you really want to pay, can you promise me something?"

"Sure." I was up for whatever he wanted.

"Let's do this again," he whispered. "Just talking...like this."

"Okay," I whispered.

"And Shadow Jade gets to destroy stuff."

I grinned. "As long as it doesn't cost you a fortune," I mumbled, kissing his chin. He chuckled. "She's still skipping out there?"

"I think so. Feels like she's multitasking and staring at the book."

"How is it entertaining for her?"

"She uses the blank pages as a way for her to imagine what could be there. I'm sure when we get home she'll start drawing in them or something. Where did you get that? It's not the hotel's book."

"I got it when you were sleeping. She appeared shortly after our last round."

"Ah," I replied. "Guess she likes you."

"Why is that?"

"She doesn't listen to others. Tanner tells her not to destroy something and she does that and more...but then again, she's like me and we love to piss Tanner off. Bad example."

"I really love you." He shook his head with a wide grin. "It's going to be fun serving you, queen."

"Baby is better," I mumbled. "Queen sounds...too important."

"You are important, Jade. My baby and Hive Queen." He winked.

"Hive Queen. I can do with that," I muttered. "Just not often."

He laughed and turned us over again, my back now pressed against the sheets while his hand slid between my legs.

I moaned, the sound muffled by his impatient lips. "Whatever you like, baby," he whispered against my lips. "But I want sex time now."

"Me too," I moaned and kissed him.

"I'll talk to Zion in the morning, all right?" he whispered as he trailed kisses down my neck and teased my pussy folds once more.

"Mhm," I breathed and moaned when his fingers slid into me. "Sure."

"You don't care now."

"You have your fingers up in my hot space,

which gives me the right not to care," I breathed. "No more talking."

"You're really hot when you're all commanding," he complimented but did as I asked while claiming my lips.

"Don't worry, baby. I'll rid you of all your troubles."

My body relaxed and I moaned in response, knowing he would do what he could to make things better. To make life better.

He wouldn't be able to solve all my troubles, but his words told me he would stick around and wasn't here just for the sex and connection.

*He was here to stay, and I hoped the others were in this for the long haul. I certainly was.*

## ᪥ 17 ᪥

## SHADOW US FROM DANGER AND DESPERATE CONNECTION

~T*WO WEEKS LATER-*

"Is it my turn to wear the prototype?" I asked, skipping around Zeus as he slowly walked down the hall to our lockers.

"Yeah. Just give me a moment to set it up. Zion's telling me the instructions because Zackery lost them."

Our outdoor session was done an hour ago, but we'd stayed behind to stretch and practice a few spells. It wasn't necessary, but when someone, as in Zeus, challenged you to a thunderstorm battle, you didn't decline.

*You playfully fight until he gets frustrated and rewards you with steamy kisses.*

My gym attire for today was a white tank top, black sports bra, and red booty shorts. I chose it because I needed the flexibility, but I also liked hearing Zeus's mumbling complaints about how revealing it was.

*I'm sure it was his way of saying he didn't want anyone enjoying my curves.*

So far, there hadn't been another incident where a student had been found dead, but we predicted the person planning all of this was studying our moves just like we were studying theirs.

My week with Zackery was spent reviewing all the student profiles and making a list of high risks. We had about fifteen people who were easy targets and another five that were maybes.

I was on the top of the list, the bait for whoever was planning all of this. They hadn't made another move to trap us, but we weren't going to take our chances.

We switched routes every day, which always threw off Calvin, who continued to stalk us and call me queen. The nickname annoyed the hell out of me, but he wasn't a bother to me in general.

I was fine with him being around because he

was a tech wiz. We may not need him now, but his annoying loyalty could aid us later on.

I'd spent the week before with Zion, and he'd begun to work on the hallucination medication. He'd done a bunch of tests, especially on Shadow Jade, since she was my strongest element.

Watching him work on that and the watch prototypes to track the weird hidden energy of our culprit was intriguing. It interested me how he could be so determined and concentrate for long periods of time.

Shadow Jade could attempt to destroy his lab-like room, and he wouldn't care until after he was done with whatever he'd been focused on.

When Zeke had asked him to begin the analysis for the medication, he hadn't asked me a bunch of questions. Just the basics: height, weight, blood type, and if I had any allergies.

When he did have to dive in for more informa-tion it was only to determine whether I had any triggers that would set off a hallucination or delusion.

His overall assessment was nowhere near the number of questions they asked in mental institutes before they made you an involuntary patient or administered the most basic medication that didn't come close to fixing your problem.

What I was excited for with Zion's medication was that it had no side effects. Since it was so specialized and created to cater to my body's needs, I wouldn't experience the numerous side effects I had with my old medications.

No dizziness, nausea, fever, the never-ending usual side effects or the serious ones like suicidal thoughts or voices.

He was going to make a trial batch that I'd be able to start tomorrow and would last through the holidays and into the second semester. That way, it would give him enough time to see if it was working or not.

If so, he'd make a large batch that would last me a good while until I was ready to taper off it. I personally felt I wouldn't need it after I left this school, seeing as I had no problems prior to attending after stopping my pills for more than six months.

His thoughtfulness and dedication to it all had brought us closer, and getting to spend the nights playing Mario Kart and other videogames was a bonus.

I was definitely taking it slow with him and Zackery, but it balanced out because my relationships with Zeus and Zeke were progressing quickly.

Since my night with Zeke, I'd honestly felt this

Hive thing would work. It wasn't something I was pressured into or that we were doing for the power and nothing more. I liked each of them and having that level of commitment start with Zeke seemed to be the foundation I needed.

Now that my week with Zeus was halfway done, I wondered if we'd go the next mile from spontaneous kissing after my playful taunts to piss him off.

I really couldn't help it. When he was mad, it was really hot, and a total turn on. I still worried about him popping a vein, but that's why there were emergency kits around the school.

*We could fix a vein or two with some gauze, right?*

"How did Zackery lose the instructions? I know he has his moments of being a klutz, but he loses things, too?" I questioned.

Zeus stopped to put the watch on my wrist, checking the size as a trial. I moved my wrist around as he responded to my question.

"He loses everything in his room. It's a war zone in there. World War III. If you give him something, make sure he's not heading into his room or it'll be lost for all eternity," Zeus explained, walking again until we reached my locker.

I skipped over to my new locker, which was right next to my guys'.

*Yes. I now claimed them as mine. Who else would be able to handle them?*

After my locker was vandalized, the four of them had nagged Tanner until he gave in and changed it in the system. I could have easily asked Alaric, but he was on an assignment with Bianca, leaving Tanner in charge until they returned next week.

"Does that mean if I go to his room, I'll be lost forever?" I inquired happily, ready to tug my locker open when Zeus's hand slammed onto it.

I blinked and slowly looked over to him, but his eyes were narrowed on my new locker. "Back up for a second."

"Zeus, there's nothing in there," I countered. "I just got it."

"Then you wouldn't care about me being over-protective," he replied, his eyes locking with mine.

With a shrug, I did what he asked, moving back to let him open it. When he did, we both looked at the empty locker before staring at one another.

"See?"

"It's better to be safe than sor—"

A flood of water burst out of the locker, drenching the both of us. We stood there in silence, glancing to our soaked attire before looking to the locker that was still spilling water onto the school's tile floor.

"So...which one of your brothers pranked us?" I inquired.

Zeus groaned, pulling out his phone, which must have been waterproof because it was working just fine. I'd given my phone to Shadow Jade, who was chilling in Tanner's office while he worked on grading our papers.

She could have come with us to check out the locker, but she was tired and was going to end up napping.

I knew for sure that this prank wasn't some random person, because Zeus would have sensed it far earlier. There wasn't a foreign energy that reminded me of the trap Zackery and I had walked into.

It honestly did feel like Zackery was the one who did it, but the water element was all Zion, which left me wondering if they did it together.

With a few taps, the phone went to speaker and rang once before Zeke spoke.

"Let me guess. You guys fell for Zackery's prank?"

"I want to kill you," Zeus growled.

"I'm masturbating right now. Can you kill me later?"

"Hi, Zeke," I chimed in. "Are you masturbating about me?"

"Everyday, baby," Zeke replied. "Come over."

"Oka—"

"Nope," Zeus interrupted. "You get her next week."

"Jelly." Zeke chuckled. "If you stopped masturbating each time you came home and made an actual move instead, you wouldn't be—"

Zeus hung up on him.

I stared at his phone and then up at him. "Wrong number?"

"He has Zackery's phone. Asshole," Zeus grumbled and clicked Zion's contact. The phone rang three times before he picked up.

"What's up, Zeus?"

"Why does Zeke have Zackery's phone?"

"Hm? Hey, Zackery? Why does Zeke have your phone?"

"He took it this morning. You know he likes switching our phones all the time. Why? Did Zeus get soaked by the trap I set up?"

"Trap? I thought you said you needed the water spell to ward off anyone trying to tamper with Jade's locker until she got the combination?" Zion questioned.

"Yes, but we installed it on Zeus's locker."

"No, we didn't," Zion blatantly pointed out.

"Yes, we did. Zeus's locker was the empty one."

"Zeus's locker is always empty because he never uses it. He only started to because it's the perfect excuse to walk with Jade and make out with her," Zion brushed off.

I glanced at Zeus, noticing his red cheeks as he gritted his teeth in frustration.

"Tell Zackery he's a fucking idiot and I'm going to flood his damn room," Zeus barked. "Also, your watch is waterproof. Still works after the fucking flood that came out of Jade's locker."

"Shit. You guys got drenched? Zackery," Zion called out. "You're an idiot!"

"Now you're angry?" Zeus groaned.

"Duh. Now everyone but me gets to see Jade all wet like that. Jade? Can we get a picture? I'm sure we'd use it wisely."

"I take it back. All three of you are idiots," Zeus complained. "I'm hanging up."

He didn't wait for them to reply, disconnecting the call and giving me an up-and-down look. "You have a change of clothes?"

"Yup. In my gym locker. I'll go change."

He reached out to stop me, the two of us staring into each other's eyes again. He didn't need to say anything for me to feel what was going on.

"You want a picture, don't you?"

He didn't say anything at first but pulled me closer. "Thunder doesn't do well with water."

"Neither does fire, but you're still holding me," I teased, going on my tiptoes to kiss him.

The mere touch was like sparks, and we pulled back.

"Shock-inducing." I giggled. "Have you ever made out with someone in the shower?"

"Do you have a death wish?" he inquired.

"Maybe." I winked. "Are you going to take a picture?"

"Only if I get to print it," he mumbled, his cheeks growing red.

I looked both ways to make sure no one else was in the hall, then moved to the opposite side of the lockers to pose for him.

The way his eyes took every inch of me in made me a little daring. As he began the little photoshoot with his phone, I lifted my white tank top up to beneath my breasts.

I could see my provocative behavior was working its charm on Zeus. When he paused in taking pictures, I walked back to him.

My hands landed on his drenched white T-shirt and slowly slid upward till they were on his shoulders.

"I want a picture of us kissing," I said innocently.

"I'll shock you again."

"It didn't hurt," I noted. "We just can't make a blackout happen this time."

His eyes proved he was considering it, glancing down to my lips and watching me slowly lick them in anticipation.

"I swear, I hate you," he growled under his breath, slamming my lips with his. His arm hooked around my waist, pulling me against him as we deepened the electrifying kiss.

Water and thunder were not good to combine, especially when we were both drenched, but how could I resist how fucking hot he looked all soaked like this?

I could tell he was taking pictures from the snap of the phone in his free hand, but we didn't pull away until the lights in the hall momentarily went off.

"We should continue this elsewhere."

"Come over."

"Really?" I grinned. "I don't think you want me getting lost in Zackery's room."

He smirked. "I have my own place."

"In this district?"

"Yup. Temporary one. The others didn't want to

invest in one seeing as theirs are in different main locations in our district. I figured having a simple one that came furnished would be manageable."

"Handy," I complimented. "Meet me at the entrance of the girls' change room then." I winked. "And make sure the lights go back on."

He snapped his fingers and the struggling lights returned to full brightness.

"There."

"Sexy." I winked.

"You make it hard to not give in to you."

I kissed him and pulled away. "No one said you couldn't give in already. You're the stubborn one in the relationship." I playfully winked and turned away, beginning to skip to the change rooms.

"Make sure no one sees you like that."

"Okay, Daddy," I called out, turning around to blow him a kiss before skipping away.

I had to call him that in bed. I could only envision all the whipping and ass slaps that could go along with the pleasurable torture.

*Yup. Zeus is as dangerous as Zeke. I love it. Imagine a threesome with them? Hmm. I should ask for an apartment for Christmas. No, a house with a spell to make sure we don't break anything with our elements. All the sex we could have. How delightful.*

Entering the change room, I got to my locker

and thanked myself for having two spare sets of clothes.

*Let me shower real quick. We did have a sweaty class and training session.*

Stripping out of my clothes and wrapping a towel around my body, I closed my locker and headed to the showers.

The lights began to flicker until they went completely out. I pouted my lips, wondering if my steaming kiss with Zeus was the cause of it.

"Zeus?" I called out. The room was silent, but it didn't give me any sense of relief.

*Someone is here.*

Tightening the towel that cloaked my naked-ness, I began to walk further into the shower area, my eyes scanning the room. I caught a glint of something shiny, and I stared at the specific shower stall.

The curtain was pulled back, allowing me to see that it was empty, but something was on the floor that caught the reflection of one of the flickering lights.

I flinched when the watch on my wrist began to vibrate, the screen turning on and off. With a slow inhale, I closed my eyes and got serious, opening them again with every intention of killing whoever was here.

I called to my ice element and an ice stake morphed in my hand, the bits of thunderous charge from my kiss with Zeus still pulsing through me and surrounding the ice weapon.

Reaching the stall, I knelt down to pick the broken mirror piece.

I stared into my reflection, noticing my black eyes were now red.

### *"You still live without regret."*

I looked over my shoulder, trying to identify the voice that spoke, but it didn't come from a specific direction.

*Those words are echoing through my own mind. Shit.*

"Not the time or place, hallucinations," I grumbled, looking back to the mirror.

### *"Is that what you think I am? A hallucination?"*

"That's what you always have been. I think you're afraid to come out of that hidey-hole of yours. Worried I might kill you?"

The voice chuckled, the irritating sound swarming my head and the entire shower area.

*"Jade. How long are you going to keep running? You're guilty as charged. Why don't you end it here and now? It would be best for both of us. You'd get to face judgment for what you did, and I'd enjoy my hidey-hole. I deserve at least that, don't you think?"*

"Stop talking rubbish." I walked away to the open showers, giving up with this hallucination.

The watch had stopped vibrating, but I kept it on. It was waterproof so I'd be able to shower no problem. I waited to remove my towel, unsure if I felt safe to do so.

Closing my eyes, I whispered, "Happy birthday to me. Happy birthday to me. Happy birthday, dear Jade. Happy birthday to me."

I sang the song over and over again, the melody slowing my speeding heart rate.

It was one of the few songs from therapy that got through to me, and though it brought back the memories of that fateful day, I'd rather experience that than deal with the hallucinations of that man.

Opening my eyes, I realized the lights were back on. With a frown, I looked back into the mirror, noticing the pure black orbs that looked back at me.

I didn't freak out, though I kind of wanted to.

My pure black eyes were normal when Shadow Jade took over or when I was casting a dark elemental spell.

*Problem was I wasn't doing a spell, and Shadow Jade was napping.*

### "How does it feel to look into the eyes of a killer?"

My whole body froze at the cool breath next to my neck. I didn't move, not out of fear, but to avoid doing anything stupid. I'd dealt with my hallucinations long enough to manage the ones that felt all too real.

*The ones that really made me feel crazy.*

The problem right now was determining if this was fake or real. Was the man I'd been after for years behind me? Or was this another mind game?

"I killed no one," I muttered, tossing the mirror to my left. I heard it shatter, the pieces skidding along the tile floor, but I didn't care.

It wasn't a weapon I could use to defend myself. Might as well free myself from the added accessory.

**"You'll drown in your lies soon enough,"** the cold voice whispered. I took a shaky breath, only to be mocked by his laughter.

**"Are you afraid of me?"**

"Afraid of what? An illusion in my mind? If you want to face me, be a man and do it," I muttered, lifting the ice stake and staring at the little bolts of electricity as a distraction.

***"Stop trying to atone for your sins and play a hero,"*** he snarled, his words sending tremors through me.

My hand trembled. "I never said I was a hero," I whispered.

***"And yet you continue to walk down these halls like you know what's going on? You hide around those boys because they make you feel worthy of their attention and love. Killers like you don't deserve an ounce of grace. You're better off sticking that stake into your wrist and bleeding to death."***

"I don't need your advice."

***"I wasn't giving you any,"*** he replied.

Things got real when he grabbed my hand with the stake in it, inching it closer to my right wrist. I hissed and tried to fight his strength, the watch suddenly going haywire as it beeped over and over again.

***"Do I feel real now?"*** He chuckled.

I couldn't move from my place, and I realized the room was dark once more. I was no longer in the showers, but in the family house I was raised in.

I stood in the middle of the dark room, but instead of the bodies of my four family members, it was the Maxwell brothers who laid in their place.

**"Realize what you're going to cause. You'll repeat what you did all those years ago,"** he whispered. **"Only this time, it'll be to these stupid men who only love you for what you are. A disgusting killer."**

I bit my lip hard, wishing to be back in the shower hall and away from the haunting, dark room. I couldn't bear staring at the four bodies on the floor, to acknowledge the image of Zackery, Zion, Zeus, and Zeke being dead.

*All because of me.*

The tip of the shard dug into my flesh, enough to make the first indent into my skin. A bead of blood formed on the spot, and I fought against the force that tried to dig it deeper.

*Snap out of it, Jade. It's just a hallucination.*

I was breathing hard, but I worried this really wasn't a hallucination. That he was here right now, trying to kill me.

*Manipulating me into doing what he wanted. Like he had back then.*

Cold water suddenly shot down on me and I shrieked. I took a step back right into someone, their arm wrapping around my waist to prevent me from slipping.

The ice stake fell to the floor, shattering into tiny bits before it faded entirely. I looked at my wrist, noticing the trail of blood that began to drip into the pooling water at our feet.

It took me seeing my own blood to realize my illness was back and that what had just happened was truly a hallucination.

*A really strong hallucination.*

"Jade."

The firm, deadpan voice had me hesitantly looking over to see Zeus's electrifying gold eyes.

To say he was pissed was an understatement. He was downright furious. Whether it was directed at me or not, I wasn't sure.

I bit my lip, knowing if I spoke right now, I'd say something stupid. The situation wasn't for silly commentary. If that was a hallucination, I needed to get back on my meds.

*That was going to be non-negotiable.*

With a shaky breath, I whispered, "I-I think I have to start taking my meds again."

I don't know what it was about that confession that made my eyes water, but with a few blinks, tears began to roll down my cheeks.

*Admitting that I had a problem in a situation like this was beyond frightening.*

Maybe I was crying because I was by Zeus and hadn't discussed my problems with him. Sure, he knew I worried about hallucinations, but I hadn't openly said, 'I have this problem' like I had with Zeke.

Or how I'd admitted the problem to Zion for the sake of the assessment.

Zeus's anger forced me to recognize what I almost did. To confront that I'd almost hurt myself.

*Something I hadn't done since...well, since my homeless and recovery years.*

"I-I'm sorry," I immediately apologized, wishing I could step away from him and hide. His obvious anger made me feel like I was the little Jade who'd woken up to Shadow Jade's destructive mess.

"It...it wasn't..." I struggled to defend myself, reliving that man's voice in my head, telling me what a liar I was.

*That I should own up to my actions. Yet...this wasn't mine. Just like before...back then.*

"Jade," Zeus said my name again. "Did your watch go off?"

I swallowed the lump in my throat, ignoring how my body shook from the cold water and the fear rushing through me.

*What would telling him achieve?*

I was more concerned that he was standing in the chilled water with me. His entire body was drenched. I noticed he wasn't wearing his shirt and he had a cut on the side of his neck.

*When did he get that?*

"Jade."

"Y-yes," I answered, trying to stay focused. "Yes."

I tried to catch my breath, or maybe I was aiming not to panic entirely. It was hard when I felt like I was freezing to death in a closed bubble and not in the open room full of showers.

"Fuck," he muttered.

"I-I-I'm sorry, Z-Zeus," I stuttered as I fought for breath.

He cursed again but immediately wrapped me in his arms. "Breathe, Jade."

I clung to him, shivering uncontrollably. The shower turned off, and within seconds, I was warmer. He walked us to the bench between the lockers, sitting down and cradling me in his arms as I kept apologizing.

"Jade. Stop apologizing. It wasn't you." He kept saying those words over and over, rocking me like a child who was crying after falling down and getting hurt.

It took time for me to calm down from what surely was a panic attack. I rested my head against Zeus's chest, noticing how warm he was. I hadn't even realized I wasn't drenched anymore until now, and even the towel around my body was toasty warm.

"Zeus?"

I leaned back to see his eyes were now a mix of gold and amber. He didn't look as angry as before, but he wasn't pleased either.

"You're not allowed to be alone anymore," he declared.

"Taking away my human rights is selfish," I muttered, unable to stop myself from saying it.

*Yes. I'd just tried to kill myself, but I wasn't going on the Maxwell's twenty-four-hour monitor plan.*

"I'm not joking, Jade."

"I never said you were. I don't need you guys to do a twenty-four-hour watch. If I did, I'd voluntarily enter a psych ward."

Lifting my right wrist, I now noticed the bandage on it. I had to blink a few times, wondering when he'd put it on my wrist. With a long sigh, I closed my eyes.

"Sorry," I whispered. "I should thank you but I'm being a bitch."

"You're not a bitch," he grumbled. "The others are coming."

"Then I should put actual clothes on," I replied sarcastically, getting off his lap and rising up to my shaky feet. "I'll be fast. You can wait outside."

Walking to the next locker row where my locker was, I reached it and tried to open the lock but my right hand was shaking again. Lowering my hand, I tried my left, but it wasn't any better.

"You seriously hate people helping you," Zeus muttered.

I realized he was behind me again.

"I don't need it."

"You were just controlled to try and kill yourself, had a full-blown panic attack, and now you're trying to act like everything is okay."

My fingers fumbled with the lock again, but it was like I couldn't even recall the simple combination with how frantic my mind was.

"You don't know that. I could have had a dumb hallucination, tried to kill myself because of it, had a panic attack for the thrill, and now be trying to remember what my stupid combo is," I argued.

Zeus let out a harsh exhale, moving to help me. I turned around and pressed my back against my locker. "I don't need your help."

"Why do you resist others caring about you?!"

"Help means favors. No one in this damn world does anything without wanting payback. There's no goodwill bullshit. I don't need your help."

"That's the biggest load of bullshit I've heard since Zackery said he'd be the first to date you," Zeus fought back. "Give me a better example."

"My Dad got help after I thunder bolted our old house and caused it to erupt in flames, and you know what that got him? The death penalty!" I snapped.

Zeus stopped, staring into my eyes.

"Good enough excuse now?" I whispered, turning my back to him as I tried again to open my locker. After a fifth attempt, I gave up.

"I might as well just walk around the damn school naked!" I raged, taking my towel off and throwing it to the floor in anger.

This emotional rollercoaster was getting annoying. I just wanted to go home, eat a bowl of ice cream, and sleep.

The sound of my lock clicking open caught my attention, and I looked to see Zeus unhooking it from its slot and opening my locker for me.

I gave him a defiant look, and he slowly took my naked body in.

"I'm not letting you go out in public naked."

"Selfish," I grumbled, blinking back tears. "Just go away."

"You say the opposite of what you mean when you're frustrated."

"Zeu—"

"You have two options. Let me dress you, take you to our mansion, give you a big tub of ice cream, and let you cry in any of our arms tonight. OR, we have makeup sex for whatever bullshit argument we're having, you still let me dress you, we head to our mansion, you get a tub of ice cream, and you can cry in my arms tonight."

I took a few seconds to repeat the two options in my head.

"All I hear is either let me manhandle you with Maxwell options or let's have sex and then I'll manhandle you," I concluded.

"Both options make sure your needs are met."

"The second one favors you more."

"I'm not here for favors," he stressed, closing the distance between us.

"Then why are you here, Zeus? Why...did you stop me back there?"

He took a deep inhale and closed his eyes. Letting the air out slowly, he opened his eyes to look into mine.

"I swear it's obvious," he muttered more to

himself as his face began to grow red. "But if it's not...I guess I should tell you."

He gently placed his hands on my hips and without hesitation, kissed me gently on the lips. It was a careful kiss, one that had very little movement but was firm enough for me to acknowledge it as one.

Inching away just slightly, he whispered, "I love you, Jade. Or at least I have a major crush on you. It could be because of Zeke and his constant wet dreams about you, but let's not dive into that foolishness."

"What about what you just saw? This just confirms I'm bait. What if...the person doing all this crazy shit is the one who killed my family?"

"Doesn't matter. It could be a person using our darkest fears against us for all we know. Not changing my feelings. As long as you agree to the twenty-four-hour Maxwell watch service."

"No."

"I'll give you and Shadow Jade cookies every single day for the rest of the semester."

"Fine."

"What kind of fluid mind fuckery is that?" he complained.

I smiled and hooked my arms around his neck. "Cookies for the rest of the semester is a hard bargain to come by. In fact, two semesters would be extra yummy," I leaned in and brushed my lips along his. "Are you sure?"

"If I wasn't sure, I would have never offered it. I'm also fine with two semesters," he whispered against my lips. "Even with your hot naked body in front of me."

"Your brothers will-mhm."

He sealed my words with those luscious lips and pressed my body against the lockers. Before I knew it, his cock was teasing my entrance, seconds from sliding right in.

"Ah!" I gasped, my head falling back against the locker's surface. He scooped my legs up, hoisted me, and slid himself deep into me.

"I hope you like it nice and fast, Jade, because we only have two minutes before Zackery's loud ass enters here."

I couldn't help but giggle, imagining the scene. "He could joi-ahh!"

My response was cut off with a moan as Zeus began to pump his cock into me. "Imagine later," he breathed as he fucked me hard and fast. "Enjoy me fucking you."

The lights began to flicker on and off, and my body shot up in temperature, my fire and thunder elements rising to his commanding declaration.

All I could do was enjoy and hold him tightly, our lips crashing against one another and muffling our joined moans and pants.

"Fuck, Jade. Your pussy is fucking magic," he growled into my mouth. I could feel the growth of his cock inside me, and I realized how close I was to climaxing.

My pussy fluttered around his cock, and I moaned his name over and over again, the sound growing louder and faster.

"Zeus! Fuck, Zeus!" Our energies were crashing against one another and the lights shut off completely, but I didn't care. I just wanted to feel the wave of my orgasm rush through me and Zeus's hot cum fill my insides.

"That's it, Jade. Let your energy burn. Let it take away all that pain," he growled against my lips. "Let me take it all away."

"Zeus!" His body was scalding hot, and yet it only made me hold onto him tightly. His warmth wasn't burning me in the slightest. It felt as though it was penetrating through my skin and really taking away the pain in my heart.

*The pain and fear of what just happened.*

"Cum, Jade!" he commanded, thrusting one last time and sending me into a screaming, shattering orgasm.

I placed my forehead against his shoulder, shaking as I rode the orgasmic high that followed.

We both caught our breath, and I heard Zackery's voice. "Why is there always a blackout at this school? I swear Alaric can afford the light bill."

"Are you an idiot?" Zion questioned.

"At least I'm not the one calling out his stupidity," Zeke declared.

"KILL!"

"AH!" the three of them screamed.

"Holy father of all things darkness, Shadow Jade!" Zackery gasped.

"I actually thought she was going to kill us," Zion admitted.

"That was unexpected. Hey, Shadow Jade. Where were you?" Zeke asked.

"Napping," she declared. "Kill. Kill. Kill."

Zeus and I leaned back to look at one another.

"Feel a little better?" he asked.

"Yeah," I whispered. "I still want ice cream...and to cuddle and cry."

"Sure," he whispered and kissed my forehead. "Anything you want."

"Including my cookies, every day starting tomorrow," I reminded.

"Mhm," he replied. "Now let me dress you." He lowered my legs and easily helped me dress while

Zeke, Zion, and Shadow Jade were focused on distracting Zackery, who wanted to come into the change room regardless of the no-light situation.

"You're just going in shorts?" I pointed out. "How did you even get those?"

"Magic." He winked. "And no one is going to see my bare chest but you and my brothers."

"Hmph." I crossed my arms over my chest. "Won't let me walk home naked but he can walk in nothing but shorts. I can see your cock."

"You can't see shit in the dark." He laughed, his eyes beginning to glow that electrifying gold. He clapped his hands.

Just like that, the lights went back on.

"Still see it," I mumbled. Zeus rolled his eyes and closed my locker, popping the padlock into place. "Let's go home."

"You keep saying that like it's mine as well," I mumbled.

"You're our queen, remember? Plus, I think our girlfriend deserves a spot in our place, which makes it yours as well."

"So weird," I muttered, a slight smile on my face.

"You love weird." He offered his hand. I took it and he led me into his arms, giving me a quick squeeze and kiss to my temple.

"We'll protect you, Jade," he whispered. "No matter what secrets any of us carry."

I closed my eyes and nodded into his chest, hoping his words were true. This was a setback, but it wouldn't stop me from what I wanted to achieve.

What we needed to achieve to save all those who could become a victim like I almost had.

*Our desperate connection really helped me today. If only it could shadow us from the approaching danger.*

## 18

### INTRODUCE YOU

"**W**hy do we need flowers?" I asked, skipping in a circle around Zackery, who was blowing into his cupped hands.

"I need them for something," he replied. "If only the florist wouldn't take so long. It's cold."

"You have the ice element. You can't be cold," I pointed out.

"Says who?" He pouted his lips.

"Says I with the same element, silly." I smirked at him. "If you want a hug to warm you up, just ask."

He blushed and stuffed his hands into his coat pockets.

"How are you so smooth? You're a girl."

"Just because I'm a girl doesn't mean I can't sweep you off your feet." I winked and twirled on one foot. "I'm totally smooth-oops!" I slipped and nearly fell onto the thin layer of snow on the ground, but my ass didn't reach the ground, hovering over it instead.

I glanced up at Zackery, who chuckled, his eyes a gorgeous glowing teal.

"Smooth, huh?" he teased, lifting me higher into the air until I hovered above his outstretched arms. The wind stopped abruptly, and I dropped right into his arms.

"You can't carry me and a bouquet of flowers," I reasoned.

"You underestimate my ability to multitas-GAH!" he began, taking a step forwards but slipping. I snapped my fingers, my wind element surging to life and stopping us from falling onto the ground.

"Yes, I'm too smooth for you." I giggled.

"Show off," he mumbled as I twirled my hand around to strengthen the gust of wind and lift him back up. Once his feet were back on the snowy surface, I snapped my fingers again to cancel it out.

I playfully kicked my feet, enjoying the comfort of still being in his arms.

"Still going to try to multitask?"

"I'll pass," he muttered with the cutest pout on his lips. He lowered me back to the ground just as the florist came out with two bouquets of roses. One was a mix of black and red roses and the other contained pure white ones.

My eyes immediately went to the red and black ones, loving the combination of the two. I was sure the black roses were dyed because it was almost impossible to get them.

"Sorry for the delay. Two bouquets of roses." She offered them to Zackery, who grinned and bowed his head in gratitude.

"Thank you very much!"

She grinned and hurried back inside, only to come out seconds later. She presented a red and black mini teddy bear to me. I blinked and stared at the cute doll, glancing up to see her smile.

"A gift for your patience. It matches your outfit," she complimented.

"Are...you sure? I can pay," I offered.

"Not at all. Think of it as an early Christmas gift. The early snow fall is bringing a merry mood to the town! You two are a lovely, patient couple," she praised, her words making me blush as I took the teddy bear from her.

"Thank you." I gave her a wide smile.

"Not at all. Get home safely, you two. Merry Early Christmas!"

"Merry Early Christmas!" We waved goodbye,

waiting for her to retreat indoors and turn the OPEN sign off. I looked to Zackery, who was watching me with a loving expression.

"I'm really glad we got here on time. Thanks, Jade."

"It wasn't a big deal," I admitted. "Traveling with dark magic is tricky but it's faster than being stuck in that traffic disaster."

I looked to the teddy bear and grinned. "Plus! I got a tedd—"

"Mine!"

"Ah!" Zackery and I flinched at Shadow Jade's sudden appearance. She was wearing just pajamas, getting odd expressions from the people across the street.

"Shadow Jade? You really appeared out of nowhere," I pointed out. "Aren't you cold?"

"No. Teddy bear!" She pointed to the bear in my hands.

"You want it for your collection, don't you?"

Her wide grin made me shake my head as I sighed. "I spoil you."

"Please?" she pleaded and blinked her eyes.

"Fine." I smiled and offered it to her. "Force Zeus to help you organize."

"Okay! Kill! Bye!" She took the bear happily, and with a little wave, she vanished in a poof of fading dark energy.

We had a moment of silence before we exchanged looks. "My teddy was kidnapped."

Zackery chuckled. "You would have given it to her anyway," he pointed out, offering me the bouquet of red and black roses. "That's why I figured you'd want these instead."

"Huh? You...bought these for me?!" I gawked at him while accepting the bouquet.

"Unexpected smooth move, huh?" He gave me a charming wink before offering his arm. I grinned from ear to ear, hooking my arm in his, giving him a little squeeze.

"Thank you, Zackery," I said as we began to walk away from the shop.

It was our second-to-last week of the semester, and Zackery had asked me to go out with him to fetch something before we went over to my place for our little snow-fall gathering.

It wasn't the holidays just yet, but the beautiful snowfall seemed to put everyone into the mood. We decided to celebrate almost finishing our first semester and the snowfall with dinner at my place.

It was the first time where I was actually inviting friends over.

*Or boyfriends, I should say.*

A week since the incident in the showers had zoomed by with no other issues.

Whether it was a hallucination or not, Zion had sped up the process of making my meds, and I had now been on them for two weeks with no side effects. Not only did they prevent hallucinations, but they were also helping me sleep better.

That and the occasional nights spent cuddled in one of the Maxwell brothers' arms did the trick. There had yet to be any more reports of students showing up dead from self-inflicted injuries, and things seemed to be back to normal at Tracker Hive Academy.

During the last week, I'd not focused on improving my elemental control but also returned to doing other exercises that I used to really enjoy.

The guys were another influence in that. Zackery loved hip hop dancing and invited me to be his dancing partner once every two weeks for his hip hop class in the other district. Zion was into yoga and meditation, which helped me improve my focus and enhance my flexibility. Zeus was all about track, from sprints to high jumps. We'd work out on the outdoor track whether it was rain or shine. Only when it started snowing did he let us go to the gym for our workout.

*Doesn't want to make himself look like a fool, or in his words, a 'Zackery.'*

Zeke was the only brother who did a wider variety of exercise, which encompassed all his brothers' favorites. He just didn't work out as often.

*Unless you counted sex as a workout. He was an expert at that.*

Having them around had helped me grow across the board, to the point even Tanner complimented me during our last training session earlier today.

The guys had asked Alaric's official permission to date me, and after a long interview process with them signing the dotted line to accept any consequences if they broke my heart — which included death — he happily approved of the relationship.

For the first time in a really long while, I was happy and doing activities that weren't solely for an assignment or to prove myself.

Continuing our quiet walk down the busy streets, we turned onto a pathway, my eyes scanning around and realizing where we were.

*A cemetery?*

Glancing at Zackery, he continued to guide me down the path, his eyes forward while he quietly hummed a holiday tune.

I held his arm a little tighter, hoping my added

comfort would ease whatever must have been going through his head.

We turned left, onto a smaller path with a row of graves, until we stopped at the one at the very end of the row. It seemed to have a double plot of space, and when I looked at the gravestone, my heart sank.

*Aurelia Maxwell. Loving Mother of Four. May Your Soul Rest In Peace.*

Zackery gently untwined our hooked arms, walking up to lay the flowers on top of the stone surface. He remained crouching, his eyes focused on the tombstone with the smiling image of their Mother.

I remained still, even though I was tempted to put my hands in my pockets out of habit. I may not have known this woman who was able to raise four amazing men before her life ended, but she deserved my utmost respect.

Whatever she taught her boys had paid off, because they were a successful group of Trackers who were definitely a part of the more respectful percentage of our population.

"Hey, Mom. It's me, Zackery. Just came to check on you. It's not Christmas yet, but all this snow is putting us all in a holiday spirit." Zackery's voice was gentle, and for the first time, I heard the aching sadness in his words.

"I would have come with the others...but you know how depressed Zion and Zeus get, even when they try not to show it. And we can't have Zeke getting his emotions all knotted up. We don't need an imbalance, especially before the end of our first semester, though we've experienced it quite a bit recently." He chuckled quietly before he trailed his finger over a specific part of the grave.

"I actually brought someone. She's our girl-friend." He looked over to me, giving me a sad smile as he continued. "I wish you could have met her face-to-face. I'm sure she'd throw you off with her intriguing responses."

I clenched my fists to hide the slight tremble in them, reminding me of my lost family who was probably looking down on me from wherever they were in heaven.

*I still wonder if they're mad at me.*

"Anyway. I didn't want Christmas to arrive without giving you the white roses you loved. The others miss you really bad, and so do I. We're working hard to get rid of all the bad in the world. Get rid of those people who took you far too soon."

He swallowed and blinked his eyes, composing himself as best as he could. "We'll be back again on Christmas, Mom. I love you. We all love you. I'll see you again...maybe all of us will come. If not, New Years for sure, kay? Stay warm for me."

Closing his eyes, he remained silent for a long moment before he rose up.

A warm breeze suddenly passed us, wrapping around the two of us and lifting the bits of snow in the air before letting it rain down upon us.

Zackery smiled, looking up to the sky and taking a few deep inhales. I knew that was his element trying to console the sadness in his heart. It was something my own wind element did when I was sad.

Though our elements were vessels of power, they each had a bit of their own personality, especially when they were main elements.

They could comfort you, even if they couldn't take a physical presence like Shadow Jade did.

I walked to Zackery's side, slipping my hand into his. It was a casual move, and I didn't pay attention when I felt his gaze on me, but he squeezed my hand in return.

We stood there for a few more minutes before Zackery spoke.

"Let's head home."

Squeezing his hand, we made our way back to the main streets, and he scheduled an Uber to pick us up.

It wasn't until we were inside the car that he spoke again.

"Our Mom died when we were ten. She died trying to protect us...specifically Zeke. We were targets of the Black Market and they found out the four of us carried two elements each. With what we know now about some organizations' intentions, I'm sure they wanted to keep us in captivity and find the queen that linked us together. Needless to say, they killed our mother during the confrontation and well...things went crazy after."

He squeezed my hand, his eyes looking out the window as the car sat in traffic.

"They tried to take us, but Zeke snapped. He hadn't unlocked his dark element fully, but that triggered it. The intensity of the attack killed the entire team that was sent to retrieve us. It also imbalanced us entirely."

"Imbalanced?" I questioned.

"The four of us are connected. It means that we basically have to balance each other out all the time. Before our mom's passing, we could be more expressive. I could be happy or sad, angry or flirty. I didn't have to maintain specific characteristics and it was the same with my brothers. When Zeke lost control, it tipped us all over, and basically, after many tests, we realized we each had to maintain specific personality traits."

"That's why you're playful and happy all the time, Zion's calm and calculative, Zeus is always angry, and Zeke is seductive and easygoing." I broke it down.

"Pretty much. We do have our times where we're sad and can't help it, but it really fucks us up if it's for too long. That's why when Zeke is all horny, it annoys us."

"Because it affects you guys, too?"

"Essentially. I'm a little more connected to Zion, and Zeus has a strong connection to Zeke. It's why Zeke's dreams or worries have a greater effect on him while I have a greater effect on Zion, and vice versa."

"That's why Zeke and Zeus move at a different pace from you and Zion?" I confirmed.

"Yup. It's not like we don't want to, but it'll fuck us up a bit. Letting Zeke and Zeus satisfy their needs first helps so that when it's our turn, they won't be too antsy about it. Not to say they won't complain, but they won't feel the need to fight or rush to be around you. It's hard to explain, but that's why we're like this."

"Is that why you guys decided to become Trackers?" I asked.

"We were recruited. They took us in before the system could. Our mom was already in the process of enrolling us into their care and protection. The process was just too late. By the time our file was reviewed, the Black Market organization had found out and sent for our retrieval. We're not mad about it, but it's the reason why we work towards getting rid of all the bad goons that reveal themselves."

"So...on days like today or closer to the holidays, you come to give flowers because you'll cause the least imbalance?" I concluded.

"Essentially," he replied. "During specific holidays like her birthday or New Years, we all go, but it really depends on how the others are feeling. I would have been fine coming by myself...but I kinda felt a little lonely." He turned his head to look at me."I thought it would be nice to introduce you before the semester ended as well."

"Zackery." I squeezed his hand. "I'm glad I could tag along."

"Me, too. It's nice having someone with me." He squeezed my hand and leaned his head down to rest on my shoulder. His eyes were closed as he whispered, "I'm just going to borrow your shoulder for a bit."

"Okay," I whispered.

He must have been emotionally drained. Taking

in his relaxed facial expression, I looked to the window, staring at the passing cars and lights.

Little by little, I was learning more about the Maxwells and I wondered when I'd be able to freely tell them all about my past. I knew I would be able to in due time, but I hoped the guys would be willing to wait for the right time for me to share.

The semester was coming to a close, and though we'd yet to truly identify the culprit behind the 'suicides' at Tracker Hive, I wasn't losing hope yet.

I was still their primary bait, and I planned to get the upper hand in it all.

*Even if it killed me.*

## 19

## NAUGHTY ZEKE AND PULL THE TRIGGER

"You overslept?"

"No. Past me thought it was smart to lie down after showering post-training session this morning with Tanner. I have a hunch that future me is going to regret it when she's being scolded for being late," I complained, sliding on my black wool tights.

Taking a quick glance in the mirror, I made sure my skirt was short as usual. It wouldn't matter since I was wearing my tights today. Even though semester one was almost done, winter was already brewing and it was freezing as usual.

I'd have to convince Alaric that wearing a skirt on mandatory class days was stupid. If we had to potentially risk freezing our asses off, so should the male population.

The thought of Zackery, Zion, Zeus, and Zeke in skirts had me snickering, even before I imagined Zackery skipping through the halls.

*Now I was laughing.*

"Why are you laughing?" Zeke inquired.

I looked at the phone on my bed, skipping over to pick it up.

"I was imagining the four of you guys wearing skirts and freezing your ass cheeks off. Then I thought about Zackery skipping. Can you imagine? His cock flopping up and down with his balls." I began to laugh again. "I hope Tanner doesn't pass by. He's going to think I'm insane. Actually, he already thinks that, but he'll emphasize it to Alaric and we can't have that."

Zeke chuckled through the speaker, and I walked over to my nightstand to take one of my hallucination pills.

"Are you taking your meds?"

"Yup!" I said, tossing the two daily pills into my mouth and grabbing the almost-empty water bottle to wash them down.

"It's been working well?"

"Very well," I replied when I finished the remaining water. "No side effects, which still baffles me. If Zion can make something like this, why the hell haven't we discovered the cure for all diseases?

Mother nature gave us all the tools and we are still slacking," I complained.

"They have, but do you expect them to give it to the public without it being a billion dollars?"

"You have a point," I reasoned.

"Kill. Kill. Kill!"

I looked at the doorway to see Shadow Jade skip into the room. I looked at her bare legs and sighed. "Shadow Jade. You're going to freeze your legs off in just a skirt. Wear tights."

"No." She skipped right out the door.

I groaned, shaking my head while Zeke began laughing again.

"What's with Shadow Jade hating tights?"

"You're asking me? She's the complete opposite of me and my likes in this department. I'll skip freezing my ass off any day. I'm happy to sacrifice comfort to prevent my poor butt cheeks from getting frostbite."

"You won't get frostbite." Zeke sounded beyond amused.

"You don't know that, and I'm not going to test the theory," I noted.

"You're wearing tights now?"

"Yup."

"What underwear are you wearing?"

"Wouldn't you like to know," I teased, picking

my phone up and taking it off the speaker. I lay back on my bed. "You really wanna know?"

"Yeah. Gives me an idea what to expect before I slide them off before the assembly today."

"Oh. Public sex? I don't think you want to lose your Tracker position, Mr. Maxwell. However, I'm down for the risk. I'll get out of the charges with my charm alone."

"Funny, because I actually believe that," he admitted with a chuckle. "Wanna have a little fun before class?"

"Depends where," I purred.

"Let's meet at my locker," he suggested.

"All right." I giggled. "We have two hours before people will start gathering in the gym. We can't take long."

"We won't," he reassured me. "Unless you want to, but I don't want your ass cheeks to get cold."

I smirked. "If you smack them hard enough, I think they'll be nice and warm."

"Wouldn't you love that?" His low chuckle had me wanting to slide my hand between my legs and masturbate to his voice.

"I would," I whispered.

"What are you doing?"

"Lying on my bed and attempting not to masturbate."

"If you make it here in five minutes, you won't have to."

"Make it ten. I'm going to try and force Shadow Jade to wear her tights."

"That's a losing battle. I bet you a threesome it's not happening."

"Oh, a threesome?" I whistled for added emphasis. "No need to bet. I've suddenly lost my urge to help her. Who are you planning to ask to join?"

"Zeus."

"You're crazy," I barked. "He'll say no."

"I'll add handcuffs and you blindfolded to the equation."

"You savage beast," I snickered. "He'll never deny that."

"I know," he growled. "I've already had a few wet dreams about it. He'll cave."

"Evil." I shook my head. "You torture him too much."

"He'll get over it." Zeke chuckled. "Hurry over here. I miss you."

"Do you now?" I sat up and sighed. "Okay. I'll be there in a bit."

"Love you," he whispered.

"Love you, too," I replied.

He hung up first, and I stared at the screen and smiled.

*He's so naughty.*

<hr/>

"QUEEN JADE!"

I came to a stop in the hall, looking over my shoulder to see Calvin and his ginormous backpack. I wondered if he carried an entire computer system in there with an external hard drive and everything.

"Morning, Calvin," I greeted.

He came to a stop next to me, putting his hands on his knees and catching his breath.

"I don't know why you run like the world is ending," I muttered, staring at him with a pout.

"I just have little legs," Calvin reasoned, rising up to give me a wide grin. "Shall I walk you to class?"

"Ah, no. I'm meeting Zeke at his locker. Seeing as we have the assembly in an hour, want to tell the others we'll be at class before we head to the gym?"

"Sure! I'll let them know." He spoke like he'd just accepted a mission, putting his hand up at attention for added emphasis.

"You're intriguing, Calvin," I admitted.

"Thank you for the compliment, Queen Jade."

*Now he looks like he's going to cry over my compliment. At least he's helpful.*

"Jade."

We both glanced to my right to see Zeke walking toward us.

"Zeke? Thought you were going to be at your locker?"

"There's a blackout there. They're trying to fix it," he explained.

"Always blackouts in this school." Calvin shook his head. "I'll go tell Zeus, Zion, and Zackery that you two will be at class before the assembly!"

"Thanks, Calvin," I replied, watching him bow down to me before he waved and ran off.

Zeke looked back at me. "Why does he carry those huge bags?"

"I'm sure he has a whole computer console and hard drive in there with his laptop and netbook," I answered.

His eyes looked me up and down, and I met his gaze.

"What?"

"Your bare legs are nice, that's all," he complimented and turned around. "Let's head to the gym. Don't want to delay our alone time."

"Okay," I sweetly commented, slipping my hands in my blazer pockets and skipping to follow him.

We reached the gym and I locked the entrance

doors. With an assembly, Bianca had explained that they always locked the doors ten minutes before starting to set things up. It didn't take long; a snap of their fingers did the trick.

The chairs were always made up of intertwining vines. It made it so we were surrounded by nature, which opened our minds more.

*Or something like that. It basically made us relaxed or whatever.*

It was those special spells that needed a combination of two or three elements to create the foundation of the chair, but it looked like Bianca had perfected it with a little of Tanner's assistance.

I was sure they would be here soon, but we had a while. A bit of foreplay and hot sex would fit the agenda.

I glanced to the upper floor balcony, wondering if I should close the doors there as well. It was where the professors would stand and watch us train and perform.

Tanner loved the balcony. He could scream and order us to do whatever and then smirk in triumph when we either failed or got all pissed to the point of wishing he could feel our wrath.

I was used to Tanner's asshole personality when it came to training, but at least I knew he meant well. The rest of the students? Not so much.

The lights suddenly went off, leaving us in the dark.

"A blackout again?" I commented. I knew this wasn't Zeus's doing, or that's what my instincts told me. Unless we were making out, he didn't see the need to shut the lights off.

Then the fire alarm went off.

"Is the school ending?" Zeke pondered.

"Maybe it's a prank," I groaned. "What's the likelihood of a blackout and a fire? Something is up. I wonder what the assembly was supposed to be about?"

We hadn't had many incidents this semester, and even if there had been, we wouldn't have had an assembly about it.

Dad and the others wanted to keep the incidents on the down low. The more people who knew about them, the trickier things would become. As Trackers, we didn't want to give our next set of moves away.

*We had to be just as sneaky and tricky as our enemy.*

"What shall we do then?" I questioned, turning my attention to Zeke, whose hands were in his pockets. He turned around, his back facing me as he took a deep breath.

"I actually wanted to ask you something."

"What? If this is about you forgetting to bring

Shadow Jade and me a cookie today like you were supposed to, it's fine. Zeus will most likely bring it...whenever we have this assembly."

Zeus was still honoring his cookie promise, but Zeke was purposely teasing him by taking our cookie share and not delivering it until Zeus nagged him.

I thought for sure Zeus would have sniped him with thunderbolt already, but he was still here, obviously.

"No." He sounded amused but continued. "How long were you going to keep it a secret?"

"What a secret?" I questioned.

"That you killed your family."

I stood completely still, not expecting him to ask that. When I didn't answer, he turned around to face me, his eyes locking onto mine.

His black orbs showed no emotion, and the silver ring that usually surrounded his irises was gone, making his eyes even duller.

"What...are you talking about, Zeke?"

"You said a person killed your family. That a man killed them because he was after you."

I held my tongue, unsure when I'd told him that. I was sure it wasn't during the night at the hotel, or the countless times he'd slept over or I'd stayed with him.

*He could be just testing me. Like Tracker Hive protocol.*

The silence between us grew, while the fire alarm continued to ring. There must have not been an alarm in the actual gym because it was nowhere near as loud as it would have been in the hall.

We both stood there, and he took a long inhale.

"Why did you lie?"

"I never lied," I honestly replied.

"Why don't I reword this," he countered. "Did the man you said killed your family really kill them with his own hands?"

I bit my lip and slid my hands into my pockets.

"You put your hands in your pockets because they shake a lot," he commented. "Is that due to your PTSD caused by killing your family?"

"I didn't kill them." I narrowed my eyes at him.

"Right. So you keep saying." He bobbed his head and pulled out his left hand. "Does Shadow Jade have something do with all of this?"

"Leave her out of it," I barked back.

"Guilty." He smirked as a ball of black magic formed in his hand. He tossed it up like a baseball, catching it and looking back at me.

"Let me guess. Shadow Jade had a little tantrum and ended up killing everyone? Was this man who is now considered a criminal just in the wrong place at the wrong time?"

"It's none of your business, Zeke." I turned around, but he was right there and the shadow ball in his hand was now a gun pressed to my forehead.

"You manipulated me. You used my brothers, and now you're trying to tell me that all of this isn't my business. Pretty two-faced, if you ask me."

"Move your gun from my head," I muttered.

"And what?" he prompted. "You'll tell me the truth? Tell my brothers the truth? No...tell all the world the truth of what you, or should I say, Shadow Jade, really did."

I pulled my right hand out of my pocket, pointing the burning red gun to his forehead.

"You're not Zeke," I whispered.

"Says who? You, the traitor?" He stared at me in defiance. "I hate dirty liars like you. Would have been better if you'd remained on the streets where you belong. Actually, you should have just been killed by those people who desperately wanted you."

My hand shook uncontrollably and my eyes grew glassy, but I fought to keep my calm.

"Are you the one telling people to kill themselves?" I whispered.

Zeke chuckled. "Really? Trying to put the blame

on me now? Last time I checked, this issue was happening before my brothers and I took the case. Try again, Jade."

He grinned and lowered his gun, but I kept mine in place.

"Why don't I ask you this? Do you love me, Jade?"

I took a steady breath, staring into his eyes. "You already know the answer to that."

"Say it," he whispered, allowing his voice to tremble.

I hurt him. I could sense it, but he didn't understand. He didn't get the situation I was in.

*We were in.*

"Yes. I love you," I confessed.

It wasn't a lie. I actually did love him and the others. I cared for each of them, even if I hadn't spent equal time with all of them. I'd spent the most time with Zeke, making the connection between us the strongest.

"Then do me this one favor. This one last challenge."

I knew what he was going to ask me to do, and I wished he wouldn't, because I wouldn't be able to deny him. I'd do anything he asked. I was sure he'd been betrayed in the past.

*Would keeping my secrets safe lead me to lose the men I*

*cared about? Lead me to lose everything in general?*

"Fine," I confidently replied, lowering the gun. "What favor am I supposed to do? Pretty two-faced yourself when you said you'd never ask a favor of me."

The second part of my statement was bitter, and I could tell from his frown that he hated it.

"Press that gun to your temple and pull the trigger."

We stared in silence, my tears rolling down my cheeks.

*Was this real? This had to be a hallucination. Was Zeke...my Zeke asking this of me?*

"You want me to take my own life? That's the favor you're asking of me?"

"Your dad asked for a favor after you fucked up. Don't you think you owe it to him to stop living a lie? You and Shadow Jade killed your entire family. You blamed it on a man because he was in the wrong place at the wrong time and fit the profile. You played the victim and took pills to shoo away the demons that haunted you on a daily basis. All while the man you blamed had to hide in the shadows because he can't clear his name. Maybe I never emphasized it, but I hate liars. I hate people like you; selfish individuals like you are the reason our mom died. I'm not dating a lying, dirty bitch.

I'm not going to let the others near you. Either you pull the trigger, or I'll go to Alaric myself and reveal all the evidence Zion and the others discovered after looking through your file in more detail."

I nervously bit my lip, glancing down to the red metallic gun I'd created with the mixture of dark and fire magic. My weapon of choice was a sword, leaving me to wonder why I'd thought a gun was the better choice. If I pulled the trigger, it wouldn't be a prank.

It was a real weapon, and the bullet would blow my brains out.

*Wasn't that something I deserved though? He'd figured out the secret I'd kept hidden my whole life. If he knew, so did the others.*

My secret was revealed, and I'd lost the game.

I slowly lifted my hand, pressing the barrel of the gun against my temple. Zeke remained where he was, not a hint of emotion on his face.

"What will this achieve?" I whispered. "It won't prove that man's innocence."

"It certainly will. I'm recording this entire thing. Your admission of guilt will be recorded and provided to the court, proving this man's innocence. Then he'll probably sue Alaric and the rest of the Tracker Hive association. Your secret is merely the beginning of the takedown of the very organization you've been busting your ass to be officially a part of. How does it feel to know you're the reason it's all going to crash and burn? Like how your entire life crashed and burned that night."

He smirked then, and the smile twinkled in his almost-pitch-black eyes.

"Your existence isn't necessary, Jade. Give in already and let us be the true Trackers we are. We don't need fakes in the organization. Disappear."

I closed my eyes, my finger on the trigger.

"You have no proof I did anything," I whispered. "The man with silver hair killed my family. He used his power, gift, whatever you want to call it. I'm the victim."

"Stop lying!" Zeke snapped.

I opened my eyes and whispered, "Last week... during the snow fall, who went to the cemetery with me and what flowers did we pick for the grave?'

He looked me right in the eye.

"Red flowers and Zeus," he answered.

I smiled. "Tell your brothers that Charles Sokolov of District A74 manipulated me to kill my entire family and is the reason I'm now dead."

His eyes went wide, realizing what I'd just said.

"N—"

*I pulled the trigger.*

## 20

# FUCK

*~Z* **EKE~**
"Where's Jade?" I asked, pulling out my phone to check the time as well as to see if I'd gotten a text from our baby.

"I brought hers and Shadow Jade's cookies early and they aren't even here," Zeus grumbled.

"Isn't that a little weird?" Zion questioned.

"Jade may hate mornings, but she's always early," Zackery added.

"I talked to her earlier. She said she was on her way. She was lying on her bed though. She could have fallen asleep again," I reasoned, beginning to text her.

I'd been a little anxious all day. It never was good for me to be anxious. It reminded me of the day our mother died.

*If I'd listened to my instincts and hadn't been a scaredy-cat weakling, she would still be here.*

"Zeke? What...are...you...jeez. I have to stop running with so much equipment."

The four of us looked over to see Calvin, who was waddling over to us. He pulled out the seat of the desk and took his bag off to settle it there, all while catching his breath.

"What?" I asked.

"Jeez, Calvin. Why do you carry all that computer shit with you?" Zackery asked.

"It's a computer for a reason. You can store everything on it and sync across all your devices. Don't need to carry three computers and that stupid external hard drive with you," Zeus added, crossing his arms.

"My equipment is important," Calvin defended, hugging his bag like it was his girlfriend. "You're just jealous."

"Of what? Old-school technology? Zion can crack any code with his phone and yet you're carrying all this shit to make notes."

"Research," Calvin stressed, pulling out his laptop and placing it on the desk. He then lowered his bag carefully to the floor and opened up his computer.

With his fingerprint identification, it was up

and running.

"Calvin," I groaned. "What were you saying?"

"Right!" He flinched like he'd just remembered. "Where did Queen Jade go? You both said you wouldn't be here until before the assembly. I was going to tell your brothers what you said."

I arched an eyebrow at him. "What are you talking about? I was waiting for Jade at our lockers. When it took her too long, I figured she'd fallen asleep and I'd meet her here."

Calvin fixed his glasses, an obvious frown on his face. It was weird to see him actually look serious about something other than technology.

"You were clearly with Jade minutes ago. Sure, I'm a slow runner and I went to piss, but you were there. I talked to you."

"I've been here. Ask my three brothers. They can tell whether this," I waved my hand in front of myself, "is the real me."

"Yeah, that's Zeke, all right," Zackery pointed out. "He's still a confident motherfucker."

"With his stupid imagination and wet dreams," Zeus grumbled.

"And we have the same connection. Are you seeing things?" Zion questioned. "If you want an assessment, let me know."

When Calvin simply stared at the four of us, I

sighed. "Calvin, I'm legit serious. Need to check my tracker app or something?"

Calvin settled in his seat, his eyes glued to the screen as his fingers began to type furiously across his light-up keyboard.

The four of us exchanged looks, the guys feeling my anxiety.

*He's making me worry.*

*"Why would he say he saw you and Jade?"* Zackery questioned through our mental communication.

We didn't use it unless there was an emergency or we were on a mission, but to me, anything about Jade was an emergency if she wasn't here.

*"His computer screens are going wild,"* Zion pointed out.

*"Who is Calvin, really?"* Zeus inquired.

*A nerd who loves to follow Jade around and call her queen, which really pisses me off. That's what we should be calling her.*

*"That's your protective ass talking,"* Zeus muttered.

*"He's harmless,"* Zackery stressed.

*"Hmm. I don't think a person who just decoded the school's security camera program and is now reversing the footage from an hour ago should be deemed harmless,"* Zion announced.

We all turned our attention to Calvin, noticing

how his eyes glowed a slight green as he focused on the screen.

We moved to gather behind him just as he reached the footage he was looking for. Pressing the enter button, he pointed his finger to the screen.

"Tell me that doesn't look exactly like Zeke?" Calvin announced.

My eyes grew wide and I moved Zackery out of the way to get closer. He wasn't joking. There I was, standing next to Jade, who was talking to Calvin. A quick conversation was exchanged before Calvin was running off as usual.

Jade turned to the Imposter Zeke, the two of them talking before moving to the hall to the gym.

"When was this, Calvin?" My voice was cold.

"Five minutes ago? I can—"

I jolted from the room, already running toward the gym at full sprint speed.

*Zeus! Lights! Zackery! Pull the alarm and get Alaric, Tanner, and Bianca to the gym now! Zion! I want every single camera and sound device on in the gym right now!*

**"ON IT!"** the three of them said in unison.

In seconds, the lights went off, only a few of the emergency lights flickering on as backup. Then the fire alarm went off.

I reached the hall to the gym with ease, skidding to a stop and pulling the door, only to realize it was locked.

"Shit!" I cursed, needing a moment to think.

*Stairs...balcony!*

I was running again, headed to the other side where the door to the stairs was. I raced through the students that were evacuating, cursing under my breath at how they were slowing me down.

I reached the door, thanking the heavens that it was unlocked. Taking the stairs three at a time, I was on the balcony in seconds.

Running to the steel railing, I skidded to a stop, gripping the cool metal before my eyes went wide and I began to shout.

"Ja—"

The sound of the gun going off seemed to ring in my ears.

My jaw went slack as I watched Jade's body fall to the side, the red gun she was holding skidding across the floor.

When it stopped it shifted to black before fading into dark smoke that ascended into the air.

My eyes trailed back to Jade's body, watching the dark red blood that began to pool beneath her head and spread like a gruesome halo.

The loud curse that echoed in the gymnasium

caught my attention, my eyes locking onto a pair of black ones.

I stared at my imposter, noticing how his eyes narrowed on me and his hair shifted to full silver. He looked furious, as though things went the wrong way as he glared daggers at me.

My mind didn't register what I was doing until I was pushing off the rail with my feet, sending both my light and dark elements toward him in a swift attack.

He swung his hand in front of him, creating a whirlwind powerful enough to send my divine body backwards.

I flipped and landed on my feet, dashing forward to counter-attack, but with a snap, his body faded into nothing but darkness.

"Fuck!" I cursed, clenching my fists as I restrained my dark element to keep it from taking over.

My heart was racing, to the point it almost felt like I was suffocating, but then my eyes lowered to Jade's unmoving body, my heart sinking faster than the damn Titanic.

"Jade..." I struggled to walk suddenly, the world swaying until I fell to my knees.

I remembered this sight. It was exactly how my

mother's body had looked as she lay in the pool of blood that grew bigger and bigger by the second.

The men around the room had laughed, their mockery their combined celebration over killing our mom.

*Our everything.*

Now I was experiencing it all over again. Seeing a woman I loved on the gym floor, the pool of blood spreading.

I knew it wasn't a dream or an illusion, or I wouldn't feel the hole of pain and guilt grow. My brothers could see what I could see.

They could feel my crushed heart and the void that was beginning to consume me. As if I couldn't believe my very eyes, I slowly rose up.

Though I struggled to walk, I did, step after step, my eyes still locked on Jade's body. She was in her usual attire. The normal black blazer that she loved to wear no matter if it was hot or cold, just so she had a place to slide her hands when she wanted to skip.

She didn't know we knew she did it to hide their trembling. That was just one of the many things in her file under the PTSD section. She didn't know that we knew about the details of the incident.

She had no idea that Alaric had spoken to the

four of us at the very beginning and explained the extent of her case.

Filled us in on the man who took control of Jade on her eighth birthday as he pretended to be an elemental analysis doctor from Tracker Hive Organization.

*The man who was still on the run.*

Her family had no idea. They knew nothing about how Tracker Hive worked. That they always sent three people to do analysis, and one was always the head of the district unless stated otherwise.

They were tricked by this man, and he was able to manipulate Jade into releasing Shadow Jade to kill her entire family.

It was why Shadow Jade constantly said 'kill.' It reminded her that she'd been a tool to kill her family and not follow orders unless Jade specifically said 'Shadow Jade.' Only those close to her knew the true significance of the nickname.

We'd known about all of this and promised that if we were going to be undercover Trackers at Tracker Hive Academy, we wouldn't tell Jade that we knew about it.

Alaric explained about the dread Jade carried. The isolation she'd experienced as a homeless child being chased at least every other day. He stressed that she didn't grow up like other kids, playing and interacting with others her age.

She was a lone wolf, reminded every day by nightmares, memories, and flashbacks of everything she'd gone through. She recalled every detail of the incident, even down to the scent of the home and clothes of the killer.

They hadn't found him because he was in hiding, and Alaric, Tanner, and Bianca believed he was the one killing students.

The Magic Council knew this, which was exactly why they were using Jade as bait, but there was more. Us being a Hive wasn't a part of the equation, and now it was starting to make sense.

This guy who killed Jade's family didn't expect us to be a Hive. Was his aim to kidnap Jade to lead us to him and his organization?

It wouldn't make sense with what had happened in the showers with Zeus, but maybe that was only a distraction. To prove that his aim was to get more students to kill themselves, even though he really only wanted Jade.

*This had been his chance...but then...she pulled the trigger.*

I reached her body, my own body practically shaking at the close-up look. My breathing was audible, the situation really sinking into every fiber of my being.

I was struggling to keep it together, to not let my darkness rage out like it had all those years ago, killing all ten of the men who tried to take us away.

Scanning Jade's body, I noticed her bare legs. It reminded me of the phone call we'd just had, which I now realized was our last.

I knelt down and pressed my shaky hand against her flesh, my tears beginning to fall when I felt how ice cold her body was.

"Jade..." I whispered, my voice trembling as I fought not to sob.

"I'm not sure if you're cute or ugly when you cry."

My head shot up to see Jade leaning against the podium of the stage.

I gawked at her, slowly taking in her extremely pale skin and weak-looking stance.

Her hands were visibly trembling, and she was leaning against the podium for dear life. She was in her normal uniform, down to the black tights she wore in winter to make sure her ass didn't freeze.

"J...Jade?"

"I'd say something cool or romantic like in the movies, but my head feels like I just shot through it and I really want to vomit right now," she admitted with a conflicted grin.

I looked back down at her apparent body, then looked back at her, still feeling speechless.

"This...can't be—"

"Real? Yeah. Sorry, Zeke. I didn't actually submit to my family's killer's suicidal command. His name is Charles, by the way. I've been around you four for how many months now? I think...I'd know...jeez. I hope Tylenol can fix my head. Give me a moment to vomit." She excused herself, attempting to move away from the podium, which only made her fall forward and collapse on the stage.

"Shit! Jade!" I was up and on the stage in seconds, falling down to her side to help her to her hands and knees.

I took off my blazer, used my dark magic to make a bowl, placing it in front of Jade, seconds before she began to vomit.

Gathering her hair so it wouldn't get in the way, I used my other hand to rub her back as she unleashed whatever she'd eaten for breakfast.

"Totally...attractive," she breathed.

"Extremely attractive," I whispered, trying to cheer her up while I fought not to continue crying in relief.

She sighed and sat back on her knees. I let go of her hair and removed my tie, offering it to her to clean her mouth.

"Are you going to strip to make me feel better?" She looked like she was going to be sick again, yet was trying to lighten the mood.

"You're insane," I huffed.

She frowned for a moment, not a reaction I was expecting.

Whenever I teased her like that, she'd have a comeback about how amazingly insane she was, but her lingering silence made me realize I could have just fucked up.

"I meant it as a joke," I whispered, reaching out to press my hand against her cheek.

She blinked a few times before she nervously laughed.

"Yeah...my bad. I think the headache isn't helping me think correctly. Jade is not processing. " She gave me the best smile she could muster, but I knew she was struggling.

She took the tie and patted her mouth, but when she tried to stand, I stopped her.

"No. Don't stand. The others will be here in a few seconds."

We hadn't communicated since I saw Jade's

body— *or the fake Jade* — but their presence was super close.

My thoughts were interrupted by a crash, the doors of the gym literally breaking open.

Zeus, Zackery, Zion, Calvin, and Alaric ran into the gym, only to skid to a stop, their eyes on dead Jade.

"Fuck!" my brothers said together while Calvin and Alaric merely stared in horror.

"Over here!" I called out, catching their attention.

I looked to Jade, who was looking down at her shaking hands. I reached out and placed my hands on hers, catching her attention.

"I'm right here. The real me. All right?"

"I'm...not dirty to you, right?" Her gaze lifted, showing the most vulnerable pair of now-red eyes I'd ever seen.

"Fuck," I cursed and kissed her with as much love I could.

She didn't react, which only made me worry about what lies that man fed into her mind, but after a few seconds, she lightly pressed back.

When I pulled away, she blushed.

"I just vomited, and you kissed me. Your commitment level is really stratospheric."

"If it reassured you that I love every part of

you and have never hated or thought of you as dirty, I'd French kiss you until you begged me to stop."

"Romantic," she sighed. "I need to lie down. My head won't stop pounding." She really looked miserable.

My brothers had snapped out of whatever shock they were in, rushing over to the stage.

Zion was there first, his athletic side always kicking in when it needed to the most.

He was at Jade's other side, his hand on her back as he leaned his head down to look at her.

"Hey, Queen. You scared us a little."

"Define 'a little.'" She gave a weak smile. "Also, can you tell Dad to stop staring? I'm over here and not on the floor."

Zackery and Zeus crowded to my right and we looked to Alaric, who was still looking at Jade's dead copy.

"Headmaster Masters! It's a fake!" Zackery declared.

Jade lifted one of her hands up and flopped it side to side. "Over...here...Dad." She sounded loopy now.

"She needs to lie down," Zion said.

I nodded and helped her onto my lap. Zeus took off his blazer and folded it. Raising her head just slightly, he placed the material under her head like a pillow before I lowered her head back.

She closed her eyes but still looked miserable.

Calvin and Alaric were finally at the stage.

"Queen Jade! Are you okay?! Let me come help," Calvin called out, attempting to raise himself onto the platform but failing miserably.

"The stairs are on the side, Calvin, but you can just stay there. We're going to move Jade once her stomach settles," Zion explained, rubbing Jade's back.

"He's gone." Alaric spoke, the sound making the four of us freeze in actual fear.

He was hiding his eyes with the reflective flare of his glasses, but I was kind of glad I couldn't see his eyes or it would have surely freaked me out.

The others looked at me and I nodded.

"He told Jade to kill herself and vanished when she did. I tried to stop him...but he deflected my attack and faded. He's skilled in wind and dark magic. That's what he used to deflect my attack and push me away far enough to run," I explained.

"Then...who is on the ground?" Zackery asked.

"Zeus?" Jade asked, catching our attention.

"Yes, Jade?" Zeus was attentive, moving closer and gently stroking Jade's cheek. "I'm right here."

"Did you...bring cookies?"

"Uh...yes?" He sounded confused by the question. "They're in my back pocket."

She was quiet for a moment.

"Shadow Jade?" she drawled out weakly. "You can...stop playing...dead now. Zeus has cookies."

"KILL!"

We all jumped at the declaration, watching Jade's dead body shoot up into sitting position. She looked at the floor before she got up.

"Blood!" she cheered and skipped over to us.

Calvin and Alaric both stared at her in horror, while the rest of us were simply speechless.

"What?" That was the only word the four of us managed to say in unison.

Shadow Jade jumped onto the stage, walking up to us before she knelt down and very gently patted Jade's head.

"Sorry. Head hurt," she said in a loving, soft manner.

"It's fine, Shadow Jade. Better...than the real thing," Jade managed to say.

Zeus stared at Shadow Jade before reaching into his back pocket and pulling out a homemade cookie.

He hadn't told them, but he'd been cooking the cookies by scratch every night since his promise.

We swore not to say anything, but I bet Jade

would have loved to know they were made by him specifically.

"Um. Good work, Shadow Jade," Zeus complimented.

"Cookie! Kill!" she cheered and accepted the cookie. "Save and eat with Jade."

That made me smile just slightly.

Shadow Jade leaned down and kissed Jade's forehead, lightly stroking her head.

"Goodnight," she whispered before she closed her eyes and her entire body faded into streams of darkness.

We exchanged a look and glanced at Jade, who remained still.

Alaric pushed off the ground and quietly landed on the stage. I was sure he used a wind spell or something, but I wasn't going to concern myself.

The others moved back just slightly, giving Alaric space as he knelt down pressed his hand to Jade's forehead.

He then pressed it against her cheek and then checked her right and left temple. He let out a long sigh, which I figured was out of relief.

"She's asleep," he announced. "We're going to my office."

"All right," the four of us replied.

I looked at Calvin, who finally took the longer

route to get onto the stage. I frowned. "What about Calvin?"

"I'll come as well," he voiced.

The four of us exchanged a look. "No."

Alaric rose up to his feet. "Calvin will join us."

"Why?" we asked in unison.

Calvin rose up and smiled. "I'll be able to help you guys."

"How so?" I questioned. "If you think you're going to be our computer whiz, we've got Zion for that."

"Nope, I'm really useful," Calvin defended.

"Again, how so? Jade doesn't need a puppy following her around," Zeus huffed.

"I'm a Tracker, just like you," he announced.

When the four of us remained silent, he grew flustered and looked at Alaric.

"I told you they wouldn't believe me."

Alaric sighed. "Talk later. Office."

"Alaric?" We heard Bianca's high-pitched voice.

"Why is there blood on the floor?" Tanner's voice called out.

We looked to see they were at the gym entrance, looking out of breath.

"Let's go." Alaric walked to the edge of the stage, dropping down to the ground with ease as his partners raced to him.

I looked at my brothers.

"This is not how I expected our first semester here to end," I admitted.

"We're not even done yet," Zeus huffed.

"Is Jade still asleep?" Zackery asked.

I looked down at her, noticing how relaxed she now looked. Her skin had gained a bit more color than before, but I still would insist she get checked by Zion and Bianca, now that she had arrived.

"Yeah," I replied.

"She made Shadow Jade be a legit copy of her, but the blow took a big hit on her body because of how she lined their energies together."

"Isn't that going to have a big effect on Shadow Jade?" Zeus questioned.

The three of them looked at me, and I looked away.

"We won't know until we examine her," Calvin interjected. "She may have mimicked her energy to make Shadow Jade play the part, but she could have easily taken the physical blow so that Shadow Jade wouldn't respond negatively to it."

"How would you know?" I grumbled, feeling rather annoyed. I was sure that was more of Zeus's energy influencing me, which only confirmed that we were unbalanced.

*Shit. This is going to be a pain to deal with.*

"I'm a Trac—"

"We know," the four of us said.

"I don't see how it matters. What would make you so special?" I muttered impatiently.

Zeus knelt down in front of Jade, lifting her up slowly from my lap. I scurried up and held Jade's head, positioning it to lay against Zeus's chest.

Zion and Zackery also rose up, and now the four of us were staring at Calvin, who gave us a confident grin.

"I've been tracking this guy for ten years! I'll definitely be of use."

"You?" Zion was the one who questioned it in a mocking manner. "You're clearly failing."

"Hmm. He could have a reason that may actually make sense," Zackery reasoned.

"You guys just switched personalities, didn't you?" Calvin asked.

The four of us glared at him, and he lifted his hands up protectively.

"Don't kill the messenger. I'm just saying. I've been one of the leads trying to track this guy down since the actual incident. I'll explain more once we get to the office, but I'll be helpful. I'm the one best-suited to track Charles down."

"Why?" I repeated firmly. "Don't tell us you

have all eight elements, because we know you don't."

"Nope." Calvin smiled and turned around, dropping down from the stage like he suddenly had no difficulty at all.

He looked back at us and fixed his glasses.

"I'm his biological son, and it's now my duty to bring my dad in," he declared.

With that, he turned and walked away, leaving the four of us truly speechless.

*Yup. This wasn't how we intended to spend our first semester in the slightest. At least we have cookies...fuck. That's a Zeus thing to say. Or is it Zackery?*

*Fuck...*

## TO BE CONTINUED.

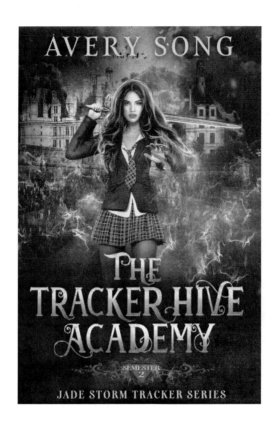

books2read.com/TRACKERHIVEACADE
MY2

# WITCHLING ACADEMY - OUT NOW

https://
books2read.com/WITCHLINGACADEMY

# FAE ROSE ACADEMY- PREORDER

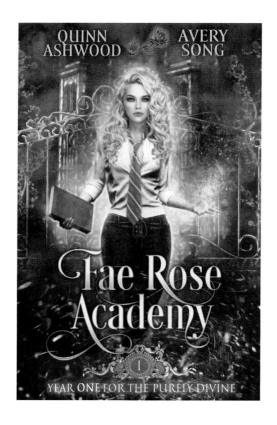

https://books2read.com/FAEROSEACADEMY

Here's a sneak peek of BLAZING
ACADEMY, coming out this MARCH 7th,
2020!

**https://
books2read.com/BLAZINGACADEMY**

### BLURB:

***When the element of fire burns within your veins, the academy for all things scorching is the best place to learn how to make that flame burn even hotter.***

Alice Blaze is my name, and I'm not exactly your typical sixteen-year-old. My mom disappeared after my birth and my dad was an alcoholic maniac, so I was raised by my protective grandparents in the single house up the hill. The one people only come to visit on Halloween.

Because, yeah, apparently, our house is haunted. Naturally.

As an orphan living in a spooky house, it's no surprise that my life has been...eventful. I've been inadvertently causing trouble since I was little and it *always* ends up with something combusting into flames. You know, lighting up the curtains, exploding vials in lab class. And don't get me started with the accidental school fire. Need I say more?

The flames really hit the fan when I'm accused of shattering all the windows in the entire school. Of course, that doesn't make sense because it has nothing to do with my burning nemesis. But it doesn't matter. Expulsion is imminent and my grandparents are fed up with my constant transfers.

But then something amazing happens: a letter of invitation lands right onto our doorstep. *Or window.*

I'm invited to Blazing Academy, the school for all things — and people — that are scorching hot. Shifters, demons, and blazing hot witches...oh, right. I almost left that part out. According to the school, that's what I am. A blazing hot witch.

*Let's hope that's all I am, and that this first semester goes a whole lot smoother than I'm imagining. Otherwise my whole life might just go up in smoke.*

# CHAPTER ONE: SWEET SIXTEEN

"Alice! You're going to be late for school!"

I turned over to hug one of my multiple pillows that crowded around the head of my bed. Even with two fans on and my window half open, I was still far too hot.

It simply wasn't bothering me because I was half asleep, but I was glad I only wore underwear to sleep because clothes were a no-no in this weather.

It was September, and I was baffled that it was still so hot. I always ran a little warm, even in the most chill days in winter, but it always left me wishing my grandparents would invest in an air conditioner.

Yes, our old, "haunted" building of a house needed a few renovations, but we were living in the time and age where we could afford a portable AC.

My grandma always gave the excuse that my room was in the attic and the hose connector to release the air pressure and water or whatever wouldn't reach the ground. It was all excuses to me.

Fans did barely anything up here. It did a bloody good job circulating the hot air, but to actually cool me off? I might as well eat ice cream every hour of the day.

Today was the third day of me going to another school that was forced to accept me. I always got a few brow raises when I'd acknowledge that I'd transferred from school twenty-something. I'd lost count, but from what I remembered, I was at school twenty-five before I made my lab vial combust.

*Seriously, it was an accident.*

People thought I was a witch. Or a red-haired, possessed female who looked like she was a part of a cult instead of a student trying to get her high school diploma.

My name was Alice Blaze, and I had a running streak of getting kicked out of every school I'd been allowed entry in.

It started in daycare and lead to grade school, and now, high school. It wasn't my fault, or at least, that's what I was told to say each time I "fucked up." See, there was something about the element of fire that hated me.

It had to be a past life vendetta or curse I had to my name because when fire was involved, I was signing off another transfer form and moving to the next school a few days later.

Lighters, fireplaces, even plain olden day matches. The spark of a flame matched with how I was currently feeling that day and either ended up with something burning to crisp or catching on fire and summoning the entire fire department to our school grounds.

*Sometimes, I could be in the happiest mood, and the flames will be all playful and try and burn the classroom down for fun.*

Due to constant fire mishaps, whenever I enrolled in a new school, the fire department was on speed dial. That was one fact that the students always found out about before the common 'Blazing Alice' nickname came to be.

How I wished to just be homeschooled. At least no one would have to deal with the fire mishaps I apparently created or stalk me all the way home to see the tall castle on the top of the hill.

Our house was literally the only one on the hill, and it gave you haunted house vibes. Totally spooky, painted in all black, and our garden and front lot were covered in thick trees and a few vines.

I wished they were nice and tall, the perfect wall of nature to shield us from the city's ridicule. The school that was thirty minutes from my house by bike was the only one that was willing to accept and tolerate all the trouble I caused.

The principal was best friends with my grandparents and was doing us this favor. It was nice of her, but I wasn't interested in the pity acceptance.

If I could be homeschooled, life would have been far easier. No more problems, no students bothering me, and it would be easier to study because no one would interrupt me.

The one problem with all of my schools was that I was an easy target to pick on. I was the tallest out of the females, standing at 5'9". I loved wearing heels or anything to bring me up to 6'0", but that merely got more attention.

Adding my small waist, wider hips, tanned skin, and extremely red hair, I was the sore spot in a bland hallway, and among my peers, I was the "weird" one.

I never asked to be this way, but I embraced it. My grandparents taught me early to love myself for who I was, and I'd thrived with that.

*Would have been nice to have contact lenses strong enough to last a day of school, but beggars can't be choosers.*

The most distinct attribute regarding my appearance was my red eyes. People thought they were contacts and that I wore them to grab attention. No one ever believed me when I said they were real and that I wasn't the Devil's daughter.

I'd gotten used to it by now, and even with knowing they were real, I lied and said they were contacts to avoid being called a trouble maker AND a liar.

*A girl could carry only so many labels.*

"Alice! Don't make me come up there!" Grandma called from the second floor.

Snuggling my pillow tightly, I wondered if I ignored her long enough, she'd let me skip school today.

*Today was my birthday after all. Did I really need to go to school?*

My sweet sixteen was here, but I didn't feel any different. No one was going to treat me a little nicer because it was the day I was born, and I surely wasn't expecting a happy birthday either.

Blazing Alice didn't have friends, because she was too dangerous to be around. That's what people liked to spread around the school, no matter how long I lasted before being kicked out.

If only I could be one of those girls who had a group of friends who cared about these milestones. To have someone sing happy birthday and present me with a cupcake with a candle on top.

With my fire problem, we weren't allowed to have candles in the classroom, but just for once, it would have been nice to experience it with good company.

"Woof?"

Something nudged my nose, and I poked an eye open to see the tiny black wolf. I hoped it was a wolf, but it very well could have been a husky breed puppy.

This little guy had been wandering through our thick trees when I came home from my first day of school. It was stuck in a patch of vines, and though I wasn't one to feel sympathy for wildlife, this mini wolf was far too adorable to ignore.

The plan was to get her out and let her be free to find her pack, but she ended up following me into my haunted house, and I basically couldn't get rid of her.

My grandparents tried and failed miserably. Thus, the reason why this cute puppy wolf thing was now chilling in my bed in a last attempt to wake me up.

"Woof!"

"I should call you Wolfie," I mumbled, and closed my eyes.

"Woof!" The light nudge to my nose, followed by the little licks, made me grin.

"Be lucky you're cute," I muttered but lifted my hand to ruffle her fur. She kept licking my face and it wasn't until her tail smacked my cheek, then I sat up.

"'Nope. Not being wolf farted on today. Your farts can kill," I groaned.

Hearing the creaky ladder steps, I groaned and lifted my blanket to cover my breasts. Soon enough, my grandma was at the entrance of the attic.

"Aren't you too old to be climbing ladders?" I whined.

She rolled her eyes. "I'm fifty-four, Alice. That's not old."

"Old to you guys is when you need a knee replacement, which I researched was seventy-five from the new statistics. However, I think it's when you have grey hair, which you do," I acknowledged.

She gave me a scowl and I merely shrugged. "You said you always want me to say the truth. I'm stating facts."

"Go get ready for school."

"Do I have to?" I whined. "Can't I skip today? Pretty please?"

"Even if it's your birthday, you need an education. I promised the principal that unless you were
super sick, you wouldn't skip school. What I will do
is drive you to school," she offered.

"That makes me sad. No thanks." I frowned and
looked at wolf pup who crawled onto my lap.

"Woof!"

"Did you give her a name?"

"No." I sighed. "Call her Cyrus. Reminds me of
a girl version of Cerberus," I suggested.

"Woof Woof!"

"Really?" My grandma gave me one of her
common 'I can't believe your logic' looks. I gave
her a nod. "She likes it! Plus, she could be a
demon from hell here to make sure I'm not
lonely."

Grandma shook her head. "I'm making breakfast. Get in the shower," she stated, and before I
could protest, headed back down the ladder.

With a pout of my lips, I mumbled, "Not fair.
She didn't even say Happy Birthday."

Deciding to get up, I petted Cyrus and picked
her up from the bed. Lowering her to the floor, she
ran around by my feet as I sat up and stretched.

After a minute of sitting almost naked on my
bed, I got up and walked over to my desk chair that
my uniform was resting on. I would have been

worried about how wrinkled it was, but I couldn't care less.

I already hated this school and couldn't wait for something to go awry. It would be the best gift a girl like me could ask for. Maybe that would convince my grandparents to let me be home-schooled.

*If Dad wasn't a recovering alcoholic getting rehab, he could have given permission for me to be homeschooled.*

My Dad was an interesting character. I sometimes wondered if he was really crazy, but basically, my grandparents hated him. They were my grandparents from my Mother's side, and the only thing they had to say about my Dad was what an irresponsible adult he was. I'd never gotten the chance to meet my Dad's parents.

Dad has been fighting with alcohol addiction for years. It hadn't been like that when he married my mom, but when she left after carrying me to full term, it left a hole in my Dad's heart.

Even after sixteen years, he still missed my Mom. He wouldn't admit it to anyone but me, and it pained me that there was nothing I could do to help him. He was in my life when I was younger, but I was mainly in my grandparents' care.

I got to visit him once in a while, but that slowly changed when his addiction got worse. He went from drinking two bottles of alcohol a day to a whole case, and when he'd get violent, my grandparents deemed him incapable of raising me.

It was only a matter of time.

The one thing I'm sure lead to my Dad drinking more was how similar I looked to my Mom. From the few pictures I carried of her, I was her mini-me and now that I was growing far too fast, I looked almost identical to her now.

With heels, we'd be at the same height, though my figure was just a little curvier than hers. My red locks were a shade brighter, but my eyes were identical, along with my lightly tanned skin.

I had no clue what my mother's background was, but my Dad was Caucasian. Whatever the combo was, it gave me a light tan mix and made it difficult for people to figure out if I was white or native.

My cultural background wasn't a big deal to me. It didn't deny who I was or give me some urge to learn where I came from.

All I wanted was to fit in at school. To learn more about myself and my studies. Not deal with the daily drama and teasing over me being far too accident prone.

*If I could even call it that.*

Regardless of my questionable ethnicity, I hadn't seen Dad in a while. He tried to show up during holidays, and at least text me once in a blue moon when he remembered he had a daughter, but the distance had really taken a stab at our Father-Daughter bond.

I didn't blame my grandparents for doing what they did, and even with the multiple school mishaps, they still took care of me and were willing to do the walk of shame to the principal's office every time I got in trouble.

They loved me, yes, but it would have been nice to have both my parents here to raise me rather than them.

*If my mom was around, maybe she'd be able to figure out what was wrong with me.*

Heading to the bathroom, I took a nice cool shower to wake me up. After that, I brushed my teeth and did a quick makeup look. I wasn't super into makeup but enjoyed a bit of a smoky eye look and red lipstick.

If my uniform could have some red to match my hair, eyes, lips, and red heels, that would make the black and white uniform less dull in comparison to my pop of color.

Leaving my lipstick for last, I gathered my single notebook, pencil case, phone, and the latest spells and fashion magazine from my wooden desk and placed it all into my red backpack.

I wasn't one to make notes or even study for long, which left me being called a smart ass. Another quality I'd taken from my mom, who was apparently a genius. I'm talking one-hundred percent, straight A-plus student genius.

My dad was more athletic, which was perfect for me since I took that trait from him and was the fastest runner at any school I attended during track season.

That reminded me of the time I'd been at one school for most of the training period for track and field, only to transfer to the opposite school they were facing in the league championships.

*Did my new school use that as an advantage? Of course. Top runner and league champion for the school's first official win. Ah, the few good times where students my age actually praised and acknowledged my existence.*

I moved onto the next school during summer break and never got a chance to make some good friends that I thought were interesting. That's why I just stopped trying.

It was disappointing to try and get along with people and then have to become long-distance friends. Those relationships barely lasted that long. No one around here was going to input that much effort into a friendship with the new transfer student.

Putting my bag on my shoulder and looking around my room, I nodded once and glanced down to Cyrus, who was sitting on my foot.

She loved doing that, which was her way of saying 'take me downstairs for food please'. Having her for three days had brightened my life just a little bit.

My grandparents may have forgotten my birthday, but the spots of love Cyrus showed me were enough to make me happy.

Leaning down, I picked her up with ease and made it down the ladder. Heading downstairs, I noticed that grandpa's brown leather coat was gone as were his matching shoes; both items usually rested against the wall near the door.

"Where's Grandpa?" I asked when I entered the kitchen. "Did he go fishing again?"

"Yes, he did," Grandma replied.

"But it's September," I reasoned. "There are barely any fish in the lakes by now."

"Doesn't stop him. You know that," she replied and lowered the plate of pancakes on the dining table. "Don't take too long to eat, I have an important meeting to go to."

"Morning bingo isn't important," I noted but headed to my spot at the table.

"It is when I can win money," Grandma countered.

"Would that money go to fixing the house?" I suggested.

"The house is in perfect condition," she argued.

"Uh huh. I think you forgot about the hole in the roof that I patched up with a metal plate from the basement. I'm sure that came from a broken appliance somewhere in the house. Then add the fact that only my toilet works properly, and the water is cold again," I explained some of the many faults in our old house.

Lowering Cyrus to the floor, she ran to her filled bowls of water and food and began to eat. Pulling out my hair, I hooked my backpack on one side and sat down.

Picking up my fork and knife, I dug right in as Grandma answered.

"Someone will come in this week to check that out, as well as the other things that need to get fixed."

"Why can't we just move somewhere else? This house makes it seem like we're dirt poor. It's like the Addam's family home. No wonder why I get made fun of all the time."

"Who's bullying you? This is a new school. It's the perfect fresh start, Alice."

"Fresh start of the new girl with the red hair, eyes, and heels. Alright," I commented with the least bit of amusement.

"Alice," Grandma said with a serious tone. "I won't hesitate to go to the school and find out."

"It's fine, Grandma. I can handle it," I vouched. "Don't need you bringing your cane around trying to hit the hot dudes."

"I would do no such thing," she huffed. "And my cane is only for when I'm tired."

"Alright," I replied and focused on my breakfast.

Once I was finished, I pushed my plate to the side to do my usual morning text message check. Turning my body to open my backpack and retrieve my phone, I turned back to see the plate with a red velvet slice of cake and a single candle that was actually lit up.

Glancing over to Grandma who had somehow placed the plate there without me noticing, I smiled back at her gleaming expression and she whispered, "Happy sweet sixteen, Alice."

"Grandma." I looked at her with teary eyes. "I thought you forgot!'

"I couldn't forget the day you were born,

Alice. I know we don't do much in terms of cele-brations, but this is extra special. Your grandpa is actually in town reserving a nice restaurant for us to have dinner tonight. The three of us. It'll be a nice, luxurious dinner with some bomb dessert."

I snickered at her attempt to use our current age "lingo". "Thanks, Grandma!"

Glancing back down at the candle, I worried about the flame that was already growing in size. "Uh. Can I blow it out now before the whole house catches on fire?"

"Make a wish before you do," Grandma urged.

I wanted to huff, but I decided to go along with it. She did get my favorite flavor of cake. Closing my eyes, I took a deep breath.

*Please let me find a school that accepts me. Not these academies that hate every unique thing about me. Most importantly, let me find some friends. Just one friend...*

Letting the air out in a stream of air, the rather large flame took a bit of blowing to put out. It finally did, but I did notice Grandma holding the fire extinguisher as back-up.

That made me giggle. "That would be pretty funny to have on a card or calendar, Grandma."

"I'd be rich if I sold photographs of me posing with this fire extinguisher," she cheered. "But your grandad would never allow it. Got to figure out another career to pursue."

"Back to the bingo drawing board," I teased.

"You can win a lot at Bingo!" she stressed.

"You haven't won in how many years? Ten? Twenty? I swear you've been on a losing streak since I was born," I emphasized.

"I'm working on it." She blushed at my statement, knowing well it was true. "Finish your cake or you're leaving it behind."

"I can't leave this beauty behind!" I exclaimed. "It gotta be in my belly first."

Staring at the cake, I took a quick picture and looked to Grandma as she picked the other plate that I'd discarded to the side.

"I can wash it."

"Nonsense. It's your birthday. You get a bit of special treatment today." Grandma winked. Staring at her with loving eyes, I whispered, "Thank you, Grandma. For putting up with everything."

She met my gaze and had a smile of her own. "Only two more years and you won't need to deal with school anymore, alright?"

Giving her a bob of my head in reply, I looked back at the cake and sliced a piece with my fork.

*She's right. Soon I'll graduate and can find a place willing to accept me. Hopefully they don't play with fire.*

# ABOUT AVERY SONG

Avery Song is the second pen name of a reverse harem author who specializes in fantasy romance.

She especially loves writing strong main characters and is excited for all the books that are approaching.

## ACADEMY FOR THE FALLEN

*Trials of the Damned - Year One*

## BLAZING ACADEMY

*Semester One (Mar 7th, 2020)*

## COWRITTEN WORKS:

## FOR THE PURELY DIVINE SERIES

*Fae Rose Academy - Year One (Feb 2020)*

## WILLA SILVER ACADEMY INVESTIGATOR

*Daggers and Smoke - Year One (Mar 2020)*

Made in United States
North Haven, CT
17 May 2023

36698234R00250